Treacherous Cruise Flirtation

Dawn Brookes

Treacherous Cruise Flirtation

A Rachel Prince Mystery

Dawn Brookes

Oakwood Publishing Ltd

Paperback Edition 2023
Kindle Edition 2023
Paperback ISBN: 978-1-913065-79-9
Hardback ISBN: 978-1-913065-80-5
Copyright © DAWN BROOKES 2023
Cover Images: Adobe Stock Images
Cover Design: John & Janet

Chapter 1

While coaxing the brush through her long blonde hair, Rachel Jacobi-Prince studied her reflection in the mirror. The person looking back at her was no longer tense and anxious, like they had been when she and Carlos left the UK for a long delayed anniversary break. They had spent the past week at the Outrigger Waikiki Beach resort in Honolulu. Rachel felt happy and optimistic about the future.

Carlos ambled out of the bathroom wearing his hotel-issued bathrobe. The sight of her handsome, hunky husband sparked a wave of affection, and butterflies rushed through her as she gazed at him. Though the intensity of her feelings had mellowed since they first met, she was more in love with him than ever before.

"What?" He grinned.

"Nothing," she replied. "I don't want this to end, that's all."

He strolled across the room, his brown eyes gleaming as he kissed her tenderly. "Me neither," he said. "But we still have one more night – let's make the most of it. Tomorrow you get to see Marjorie, and she's been looking forward to cruising with you for just as long as I've looked forward to this week."

Carlos was right. The pandemic had hit Rachel's octogenarian friend hard. Marjorie's son, Jeremy, had insisted she remained isolated, although her housekeeper, Gina, and Johnson, her chauffeur, both refused to abandon her.

Rachel felt her face light up at the thought of meeting her dear friend again. "I can't wait to see her."

Carlos hurriedly dressed, looking dashing in his tux. Rachel was wearing the red dress he had bought for her when she last cruised with Marjorie. She tried not to think of her most recent cruise to India. Although she had enjoyed it immensely, the holiday had been marred by her fretting about Carlos being on a secret mission in China. As it turned out, she had been grateful that the Chinese government had not harmed him and he hadn't succumbed to the deadly virus that had just begun spreading.

Rachel shuddered at the recollections, pausing for a moment before applying her mascara.

"Come along, Mrs Jacobi-Prince. I don't want to be told off by Pearl for being late."

Rachel flashed him a grin. "As if. You've got her wrapped around your little finger. The woman's besotted with you."

He extended his arm, and she gladly took it. "But she knows my heart belongs to you."

Holding his arm, she felt her own heart would burst. All the doubts and fears she had entertained before they married a few years earlier seemed an age away. Her husband filled the role of lover, friend, and soulmate, all rolled into one. Yet somehow, they managed to live together without blurring the boundaries of their independence.

Duke's restaurant buzzed with activity. It was infused with aromas of freshly cooked food. Rachel's attention was drawn to a group of noisy people. Three women wore nurses' hats, but they weren't wearing uniforms. Their colourful dresses blended in with those worn by the Hawaiian people.

Seeing the nurses reminded her of her best friend, Sarah, who she was looking forward to seeing when the *Coral Queen* docked the next day. Since the pandemic, Sarah and her husband Jason had returned to the cruise ship where she worked as a nurse and he was a security guard.

"Aloha, Mr and Mrs Jacobi," Pearl greeted them, her doe eyes fixed only on Carlos. Rachel had spent the first few days of their holiday trying to correct Pearl into using their double-barrelled surname but had decided it wasn't worth the effort. She could only imagine what Pearl would think if she knew Rachel went by her maiden name at work.

She giggled while they followed Pearl to their table. Carlos's eyes shone as he grinned. He could always read her.

Pearl led them to a table overlooking the stunning beach. A bottle of champagne sat in a bucket of ice. Rachel raised a quizzical eyebrow.

"It's our last night. We must celebrate," Carlos said.

"You earn too much money," Rachel replied, pleased with the surprise. Carlos's private investigation business was thriving, and he'd taken on some well-paid jobs during the pandemic. Rachel now worked as a detective inspector, which meant a salary increase, although her work life had got harder. When Carlos was in his Leicester office, their professional paths crossed occasionally.

A waiter poured their champagne, and Carlos raised his glass. "To my wife… and to many more lucrative jobs." He winked.

"Don't get above yourself, Mr Jacobi-*Prince,*" she mouthed the latter in Pearl's direction, but then laughed. An angry-looking older woman in a wheelchair preoccupied Pearl, who was trying to dodge the stick the woman was waving in the air.

Carlos followed her gaze. "Ooh looks like there could be trouble ahead. I bet that lady's on your cruise," he said with a smirk.

At that moment, a loud peal of laughter rang across the room from the nurses' group. "Do you think they're on a hen night?" she asked.

"You'll know the answer to that if you look closer," Carlos replied.

Rachel's stomach dropped when she studied the nurses. There were four of them: three women wearing the hats and a younger man with a lanyard around his neck. They were sitting with four other people, one of whom was the stick-brandishing woman of a few moments ago.

"Looks like your cruise is going to be…" Carlos cleared his throat, "…interesting."

Rachel frowned. "Even if they are joining the *Coral*, it's a big ship. Seeing them, though, has reminded me of something. Jeremy's been wondering if Marjorie should hire a private nurse or companion."

Carlos's eyes widened. "I hope he hasn't dared mention that to her."

"He hasn't because, guess what? He's asked me to."

Carlos almost choked on the sip of champagne he was about to swallow. "What did you say to that? I hope you refused."

"Not exactly." Rachel thought about the conversation she'd had with Marjorie's son the week before she and

Carlos flew out to Honolulu via Vancouver. "I haven't mentioned it before, because I didn't want to ruin our holiday, but Jeremy says Marjorie is a lot frailer, and he thinks she could be losing her memory."

"Nonsense. You speak to her every week and haven't noticed anything, or you would have told me."

"Sometimes she repeats things," said Rachel.

"Well, if that's the criterion, we're all demented, especially you, my darling." Carlos laughed.

"I do not repeat things!" Rachel exclaimed.

"You do when we're arguing."

"Debating…" she grinned, "and that's to make sure you've heard my side of the arg… erm… debate."

"Saying something in triplicate doesn't make the argument any stronger," he said, his teasing eyes dancing under the lights of the restaurant.

"If you're not careful, this might be one of those occasions," she retorted playfully.

"Anyway, back to the Marjorie thing. You should make your own mind up when you see her. Can you imagine her being in the care of any of those people?"

As if to prove his point, further loud guffaws travelled across the room from the rowdy group.

She shook her head. "Perhaps Jeremy's being overprotective."

"More likely the extravagant Octavia won't allow him enough time to visit his mother and he's feeling guilty about it."

Rachel felt Carlos had a valid point. They were both aware of Octavia Snellthorpe's love of the highlife. "I'm surprised they stayed together after their last cruise," she said. "The woman threw herself into another man's arms."

"They understand each other. Besides, he loves her, despite her misdemeanours," said Carlos.

There was a break in the conversation when Kapena, the waiter, arrived to take their dinner order. "Aloha, Carlos, Aloha, Rachel. What can I get for you this evening?"

Kapena had been on duty every evening Rachel and Carlos had dined in at Duke's. She was pleased he was here for their last night.

"Aloha. I don't even need to look at the menu," she said. "No starter for me. I'll have the coconut ginger braised seafood, please." Unlike her husband, Rachel preferred fish and vegetables to meat and pasta, and the Hawaiians excelled in the variety of fish dishes on offer.

"It's teriyaki steak for me," said Carlos. "Medium cooked."

"Any cocktails for you this evening?"

"We'll stick with the champagne for now," said Carlos. "I'm flying back to England tomorrow and Rachel's joining the *Coral Queen* for a cruise around the islands."

7

"You will love it, Rachel. Ask for Malia, my sister; she's a cocktail mixer on board that ship."

"I will. Thanks, Kapena."

Carlos reached across the table for Rachel's hand before putting his other hand in his pocket. "Happy anniversary, my love," he said, handing her a rectangular box.

They had both put aside funds to buy a special gift for each other when they eventually travelled to Hawaii for the anniversary break, a holiday they had been forced to cancel and rebook twice before they finally made it. It was spring, and their real anniversary wasn't until the summer, but they had waited long enough for this special moment. Rachel reached into the box and took out a ruby studded necklace, perfectly matching the dress she was wearing. Light caught the gems, which reflected flashes of orange and red.

"Carlos, it's beautiful."

"I meant to give it to you while you were dressing, but we were running late."

They had taken a surfing lesson that afternoon and became so engrossed they'd been rushing around before coming down for dinner. She took the necklace from the box and Carlos moved from the other side of the table to fasten it around her neck, removing her gold chain first. Rachel slipped the chain into the box and placed it in her handbag.

"I'm afraid my gift isn't as beautiful, but here it is." She handed him a box.

Carlos's eyes lit up. It was the smartwatch he had been pining for and which she had bought after the second lockdown. She had kept it hidden away in a locked drawer at work, longing for this moment.

"It's perfect," he said, kissing her tenderly before returning to his seat.

Kapena arrived soon afterwards and served them dinner: a large platter of steak teriyaki for Carlos and a smaller plate of Rachel's coconut ginger braised seafood. Both dishes smelled wonderful as the aromas wafted across the table between them.

They chatted while they ate, discussing the plans for the next day. While Carlos was going to fly back to England, Rachel was due to meet Marjorie at the airport before boarding the *Coral Queen* in the afternoon. A warm atmosphere settled over the dinner table while they ate the delicious food and listened to the live band playing in the background. The nurses and the people Rachel assumed were their patients or clients had settled down, thankfully, and were quieter.

After she had eaten, Rachel cast her eye around the restaurant. Exercising her people-watching skills was a practice that came in handy when she was policing in England. The nurses and their clients were American, which was obvious from their accents. Rachel guessed the nurses' ages ranged from mid-twenties to early forties. She wondered whether they had arrived together or just met up as part of a package tour. The stick-waver was in her seventies and remained in her wheelchair for dinner. Rachel couldn't see the others clearly, as a large pillar blocked her view.

Kapena returned to clear the table. "Can I get you any desserts?" he asked.

"Not for me, thank you," said Rachel.

Carlos patted his belly. "Nor me tonight. Please give our compliments to the chef."

"I will," said Kapena.

"Do you know whether those nurses are staying here for a holiday or joining the cruise tomorrow? My best friend is a cruise ship nurse on the *Coral*." Rachel's curiosity was getting the better of her.

"They arrived this afternoon and are accompanying the guests who are with them at the table. They have only booked in for the one night, so they might well be joining your cruise."

Rachel couldn't understand why the idea jangled warning bells in her head, but it did.

"If you're going to broach the subject of a private nurse with Marjorie," Carlos said, as if reading her mind, "maybe you could get her to chat to their patients."

Rachel snapped out of her anxious thoughts. "That would hardly be subtle, Carlos."

Carlos had been teasing, but his face became more serious as he looked from Rachel to the nurses and back again. "I was joking when I said there might be trouble ahead. You haven't taken it to heart, have you?"

"Of course not!" Rachel hoped her snappy response wasn't a giveaway, but she yearned for a peaceful cruise. She wanted no repetition of previous voyages where she'd earned the reputation of being a murder magnet.

Chapter 2

A sea breeze blew gently through Rachel's hair as she and Carlos got out of a taxi. Carlos retrieved their luggage from the driver and they entered Honolulu airport. Her eyes were watering with a mixture of excitement and sadness.

"Promise me you'll try to relax and stay away from trouble," pleaded Carlos, his voice tinged with concern. He knew all too well how fiercely dedicated she was to her work and how it had taken its toll over the past few years.

Rachel pulled him into a tight embrace, feeling the warmth of his body against hers. "I promise," she whispered, her voice barely audible above the noise of people clamouring to get to the check-in desks. She felt the weight of recent cases lingering in the corners of her mind, but she was determined to set them aside.

"That's good enough for me," Carlos said, giving her one last squeeze before reluctantly pulling away. "It's hard to part after a memorable week, Rachel, but you need this extra break. Enjoy the Hawaiian sun and take plenty of photos of the islands. Most important of all, have fun with Marjorie."

Thinking of Marjorie brought a smile to Rachel's face. She nodded. "I'll do my best to let go of work and just... be me. Besides," she added with a playful grin, "I have a feeling Marjorie will keep me entertained."

Carlos laughed, shaking his head. "Of that I am in no doubt," he agreed, taking her hands in his. "I'd better go. You need to find her before she wanders off to hire a private nurse." He winked. "Go on, you don't want to keep her waiting any longer."

"Thank you for arranging all of this," Rachel murmured, giving his hands a gentle squeeze, not wanting to let go. "The past week has been so special." She touched the ruby necklace still hanging around her neck. "I love you, Carlos Jacobi-Prince."

"I love you too, darling," he replied, his eyes shining with affection. "Now go. Your adventure awaits!"

The airport terminal became noisier, a sure sign that Marjorie's plane must be disembarking. With a last wave to Carlos, she walked towards the cacophony of excited chatter and the rumble of suitcases rolling across the tiled floor. Rachel scanned the bustling crowd, her heart pounding in anticipation.

And then she saw her. Marjorie looked resplendent in a vibrant peacock-blue dress, her snow-white permed hair making her stand out, despite her small stature.

"Rachel, my dear!" Marjorie exclaimed, beaming as she opened her arms wide for an embrace.

"Marjorie!" Rachel rushed forward, bending to wrap her arms around her friend. The familiar scent of Marjorie's perfume filled her nostrils as they hugged, and she felt a wave of warmth and affection wash over her.

"My dear," Marjorie said, pulling back to look at Rachel with twinkling eyes, "I can tell you've had an enjoyable week. You look radiant."

"Thank you, it was magnificent," Rachel replied, feeling a blush creep up her cheeks. "It's been far too long since Carlos and I spent quality time together, and now, seeing you is the cream on top of the cake."

"Likewise." A porter who was with Marjorie took Rachel's suitcase and placed it onto his trolley. Marjorie looped her arm through Rachel's and guided her towards the exit. "Now, tell me all about your expectations for this Hawaiian adventure of ours."

Rachel smiled as they stepped out of the terminal into the bright sunlight. As soon as she turned her back on the airport and stared into the distance, she felt a mixture of emotions: the lingering worry over recent cases; the bitter sadness of parting from Carlos; and the excitement of the voyage ahead. The porter handed their luggage to a taxi driver and they climbed into the vehicle. Soon afterwards they were headed towards the port.

When they exited the taxi, the driver removed their luggage. The towering cruise liner loomed in front of them, casting its shadow over the throngs of passengers eagerly waiting to board. Once they were separated from their luggage and checked in, they made their way onto the gangway, arm in arm. The *Coral Queen* beckoned them forward.

"I can hardly wait to explore the other islands, soak up some more sun, and maybe even learn a bit of hula dancing," Rachel said.

"Really?" Marjorie's eyes sparkled, mirroring Rachel's enthusiasm. "I'm looking forward to the tropical air, exotic flowers, and the thrill of discovering exciting places. Exploring is what keeps life fresh after being locked away for far too long." A sadness crossed Marjorie's face for a moment.

"Absolutely," Rachel agreed with the sentiment. "And there's no-one I'd rather be exploring with."

"Nor I, my dear." Marjorie patted her hand gently. "You know, even though we've done that video calling thing, I've missed seeing you. This holiday will bring out your adventurous spirit because you never shy away from a challenge."

"Uh-oh," Rachel murmured. "That sounds like you've cooked something up that I might not like." She knew well that beneath Marjorie's refined exterior there beat the heart of a true adventurer.

"Would I do such a thing?"

"The answer to that is yes," said Rachel, chuckling nervously.

They continued chatting, both animated about their upcoming voyage, and Rachel felt a happy sense of anticipation. Seeing Marjorie made her realise just how much she cherished her friend. This cruise would be an unforgettable experience and a much-needed escape for both of them.

"Here's to adventure," Rachel said, raising an imaginary glass in toast while they walked.

"Adventure," Marjorie repeated, her eyes shining. "To new horizons."

Once they stepped inside the ship, Rachel thought back to some of their previous cruises. She turned to Marjorie.

"Let's try to avoid murder on this one, shall we?"

"If you insist," Marjorie tittered, "although I could do with something to sharpen up my brain cells. Nevertheless, I accept you might like to give yours a rest."

"If that's possible, Marjorie," Rachel replied. "We'll just have to reminisce about your invaluable contributions and unswerving dedication. You're quite the sleuth."

"Flattery will get you everywhere, dear," Marjorie quipped. "Speaking of dedication, do you still run every day?"

"I do," Rachel said, a sheepish smile crossing her face. "It's a great way to clear my head, and it keeps me sharp."

"And I suppose you still go to the gym? Perhaps I should take a leaf out of your book and try it." Marjorie giggled. "Although I daresay I might need resuscitating afterwards."

Rachel laughed, imagining her elegant friend donning athletic gear and joining her for a morning workout. "Just say the word and I'll be there."

"Goodness, what a sight that would be." Marjorie giggled again, shaking her head in mock horror. "But who knows? Never say never."

"Nothing's impossible, but perhaps we'll just enjoy pleasant strolls around the decks and the odd cocktail."

"Now you're talking," said Marjorie.

The vibrant colours of the atrium seemed to come alive as Rachel and Marjorie strolled arm in arm, taking in the lush greenery. The sound of tinkling water from the familiar ornamental fountain in the centre was musical, and the scent of fresh flowers filled the air.

"I'm looking forward to seeing Sarah and Jason. I haven't seen them since their wedding. They are on board, aren't they?" Marjorie said.

"Yes, that's one reason for choosing this cruise," Rachel replied, her thoughts turning to her best friend. "They'll be just as eager to see you as you are to see them."

Marjorie sighed, a fond smile playing on her lips. "You said she'd been working on land when cruising was cancelled."

"Yes, she took a contract in accident and emergency after they anchored the *Coral Queen* close to Southampton," Rachel said.

"Have the rest of the medical team returned?" Marjorie enquired.

"I think so. Sarah said that Bernard rejoined the ship straight away and as far as I know, Dr Bentley is back on board along with Gwen. I'm not sure about the junior doctor, Janet Plover, or Brigitte." Marjorie was fond of the chief medical officer, Dr Graham Bentley, and they had both become friends with the chief nurse, Gwen Sumner.

"The ship wouldn't be the same without the cheeky Bernard and his wicked sense of humour," Marjorie said.

"You're right there," Rachel replied. Her thoughts drifted to the sometimes borderline humour of her favourite Filipino nurse.

They continued their leisurely stroll through the atrium and sat down to wait until they could go to their rooms. Marjorie leaned in closer, her voice dropping to a conspiratorial whisper.

"I must confess, I was rather excited about the prospect of joining you in another mystery."

"Marjorie, the plan is to relax," Rachel chided, her lips curling into a smile despite herself.

"Of course, dear," Marjorie said, her voice tinged with amusement. "But should the need arise, you know you can always count on this old girl for help."

Rachel laughed. "Whilst your enthusiasm is comforting, Marjorie, let's hope we encounter nothing more nefarious than sunburn on this voyage. It would be wonderful to enjoy a peaceful cruise for once."

"If you insist," Marjorie conceded, her eyes still holding a mischievous glint.

Rachel giggled, but felt a pang of anxiety rising within her chest.

***

After unpacking in the familiar suite at the rear of deck fifteen, Rachel made her way to the matching suite on the port side. She knocked on the door.

Marjorie answered, bursting with enthusiasm.

"Come in. Mario's already spoiling me."

"Me too," said Rachel. The two suites Marjorie always booked for them came with their own personal butler and they had got to know him over the years.

"Did you see the itinerary for tonight?" Marjorie asked. "There's a Hawaiian-themed party on the pool deck. I can hardly wait!"

"Right, but don't you think you should rest? You've had a long flight," Rachel said, worried her friend might overdo it.

"Not at all. Didn't I tell you? I decided to stay in Los Angeles for two nights before getting a comparatively shorter flight today. Only six hours; I'm full of energy."

"That explains why you look so fresh," said Rachel. She too had hoped to go to the party and was already imagining the rhythm of traditional island music amid a sea of brightly coloured leis and grass skirts. She and Carlos had enjoyed dancing at Duke's during their stay. "As you're so full of energy, it will be a wonderful way to kick off our holiday."

"Exactly," said Marjorie, her childlike enthusiasm contagious. "And do you have any plans for our stops in Maui and the Big Island?"

"If you wouldn't mind, I've been thinking about taking a guided hike or something similar through the lush rainforests," Rachel said. "I'm yearning for the chance to explore the landscapes that make up the islands."

"Of course I don't mind," Marjorie replied.

"How about you?"

"I would like to go on one of those thrilling helicopter tours. Can you imagine soaring over the majestic Na Pali Coast or getting an aerial view of the volcanoes?"

"Sounds spectacular," Rachel said, feeling a twinge of envy at her friend's daring choice of excursion.

"I'm glad you think so, because I've booked us two tickets."

Rachel burst out laughing. "You never fail to amaze me, Marjorie Snellthorpe. I guess I won't be needing that guided hike after all."

They continued discussing their plans, but Rachel felt the weight of a lingering concern tugging at the back of her mind. Jeremy's request for her to broach the subject of employing a private nurse for his mother seemed premature. Although she could understand his worry, looking at her energetic friend now, Rachel found it difficult to imagine that Marjorie might need such help.

"Marjorie, before we go anywhere, I was wondering about your health?"

Marjorie's eyes widened before she let out a hearty laugh. "I'm in perfect health, Rachel. You mustn't worry about me."

"It's just that Jeremy is concerned about you."

"I'm surprised Jeremy's had time to be concerned about anything now he and Octavia are back wooing the socialites."

"He cares about you," Rachel replied, relief washing over her.

"That may be, but I'm not on my way out just yet." Marjorie's lips tightened.

Rachel took the hint to drop the subject, and they stepped out onto the balcony to sit and watch the ship pull away from the port.

Chapter 3

The tantalising scent of freshly baked cinnamon swirls filled the air as Sarah stood in the lavish lobby off the main atrium. About to escort four guests and their accompanying private nurses on a tour of the ship, Sarah smiled at passengers joining a snakelike queue around rope barriers to speak to someone at guest services.

The nurses were easy to recognise when they arrived, as the three women wore starched linen hats and the male had a lanyard with a photo ID hung around his neck. Two of the passengers drove motorised wheelchairs, another walked with a stick, and the fourth – a younger man – had his plastered left arm in a sling. Once they were all assembled, Sarah took a deep breath, preparing herself for guiding the tour of the magnificent vessel.

"Good evening," she said brightly, her voice cutting through the quiet murmur of conversation. "I'm one of the ship's nurses, Sarah Bradshaw. It's going to be my pleasure to show you around the *Coral Queen*." She flashed a reassuring smile at them. "My husband, Jason Goodridge, is a member of the ship's security team, so you can rest assured you're in safe hands."

The nurses and their patients exchanged polite smiles. Sarah hoped what she was sensing behind their expressions was a subtle curiosity rather than barely concealed hostility. Prior to meeting them, she had studied each of the nurses' names along with the passengers' medical conditions, only one of which, in her opinion, warranted a private nurse. But it was their prerogative to employ whoever they wished. Eager to foster a healthy working relationship while the nurses were on board, Sarah dived into friendly conversation as they set off.

"Please let me know if you have questions as we go along."

One nurse had introduced herself as Margaret Green. She stood out, wearing a red blouse and a bright yellow skirt with red high-heeled sandals. Although she wore a hat, her long black hair hung loosely below her shoulders. She was yawning already and appeared disinterested.

"Thanks for doing this," said the youngest of the nurses, a Black man with a loose wavy afro, and a smile that caused his face to glow. "I'm Preston Smith." He was accompanying thirty-five-year-old Bradley Roberts, the man with the forearm in plaster. The other nurses seemed to exclude Preston, who came across as more timid than them.

"It's my pleasure," said Sarah while they waited for a lift to take them up one floor. "How long have you been nursing?" she asked.

"Only two years since qualifying. I trained in Chicago before moving to New York City. That's when I joined the agency. I'm new to all this. They only gave me the job because it was last-minute and nobody else was available at such short notice. Brad broke his arm skiing last week and wanted someone around to help him out."

"Well, I'm sure you'll both enjoy the cruise." Sarah resisted the temptation to say it looked as though he would have an easy ride as Brad was quite happy attaching himself to Margaret, who was accompanying the elderly Stephen Williams, one of the two travelling in electric wheelchairs.

When they got out of the lift, or elevator as her American entourage called it, they continued along the plush corridors. Sarah attempted to engage with each member of the party, but only a few responded. The rest seemed in a hurry to get the tour over with. It was almost as if it was a box to tick off on their itinerary.

"This is the ship's library," Sarah announced as they entered a large room filled with classics and modern books of every genre, along with a few leather-bound tomes. Plush armchairs were scattered around and there was a selection of games passengers could borrow. "If you enjoy reading, this might be a spot for you to unwind or come to for some peace. You can borrow books during your stay." Sarah couldn't help staring at a spot where, a few years before, an elderly woman had been murdered. Her best friend Rachel had tracked down the killer and brought the person to justice. She shuddered before shaking the recollection from her memory.

"I like a good mystery," said the nurse named Amelia Hastings. "But being on a cruise ship makes me crave a romantic novel. Perhaps it's the sea air?" Amelia was quieter than the other two women, and more serious. Laughter bubbled up sporadically from her two female colleagues.

"Or perhaps it's the handsome sailors," Olga Stone, the fourth nurse, quipped. She hadn't introduced herself, but thanks to her preparation, Sarah knew who she was. Olga and Margaret exchanged suggestive glances, making Sarah feel uncomfortable, especially with their patients present.

"There'll be no time for that; you've got work to do." Emma Johnson was a retired actress who had been involved in a serious car accident a few years before and walked with a limp. Sarah had seen none of the films she'd been in.

Olga and Margaret rolled their eyes while Amelia continued looking at the books. Although they were talking to each other, the female nurses didn't convince Sarah they got along as well as they made out.

Sarah led them out of the library and continued the tour. Heading to the lifts again, she took them down to deck two.

"Okay, everyone," she announced as they approached a set of double doors. "Welcome to our state-of-the-art medical facilities." Upon entering, the group was greeted by the pristine waiting room. A few people were sitting in seats, ready to attend evening surgery.

"We hold two surgeries each day, one in the morning and one in the evening. I can't introduce you to the staff just now because they are busy consulting. There's always a doctor and a nurse on call in case of emergencies, and we even have an intensive care bed." The group followed Sarah along the corridor away from the waiting room, where she opened the doors to the infirmary and led them into a room on the far side. The brand new ventilator stood in a corner.

"That's impressive," said Amelia. "Is it used much?"

"I'd be happy if it was never required, but yes, we have to admit people to the infirmary and to this room from time to time." Moving away from the high-dependency area, she showed them around the infirmary where there were four beds. "We have X-ray facilities and can treat most things on board, although sometimes medical evacuation is required. Don't hesitate to reach out to any of the team if you have any concerns."

A murmur rippled through the air from the passengers, and Sarah felt proud. The ship's facilities even impressed the hostile nurses.

"Dr Bentley is our chief medical officer," she continued, "but he's not here at the moment. He'll be doing his rounds. All medical and nursing staff on board a cruise ship hold officer status and Dr Bentley is a senior officer. We also have a second-in-command doctor as well as three other nurses, including a senior nurse. Hopefully you won't need us, but we are always happy to address any medical issues should they arise during the voyage."

"How old are the doctors?" Margaret asked, sniggering.

Sarah frowned. "We don't divulge personal information about our staff. Perhaps we should continue our tour," she said, motioning for the group to follow her out. "Our next stop will be the ship's premier restaurant. You may have already eaten in there." Sarah led the group to board a lift again, which took them up to deck four, and then along a corridor adorned with vibrant paintings. "I'll take you through the art gallery along the way. There are regular art auctions if any of you are interested."

The corridor leading to the ship's main restaurant was alive with the gentle hum of conversation, punctuated by bursts of laughter. Sarah tried her best to engage her group in small talk as they walked, but she was developing a headache, making it difficult to concentrate.

"Did any of you know each other before the cruise?" she asked.

"Sure did," said Margaret, nudging Amelia, who forced a laugh, but didn't seem amused.

Victoria Hayes, the other wheelchair user, narrowed her left eye, the other was covered with an eye patch, and glanced at Stephen, who seemed anxious to avoid her gaze.

"Stephen and I have crossed paths a time or two in the past," she replied curtly, her tone icy.

"I see," Sarah said, sensing tension between them. She couldn't tell if their prickly attitude towards each other was an act or if there was genuine animosity there. Deciding it was best not to dwell on it, she redirected her attention to the task at hand. "Here we are," she announced as they reached the entrance to the grand dining room. A maître d', dressed in a crisp black suit, greeted them with a warm smile.

"Welcome to the *Coral Queen's* premier restaurant," he said, smiling at Sarah before turning to the group. "I'm Charles, the maître d'. It's a pleasure to meet you."

"Thank you, Charles." Sarah turned to face her group, moving them away from guests trying to enter or leave. She gestured towards the elegant room packed with diners seated at elaborately laid white-clothed tables. Overhead, sparkling chandeliers provided ample light. "This is where you'll enjoy your breakfast, lunch and dinner during our voyage."

Charles joined them. "Have you chosen set dining?" he asked.

"Yeah, us oldies are taking early dining, although we ate at the buffet tonight. Brad there is eating on his own at eight, and the nurses will do what they like," said Stephen.

"Of course, if you have any dietary restrictions or special requests, our chefs will be more than happy to accommodate them."

"Thank you for your time, Charles," said Sarah. "We'll let you get back to work."

"Always a pleasure, Sarah. I hope you all have a wonderful dining experience aboard the *Coral Queen*," Charles replied before returning to his post.

As the tour continued, Sarah found it increasingly difficult to warm to her group. Their private conversations were hushed and guarded, making her feel like an outsider.

The only person who seemed genuinely grateful for her efforts was Preston, the inexperienced nurse. She noticed him fidgeting with his lanyard and stealing nervous glances at the others, clearly uncomfortable.

"Are you okay?" she asked quietly, falling into step beside him.

"Yes, thank you, Sarah," he stammered, his cheeks darkening with embarrassment. "I just want to make a good impression on everyone. I'm not used to working outside of the hospital setting. And I probably shouldn't say this," he lowered his voice, "but that woman's rude." Preston nodded towards Victoria.

"Oh dear," she said, sympathising. "Look, feel free to ask for help if you need it. You'll do a great job." Sarah noticed Victoria scowled the whole time.

"Thanks. I appreciate that," Preston replied.

Sarah glanced around at the rest of them, her unease growing with every passing moment. Her headache intensified as she led the group through the ship's entertainment venues. The dazzling lights and noise in the casino and the pulsating beats of the nightclub pierced through her skull. It was difficult to focus on the tour, let alone consider their group dynamics. She closed her eyes briefly, wishing she had brought some painkillers with her.

"Over here," she said, raising her voice above the cacophony, "we have our modern theatre, where you can enjoy performances ranging from Broadway-style shows to comedy acts every night." She gestured at the grand entrance, trying to muster enthusiasm despite her throbbing head.

"Sounds delightful," Victoria Hayes remarked, her scathing tone only exacerbating Sarah's discomfort. "I do hope they have something more sophisticated than those dreadful amateur productions one hears about."

"Our performers are all professionals, handpicked from around the world," Sarah replied, forcing a smile. Stephen Williams remained silent, his brow furrowed as he appeared lost in thought. Emma Johnson had barely spoken a word while Brad seemed more intent on ingratiating himself with Margaret and Olga than concentrating on the tour. The two women weren't paying him much attention.

As they continued walking, Sarah tried not to eavesdrop, but occasionally she caught snippets of hushed conversations. Victoria and Stephen's seemed far from friendly.

"Your past is irrelevant on this trip, Vicky," Stephen hissed at one point, causing Sarah to glance over in concern.

"It's Victoria! And let's keep it that way," Victoria retorted, avoiding eye contact with anyone else in the group.

Sarah's headache continued to worsen as they approached the lido deck, where the lively sounds of laughter and splashing in the water greeted them. She paused momentarily, rubbing her temples, and took a deep breath before addressing the group again.

"Through those doors is our lido deck, complete with swimming pool, jacuzzi, children's pool, hot tubs, and plenty of sun loungers for relaxing." Her voice wavered slightly. "We also have a poolside bar and grill should you get hungry or thirsty."

"Marvellous," Victoria muttered under her breath, rolling the visible eye.

As Sarah opened the doors and they went outside, they were each given flower leis to wear around their necks. All but Victoria took one. She swatted hers away with a flick of the wrist.

Sarah stepped to one side while the crew welcomed the group to the Hawaiian-themed party. Leaning against a nearby wall and closing her eyes, praying that her headache would subside soon, she overheard another heated conversation between Victoria and Stephen.

"Listen, Stephen," Victoria said, her voice low and icy, "let's leave the past behind us and we'll get along just fine."

"That's okay with me," he snapped. "Don't worry, I won't bring it up, as long as you keep your end of the bargain." His voice was tense. "But don't forget, I'm not the only one who knows about your sordid history."

"Touché," she replied.

Once most of the group had their leis in place, they moved along the pool deck. The party was in full swing, with vibrant decorations, live music, and laughter filling the air. Despite her headache, Sarah smiled at the lively atmosphere.

"This way," she called to the group, leading them towards waiters carrying cocktail trays. She scanned the crowd for familiar faces and spotted Rachel and Marjorie near the edge of the pool, sipping tropical drinks decorated with tiny umbrellas. Sarah's heart lifted.

Chapter 4

The balmy evening air was filled with the scent from two large pot plants. Rachel moved in to savour the distinct fragrance from the flowers. The gentle breeze mixed the scents together, creating a delicate perfume.

"These flowers smell like jasmine, but it isn't jasmine," she remarked.

"That's plumeria," said Marjorie. "It grows everywhere in Hawaii. I believe it's known by another name here, but I can't remember what that is."

"Good evening, ladies." An officer gave them a welcoming smile while draping flower leis around their necks. The silky petals felt cool against Rachel's skin.

"Mahalo," Marjorie said, offering the young woman a warm smile before linking her arm through Rachel's.

Rachel had picked up a few Hawaiian words during the week and knew that *mahalo* meant thank you. Aloha was the widely used greeting for hello or goodbye, and also meant love.

Rachel and Marjorie strolled around the pool on deck fourteen where the party was in full swing, navigating their way through the lively crowd. Every so often, Marjorie exchanged pleasantries with fellow passengers. The sun had dipped below the horizon, and a smattering of stars shone like jewels in the navy-blue sky.

The lively and vibrant beat of percussion resounded in the night air. The music contained a hint of the exotic tropics. Rachel felt the energy reverberating through her feet and moved her head to the rhythm.

"It's a little loud for my taste, but the atmosphere here's quite marvellous," said Marjorie, her blue eyes shining.

Solar-powered torches, which glowed softly on bamboo poles, illuminated the deck, but most of the glow came from coloured disco lights flashing on the outdoor stage. Rachel enjoyed watching people dancing. Others, like her, moved to the beat while standing in groups, drinking cocktails and chattering happily. Both she and Marjorie had dressed for the occasion, with Rachel wearing a brightly patterned sundress while Marjorie's was billowy and floral.

As they mingled, Rachel's thoughts turned to Carlos. He would have changed flights by now and would be flying across the Atlantic towards home. She looked up at the sky.

"Is everything all right, dear?" Marjorie asked, arching a delicate eyebrow.

"I was just thinking of Carlos."

"Ah, when will he be home?" Marjorie squeezed her arm.

"Not until the early hours here; around 4am, I would have thought. He had a three-hour transit stop but should be well on the way by now."

"Have you ever seen so many people wearing grass skirts in one place?" Marjorie said.

Rachel chuckled despite the heart wrench she had just felt. "They look lovely, don't they?"

A group of men and women in front of the stage had begun a traditional Hawaiian hula dance, and the crowd surged forward to watch. Others watched from the deck above that overlooked the pool. Shaking off her mood, Rachel felt glad to be back on board the *Coral Queen* and she couldn't wait to see Sarah.

A waitress passed nearby with a tray of cocktails. Marjorie took two, handing one to Rachel.

"They're complimentary," she said, winking. "Savour it because, as you know, it will be the only free drink you enjoy this week."

Rachel took the Blue Hawaiian cocktail from her friend and sipped the tasty drink through a straw.

"Rachel, Marjorie!" Sarah's voice cut through the warm evening air. Rachel turned to see her best friend hurrying over with a group of people she recognised trailing behind.

Rachel beamed while they hugged. "Am I pleased to see you!"

"Oh, me too. We'll talk properly tomorrow. Jason and I have got tomorrow evening off. I'm on call tonight." Sarah released Rachel and leaned down to embrace Marjorie before stepping back.

Rachel looked at the nursing group that appeared to be popping up everywhere. They were standing behind Sarah, along with the group of four patients that included the aggressive woman from the hotel on Waikiki beach. She and an elderly man were in wheelchairs. The other two were ambulatory.

"I've just finished giving these passengers and their nurses a tour of the ship." Sarah inclined her head towards the group, smiling.

"And did you enjoy your tour?" Marjorie asked, scrutinising the group while Rachel scanned them with curiosity. The nurses, as had been the case the night before, were not in uniform, but the women were still wearing their hats and the male nurse his lanyard. Sarah wore her crisp white officer's uniform, which stood out against the backdrop of the colourful party attire.

"It's an enormous ship," replied the elderly man. In fact, three of the patients were elderly, although younger than Marjorie. The fourth was a man in his thirties with an arm in plaster protected by a sling. The stick-brandishing woman appeared to be recovering from eye surgery, as she had a pad over her right eye. A tall, skinny woman, carrying her own stick with more poise, had a familiar face.

Marjorie smiled at them before speaking to the man in the wheelchair. "Once you get your bearings, I'm sure you'll enjoy a wonderful holiday."

Sarah interjected, "These are my friends, Rachel Jacobi-Prince and Lady Marjorie Snellthorpe."

"Oh, please dispense with the lady bit. I'm Marjorie."

"Stephen Williams," the man replied. "That's Vicky," he nodded towards the angry woman.

"Victoria," she snapped, not acknowledging Rachel or Marjorie.

At that moment, Sarah's radio chimed into life. "Excuse me, I have to go back to work," she said, disappearing a little too hastily. Rachel didn't miss the fact she looked relieved to escape.

"Thanks for the tour," Stephen Williams called after her.

Rachel and Marjorie attempted to make polite conversation with the four guests, but it was all rather awkward. None of them, other than the man called Stephen, showed any inclination to engage. The female nurses' attention had shifted to a group of wealthy-looking men while the male nurse hopped from one foot to another as if he needed the toilet. He couldn't be more than twenty-three. Rachel suspected he was out of his comfort zone.

When the group finally moved away, Rachel and Marjorie sat in two vacated seats at a table.

"Thank goodness they've gone. Poor Sarah. Did you notice how delighted she was to be called away?" Marjorie remarked.

Rachel smiled. "I don't blame her. Apart from Stephen, it was like pulling teeth."

"And as for those two," Marjorie motioned her head towards two of the female nurses, "what a pair of flirts."

Stephen's nurse, wearing a yellow miniskirt and a tight-fitting red blouse, seemed to be getting rather too overfamiliar with a young male officer, who blushed several times. The other flirty one, who had wavy blonde hair, focussed on a trio of male passengers, dragging the third of the female nurses along with her. As Rachel observed the three nurses, the one in the yellow skirt and the blonde laughed loudly and batted their eyelashes at every opportunity.

"I get the impression the redhead's heart isn't in it," said Marjorie.

Rachel nodded. "You're right. She's playing along with the others, but she's more reserved, and the guy looks downright uncomfortable." Rachel had noticed the male nurse's eyes darting nervously around the deck.

"No wonder Sarah wasn't impressed with them," said Marjorie. "She's such a professional and their behaviour is the exact opposite. One expects decorum from medics when they are on duty."

"Perhaps their employers have given them leave to enjoy themselves," said Rachel. "The patients don't seem too bothered about it. With the amount of booze those two girls are consuming, I hope neither of their charges takes ill." Rachel watched as Stephen's nurse draped herself over yet another crew member's arm, giggling while sipping her cocktail.

"That might be the case, but it doesn't feel right," said Marjorie. "Thank heavens for the ship's medical team."

"Let's forget about them," Rachel suggested. She held her glass up. "Cheers, Marjorie."

"Cheers to you, too."

Rachel and Marjorie enjoyed their cocktails while the party buzzed around them. The scent from the plumeria mingled with perfumes worn by passengers and food from the grill. From her vantage point, Rachel watched as the woman called Victoria glared at Stephen's nurse flirting shamelessly with a crewman. Victoria's fists were clasped around her stick, her lips pressed into a thin line. Rachel hoped she would not give a repeat performance of the previous night.

"As we don't know their names, I think I'll call her Nurse 1," said Rachel.

"Who?" Marjorie looked confused.

"It must be the yellow skirt grabbing my attention. I mean the nurse who is supposed to be with Stephen. Victoria, the woman wearing the eye patch, isn't thrilled with her, that's for sure. Did I tell you she had a to-do with the head waiter at our hotel restaurant last night? I'd steer clear of that stick if I were you."

Marjorie's eyes widened. "Thank you for the warning, I will." Marjorie's gaze followed Rachel's. "And it appears she's not the only one getting fed up. Look at the young man wearing the plaster."

Rachel saw what Marjorie was referring to. The man with the plastered forearm shifted uncomfortably in his seat where he sat with the other patients. His eyes darted between the flirtatious nurses, a scowl fixed firmly on his face. As always when alcohol was involved, tension was escalating, and Rachel had to wonder what had made these passengers choose the nurses in the first place.

"They are a mismatched bunch, aren't they?" Marjorie said, her sharp eyes fixed on the group.

"I'll ask Sarah what she's found out about them," said Rachel.

"Excellent idea," Marjorie concurred, adjusting her lei. "It will be interesting to know what brought them together. However, I expect it will be nothing more than a group of highly paid nursing professionals taking advantage of an all-expenses-paid holiday."

Rachel relaxed. "I'm sure you're right." She forced her eyes away from the nurses and their patients and focussed on the lively party instead.

Marjorie leaned in close, her voice just audible above the hum of conversation and laughter. "It's just occurred to me. One of their patients is... or rather was... an actress."

"The tall, skinny one? I thought I recognised her," Rachel replied.

"Her name will come to me in a moment. The old brain doesn't function so well these days."

"You don't fool me. You're still as sharp as a razor, Marjorie Snellthorpe."

Marjorie's eyes crinkled as she gave a cheeky grin. "Perhaps, but there are advantages to being old. At my age, I can say what I want to and people can like it or not... I've got it! Emma Johnson, that's her name. She was in an American soap before getting a big break in Hollywood. If I remember correctly, she's a drinker and lives in chronic pain following an awful car accident. She's lucky to be alive."

"How do you know all this?" Rachel's eyes widened, impressed.

"Elsa, my housemaid, is a fan, and she reads everything she can about American celebrities. There was an article in one of those magazines that discusses celebrity gossip."

Rachel noticed Emma Johnson was sticking to bottled water. "Perhaps she's learned her lesson."

"I hope so. I fear it's taken its toll, though, hasn't it? She looks a lot older than she is."

"Which is?"

Marjorie shrugged. "How should I know? But not as old as she looks, of that I'm certain."

Rachel grinned. While she and Marjorie chatted, it reassured Rachel her friend was healthy in mind and body.

Out of the corner of her eye, Rachel spotted Stephen summoning Nurse 1 away from the crowded party. "I'll be back in a minute," she said to Marjorie, her curiosity piqued. She drew close to where Stephen and Nurse 1 were having an intense conversation, keeping a discreet distance between herself and them.

"Listen here, Maggie. I know what you've been up to, and it's got to stop," Stephen hissed, his voice strained. They had moved to a dimly lit area. "Do you think I'm blind? If you imagine I don't see the way you're trying to manipulate everyone around you, you're very much mistaken."

"Keep your voice down, Stephen, and I've told you before, my name's Margaret, not Maggie." The nurse's eyes darted around. "Anyway, I don't know what you're talking about."

"Like hell you don't," Stephen retorted, his anger rising. "You may have fooled some of these people, but not me.

You'd better watch your step, or I'll make sure everyone on this ship knows what you're up to."

Rachel's heart raced while she listened to the heated exchange, her gut screaming that it could be a catalyst for something more dangerous than just unprofessional behaviour. If Stephen was right, the nurse called Margaret had an agenda, but what was it?

She left the two of them to battle it out and returned to her seat. "I've just witnessed a confrontation between Nurse 1, who's name is Margaret, and Stephen. He accused her of being manipulative and threatened to expose her."

"Expose her for what?" Marjorie asked, concern etched on her face.

"He didn't go into details, and she denied any wrongdoing, but he sounded quite threatening."

"Oh dear," said Marjorie. "Let's hope it's just tittle-tattle and nothing more."

Rachel wasn't sure. She had observed a dangerous side to the otherwise amicable patient called Stephen. That said, he'd looked worn out when she left, gasping for breath, so she doubted he could do Margaret any physical harm. She decided to put the altercation to one side and enjoy the party until Marjorie called it a night.

"I'm afraid I must retire, Rachel," Marjorie said, stifling a yawn. "Do you mind?"

"Not at all. It's a wonderful party, but I'm happy to leave." Rachel gave her friend's arm a reassuring squeeze. "Come on. I'll walk you to your suite."

Chapter 5

After leaving Marjorie in her suite, Rachel found her mind was still too active to go to bed. She considered trying to track Sarah down.

"No. Sarah's on call, remember?" she told herself. Then she recalled the conversation with Kapena at Duke's, and his suggesting she look his sister Malia up. In need of the distraction, Rachel made her way to the Sky Bar. If Malia wasn't on duty, she would head down to the medical centre to see if any of the team were around.

Upon entering the dimly lit lounge, Rachel asked the man behind the bar if he knew anyone called Malia.

"She's just coming back now," he said.

An attractive young woman with jet-black hair and wide eyes, carrying a tray of empty glasses, moved behind the counter. She placed the glasses on a shelf where another bartender collected them. Rachel watched as Malia took an order and deftly mixed cocktails for a small group of passengers.

Once she'd finished serving them, Rachel took her opportunity. "Excuse me, I understand you're Malia," she said. "I'm Rachel. I met your brother while my husband and I were staying at the Waikiki Beach Resort. He suggested I say aloha."

Malia looked at Rachel, her eyes lighting up. "I saw Kapena this afternoon. Did he look after you during your stay?"

Rachel got the impression Malia was the older sister from the way she spoke. "He did, and he said you were an expert mixologist."

"Did he now? I suppose I'm okay." Rachel warmed to the open Malia. She was beautiful up close, yet unassuming. "Is this your first cruise, Rachel?"

"No. I've sailed on this ship many times. Sarah Bradshaw – I think she still goes by her maiden name at work – is a good friend. We grew up together."

Malia's wide smile could light up a room. "Sarah and Jason. Yes, she does still use Bradshaw for work. They are both very popular. Can I mix you a cocktail?"

"Yes please. Something fruity and non-alcoholic would be nice. I've already had two alcoholic cocktails." Settling onto a barstool, Rachel watched Malia work her magic. They chatted amiably for a while, sharing stories about their respective travels and experiences. Malia's laughter was infectious. It filled the air with a warmth that seemed to dispel the lingering unease that had settled over Rachel during the Hawaiian party.

Once she'd finished her drink, her thirst quenched, Rachel said goodnight before moving outside for some fresh air. Stepping out onto the deck, she inhaled a deep breath, enjoying the salty sea air filling her lungs. The moon cast a soft glow over the rippling water, its surface dotted with stars.

As she moved along the railing, something caught her eye. A white nurse's hat with a red cross lay crumpled and discarded in one of the drainage gulleys.

"How strange," she murmured, retrieving the hat and examining it. It was made of starched cotton and was definitely one of the hats worn by the private nurses earlier that evening. What was it doing here?

A shiver ran down her spine as she looked around, but she couldn't see anything in the immediate vicinity. Perhaps one of the flirty nurses had drunk too much and dropped it, or, more likely, lost it during a liaison. She would hand the hat in at guest services.

With the discarded nurse's hat in her hand, Rachel ventured further along the deck. The gentle lapping of waves against the ship's hull drowned the soft sound of her sandals on the floor. She tried to shake off the sudden chill that gripped her, despite the lingering warmth of the tropical evening.

Shaking her head for letting her imagination get the better of her, Rachel walked on. A cluster of sunbeds bathed in moonlight drew her attention, on one of them a flash of yellow. As she approached, her heart pounded in her chest. A figure lay face down on the lounger, motionless and eerily silent.

"Miss?" Rachel called. "Margaret?" she said tentatively, recognising the clothes the woman was wearing. Then Rachel raised her voice over the pounding of her heart. "Are you all right?"

When there was no response, she stepped closer, dread building in the pit of her stomach. She reached out a hand to touch the woman, realising with horror Margaret hadn't just passed out.

"No, this can't be happening," Rachel exhaled, her mind racing. Clutching the incriminating hat tighter, she went through the motions, checking for a pulse in the neck of the lifeless form.

"Rachel?" Malia's voice cut through the night. Concern was etched in her features as she hurried towards her. "What's wrong? What happened?"

"Call security," Rachel choked out, her gaze never leaving Margaret's still form. "And the medical team — quick!"

"What – oh," Malia gasped, following Rachel's line of sight. Without another word, she raced back inside the Sky Bar, shouting for help. As the urgent cries of staff echoed around her, Rachel forced herself to focus, her training kicking in. She noted the disarray around the sunbed. A faint scent of alcohol lingered in the air. There were finger marks on the back of Margaret's neck.

Dr Graham Bentley arrived first, soon followed by Sarah, who shot Rachel a concerned look. Dr Bentley examined the body briefly before shooing people back. Rachel was sitting on a nearby sunbed, scarcely able to believe what had happened, when Chief Security Officer Jack Waverley and Sarah's husband Jason Goodridge arrived.

"What happened here?" Waverley asked.

"Erm…" Dr Bentley steered Waverley to one side. "First impression is that someone strangled her. It's your scene for now. There's nothing I can do for her. I'll be able to tell you more once I get her downstairs."

"Who found her?"

Rachel felt Sarah and Dr Bentley's eyes swivel in her direction. Waverley's own eyes were wide when he cleared his throat.

"You can't be serious?"

Rachel held her palms out, helpless. "Sorry," she said. Feeling the chief's stress emanating from every pore and worrying about his blood pressure, Rachel put her head in her hands.

"Rachel's had a shock, Jack. I think we should let her get some rest," said Dr Bentley. "She can come down to the medical centre for a coffee while you start your preliminaries."

"Yes. You're quite right, Graham. Do we know who this young woman is?"

"Her name's Margaret Green," said Sarah. "She's one of four private nurses employed to accompany four passengers for the duration of the cruise. Her patient is called Stephen Williams. I gave them a tour of the ship earlier and can let you have the details when you've finished here."

"Were they travelling together?" Waverley asked.

"From what I could gather, the nurses knew each other, although the male nurse is new." Sarah's eyes filled with water threatening to spill over.

"Come on, Sarah. Best leave them to it," said Rachel, taking her friend's arm. She saw a brief look of concern cross Jason's face before Waverley called him back to the body.

"Find out if anyone saw her up here, Goodridge."

"Yes, sir."

"I'd better break the news to her patient," said Dr Bentley. "And find out whether he needs any help from us."

"Don't tell him how she died for now," said Waverley. "Just in case."

Dr Bentley exhaled a long breath. "Right. Would you like one of your team to accompany me?" Rachel got the impression the chief medical officer was being sarcastic, but Waverley took him at his word.

"Good idea. Goodridge, you go with Graham. I'll get Ravanos and Inglis to question people up here."

"Right, sir," said Jason.

"And get these people away from here. Unless any of them have anything to tell me, send them away."

Rachel thought poor Jason was in for a long night. The death, and the fact she found the body, had put Waverley in a foul mood.

The lights were on in the medical centre when Rachel and Sarah arrived. Bernard and Gwen Sumner were in the senior nurse's office.

"Words fail me," Gwen said on seeing Rachel.

"You can't talk, boss," said Bernard, giving Rachel a hug.

"Oh?" Rachel quizzed.

"We won't talk about that now, Bernard," warned Gwen. "Sarah, sit down. You look pale. I'll get Raggie to order something up from the kitchens. Bernard, get Sarah a strong coffee. What about you, Rachel?"

"The same, please," she said. "What are you both doing still on duty?"

"We're not, but we heard the alert and were on our way to the emergency when Graham called to tell us what happened and to stand down. Is he still up there?" Gwen asked.

"He's gone to let Stephen Williams know what happened and to see if he needs any medical help," said Sarah, trembling.

"What is it, Sarah?" Rachel asked as they all sat around a coffee table.

Sarah's eyes filled once more. "I... I... know... knew her brother."

"I'm so sorry, Sarah," said Gwen, patting her hand. "Did you know the dead woman?"

Sarah shook her head. "No. While I was giving them the tour, I heard her mention that her brother used to work on this ship and when I left them, I remembered. He still works for Queen Cruises, apparently. We erm... almost... well... we knew each other, but he was engaged."

Rachel felt her eyes widen. "You went out with him?"

"Almost, but your ex, Robert had not long done the dirty on you and I couldn't do the same to someone else. He left the ship on the day of your first cruise and the day Gwen joined us. Remember, Bernard?"

"Ah yes, I do. The engineer? You asked me to stay with you when he tried to get you alone."

"Have you kept in touch?" Gwen asked.

"No. It's just sad knowing he's going to get the call telling him his sister's been murdered, that's all. Who could do such a thing?"

Rachel's thoughts went back to the nurse's inappropriate behaviour earlier in the evening and the heated conversation she overheard. "I heard Stephen accusing her of being manipulative, and she was putting herself about a bit at the party," she said. "Sorry, Sarah."

"Don't be. I didn't warm to her, but that doesn't mean I'm not sorry she's dead."

Bernard tutted, shaking his head. "You've been on board this ship for two minutes, Rachel, and there's a murder. Plus, you have already discovered a motive."

"Not to mention it was me who found the poor woman," said Rachel, grimacing.

"I take it Marjorie doesn't know about any of this yet?" Gwen said.

"She went to bed," said Rachel. "I wasn't tired, so I went to the Sky Bar to introduce myself to someone."

They heard the door to the medical centre opening. Bernard got up to check who was coming.

"Looks like the chief released the body," he said, leaving the room. "This way, boys."

A few minutes later, Dr Bentley and Jason arrived. Gwen poured more coffee and Jason kissed Sarah's head before sitting down next to her. Gwen sat in another chair.

"That Stephen Williams is a cool customer; didn't bat an eyelid when we told him his nurse was dead."

"It could have been shock," said Dr Bentley. "Although I'd say he's got the skin of a rhino."

"Is he going to need anything from us?" Gwen asked.

"No. Seems he knows Mrs Hayes and says he's sure she'll share her nurse with him."

"The aggressive woman with the eye patch?" Rachel asked.

"Yes," explained Sarah. "Victoria Hayes. They seem to have a bristly relationship, but know each other well enough to be rude. She's a retired politician."

"What about him?" Rachel asked.

"I don't know. He was quite secretive and changed the subject whenever I asked."

"Shady then," said Jason.

"Or just private," said Gwen.

"Did you sense any friction between the group members earlier?" Jason asked.

Sarah finished her coffee before placing the cup down and rubbing her forehead. "To be honest, I had a headache and was pleased to get away from them, so it could have been me. I took a couple of painkillers after the tour."

"But?" Rachel coaxed.

"The nurses weren't that nice to each other, or to their employers, for that matter. Preston was okay, but quiet. He told me he was new. His client – Bradley Roberts, who likes to be called Brad – is some sort of businessperson from New York. He broke his arm skiing the week before the trip, which is how Preston got the job at short notice. Brad spent most of the time talking to Margaret and Olga. The latter is the actress's nurse. They ignored him at first, but then Olga kept making suggestive remarks to him, and to anyone else who would listen. I thought maybe they knew him, but they were the same with all the younger men. As I mentioned, Stephen Williams and Victoria Hayes have a weird relationship, but they are both in wheelchairs, so I can't see either of them being involved."

"Victoria and the man named Brad disapproved of Margaret's behaviour at the party," said Rachel. "And I overheard Stephen accusing her of something, but I agree with Sarah. He's too frail to have done her any damage."

"Well, I think that's enough for tonight," said Dr Bentley. "I've got the next of kin to inform and a body to examine. Gwen, can you help me? Bernard, there's a patient in 9624 needing these." He handed over a packet of tablets. "Sarah's done enough for now and she's still got a few more people to attend to."

"Hopefully we'll catch up tomorrow," Rachel said to Sarah as she stood up.

"The boss called and asked if you and I could meet him in the main ballroom around 10am, Rachel," said Jason. "There's a computer upgrade going on in his office and he's not sure what time it's going to be finished. He said to tell you to go to bed for now, and to stay out of the investigation. His words, not mine."

"Good to see you, Jason," Rachel smirked as she gave him a hug.

"Likewise, Rachel," he said. "See you later."

Chapter 6

Marjorie tossed and turned, struggling to fall asleep. The room was cool enough, but the air was dry and filled with the constant hum from the air conditioning. Wide awake, she glanced at the clock and saw that it was only just past midnight, yet she felt as if it was already morning and time to get up.

"Jet lag," she muttered to herself in frustration, finally throwing the covers off and switching on the overhead light. Ever since the flight to Los Angeles, she had struggled with this problem. Marjorie got out of bed, quickly dressed, and left the suite. The corridor was silent, except for the gentle sound from the waves lapping against the side of the ship and the quiet hum of the engines.

She made her way to the lifts, deciding to go in search of a nightcap. She could have had one from the minibar, but knew that the ship's bars were open most of the night. A walk coupled with a glass of brandy would help settle her before she got back to bed and into a deep slumber.

Once downstairs, Marjorie saw that the ship's bars were busy despite the time. She wandered around for a little while before entering a quieter bar where passengers like her were enjoying a nightcap. Some, she noticed, were drinking coffee liqueurs. Looking around for a seat, Marjorie spotted the actress, Emma Johnson, sitting alone in a corner, so she headed in that direction.

"Hello," she said.

Emma shot her a wary stare, not replying but giving a sort of nod.

"I think I saw you earlier with a friend of mine, Sarah?"

"Oh, yes. She showed us around the ship." Emma appeared to relax a little.

"I couldn't sleep… jet lag," said Marjorie. "It's late morning where I come from and despite a few nights in Los Angeles, my body wants to go back to it. My circadian rhythm is still on London time and refuses to acknowledge that it should sleep right now."

Emma half-smiled and shook her head. "Mine neither, but it's nothing to do with jet lag. Darned pain in my back gives me hell. I had a car accident a while back, which has left me a virtual cripple."

"Sorry to hear that," said Marjorie, thinking Emma looked far from what she described, but perhaps her disability was more internal. "I'm Marjorie. Do you mind if I join you?"

"Go ahead," said Emma, gesturing to the chair opposite. "I'm Emma."

Marjorie smiled, holding out her hand. Emma reached out and shook it. Marjorie noted the softness of Emma's hand before the other woman snatched it back.

"Thank you," she said, taking the seat. Emma was drinking a mug of hot chocolate. Marjorie wondered if she should settle for the same, bearing in mind the article Elsa had shown her about the woman's alcohol problems. Marjorie didn't want to put temptation in Emma's way if she was trying to abstain.

She decided when the waiter arrived.

"What can I get you, ma'am?"

"Something to help me sleep, please," she said.

The waiter smiled. "Alcoholic or non-alcoholic?"

"A hot chocolate will do nicely."

"Who are you travelling with?" Emma asked roughly after the waiter walked back to the bar.

Marjorie resisted the temptation to remind Emma that they had been introduced earlier. Instead, she replied, "A young friend called Rachel. She's Sarah's best friend... they grew up together in a small English village. We met when she was on her first cruise." Marjorie thought back to the cruise when her life had been in danger and recalled how Rachel had stepped in to protect her. They had been firm friends ever since. "I look upon her as the granddaughter I never had. My son doesn't have children."

"Children are overrated," Emma said, a bitter tone entering her voice. "I've got two boys and don't see them from one year to the next."

"I'm sorry to hear that," said Marjorie, noticing Emma's expression. Her face clouded over and her lips tightened when she spoke of her family. "What about your husband?"

"Divorced," she answered, eyes cold and sharp when she lifted her head to look at Marjorie. "He's better off without me. I was never the marrying kind, but, hey…"

"I expect your work took up a lot of time."

"Yeah, it did. Thanks for not asking for an autograph. I get sick of people harking on about how good I was. *Was* meaning has-been." It was impossible to miss the resentment and underlying anger in Emma's tone.

"It can be hard to accept retirement," Marjorie said.

Emma shook her head. "Especially when it's forced upon you by some stupid accident."

Marjorie wanted to probe further but resisted. She didn't want to pry into a personal matter that was obviously painful and was pleased when the smiling waiter returned with her drink. She might need that brandy when she got back to her room. Thank heavens for the minibar.

"Have you cruised before?"

"Surprisingly not," Emma said. "This is one gigantic vessel."

"Yes, it is. I only ever cruise on the *Coral Queen*. Apart from a few river cruises, that is. What made you decide to try cruising out now?"

Emma looked away for a moment before speaking. "I guess I just wanted to get away from everything. My agent told me about this cruise, so I thought why not? It seemed like an opportunity to try something new, or at least try to forget some things. So here I am... setting sail for fresh adventures."

Marjorie nodded at Emma's explanation and smiled before taking a sip of her hot chocolate. The warmth of the drink settled in her stomach and gave her a sense of peace.

"Where are your friends?"

"Who? Oh... you mean the people I came aboard with? I wouldn't call them friends. We meet up from time to time, but this is our first vacation as a group. When I mentioned it to them, they decided it would be fun to combine forces. The young guy, Brad, I don't know him at all."

"How did you meet the others?" asked Marjorie, intrigued.

"We share the same physical therapist. He recommended some joint outings, and they pass the time.

Although I don't go out with them that often. I prefer to stay home these days."

And wallow, no doubt, thought Marjorie, but said, "Still, it's good to have company when travelling. Is your nurse permanent?"

"Sort of, but only for the past few months. We got them from the same agency. It's the first time I've met the others."

Marjorie had to force the image of nurses sitting on a shelf ready to be picked like a new handbag out of her head, otherwise she would have burst out laughing. "It must help with them being employed by the same place. I suppose the nurses know each other well."

"Yeah, I guess they do." Emma shrugged. She seemed disinterested in talking about her employee, so Marjorie tried a different topic.

"You must have met some famous people in your time. I'm not really up on the who's who of this world, but I remember seeing a photo of you with that actor. What's his name? Brett something…"

Emma smiled at the memory and nodded. "Brett Matthews. We starred in a few films together. He's down-to-earth despite his fame. We keep in touch, but he and his wife moved to California, so it's just the odd phone call nowadays…"

The ensuing silence gave the impression Emma didn't wish to dwell on her former life or celebrity acquaintances, so Marjorie asked, "Are your travelling companions famous?"

"Stephen and Victoria?" Emma spluttered what was supposed to be a laugh, but turned into a coughing fit. Marjorie wondered if she might need to call for help when the other woman's colour turned bright red. A few people turned their heads towards the choking sounds.

"Are you all right?"

Emma held a hand out. "I'm fine. Just a spasm. I get them now and then."

Relieved when Emma's colour returned to normal, Marjorie felt sorry for the woman. Emma must be twenty or more years her junior, but far less fit.

"Should I ask the waiter to bring some water?"

"Thanks."

Marjorie called the waiter who had brought her drink and asked him to bring a bottle of mineral water for Emma. When he returned, she thanked him, noting Emma didn't.

"Is your nurse still around?"

"Olga? Who knows? The four of them are most likely partying the night away. It's what I'd do if I was their age. Anyway, I gave her the night off once she'd sorted out my meds. I expect she thinks I'm in bed."

"Yes, I expect Rachel thinks the same about me."

"You were asking about my travelling companions. As I mentioned, Brad I don't know, but Stephen is rich – not famous, but rich. He's got property on Caribbean islands, but he's coy about what he did exactly. He's not modest, so I assume he made his fortune in ways he'd rather not mention."

"Unless he was born into money," said Marjorie.

"Nope, that much I know," said Emma, her voice cutting through the air like a knife. "Victoria's unique. She was a senator and retired when she lost her place. I know little more about her than I do about Stephen, to be honest, but then again, who cares? We're all has-beens with money."

"That's rather a sad way to look at things," said Marjorie.

"Realistic, I call it," Emma snapped. "What about you? I take it you don't consider yourself one of us?"

"I certainly don't consider myself a has-been," replied Marjorie with conviction. "My life, while not exciting, is satisfying, although I miss my late husband. I try not to dwell on the past."

"Me neither. Too many memories of what I can no longer do," said Emma. "You must feel the same sometimes."

"Perhaps," said Marjorie. She didn't know how else to react, so opted to finish her hot chocolate. "Well, I think it's time to get back to bed and see if I can sleep."

"Good luck," said Emma.

"Thank you. It's been nice speaking with you. Goodnight. I hope you enjoy your cruise."

"Yeah, you too."

Marjorie left her rather bitter companion to herself, imagining it must be a sad world of thoughts Emma would return to.

But for the grace of God, she thought as she entered the lift.

Chapter 7

The morning sun bathed the *Coral Queen*'s main restaurant in a golden glow as Rachel and Marjorie settled into their chairs next to a window. Rachel had been up for hours, having gone for an early morning run after receiving a text from Carlos letting her know he was home, long before getting ready to meet Marjorie. She had already taken in the breathtaking view of Lahaina harbour and spent some time transfixed by the azure waters. The harbour was dotted with sleek yachts, their sails swaying in a light breeze. It would have been the perfect backdrop for a leisurely breakfast had Rachel not got the weight of what had happened the night before pressing down on her. She was working up to breaking the news to Marjorie.

"Isn't this marvellous?" Marjorie remarked, her bright blue eyes twinkling with delight as she gazed out. "Ralph and I never made it to exotic places like this, although we travelled a lot. A sight like this could almost make one forget time."

Rachel gave her dear friend a wry smile. "I suppose there are worse places to be," she agreed, reaching for the pot of freshly brewed coffee once the waiter had left with their breakfast requests. As she poured the steaming liquid into her cup, and filled another cup with tea for Marjorie, she readied herself for the conversation to come.

Waiting until after their breakfasts had arrived, Rachel broke the comfortable silence. "Marjorie, there's something I need to tell you."

"That sounds ominous," said Marjorie.

"After you went to bed last night, I wasn't tired, so I went to the Sky Bar to meet the sister of a waiter who had looked after me and Carlos when we were staying at the Outrigger resort."

"Don't tell me: she's another private nurse with a difficult patient?"

"Be serious, Marjorie!" Rachel grinned. "Actually, Malia's a nice person – not that the nurses aren't. Anyway, she's a mixologist in the Sky Bar, and just as friendly as her brother. But after I left the bar and went outside, things got complicated. It all started when I found a nurse's hat."

"Belonging to one of the flirtatious four, I suppose?"

"Great name, Marjorie," said Rachel, "although the guy didn't seem at all flirtatious, nor did he have a hat, and one of the girls wasn't as bad as the others. Maybe the teasing two. Anyway, back to last night. I felt it odd, finding the hat in a gulley like that, so I had a look around. That's when I discovered Margaret Green."

"Go on," said Marjorie.

Rachel looked into her friend's blue eyes. "She was face down on a sun lounger."

Marjorie's eyes widened as she placed her fork down. "Good grief! Are you telling me she's dead?"

Rachel nodded. "I'm afraid so."

"How?"

"I don't have all the details yet." Rachel looked around to check they weren't being overheard, took a large mouthful of coffee and lowered her voice. "Dr Bentley's first impression – and mine, judging by the fact she had finger marks at the back of her neck – was that someone strangled her."

"My goodness," said Marjorie, her brow furrowing. "She wasn't the most dedicated nurse I'd ever laid eyes on, but it's dreadful to think that one so full of life is so soon afterwards… well… dead."

Rachel sighed before taking a large spoonful of fresh fruit and placing it in her mouth. "There's more," she said after swallowing the fruit. "We… well… I've been summoned to meet Waverley in the large ballroom at ten."

"And how did His Lordship take this development?" Marjorie asked, her grin wide.

Rachel chuckled at Marjorie's nickname for the long-suffering chief of security. "Well, let's just say it was a shock. He was horrified it was me who found her."

"I bet he was," said Marjorie, still grinning. "Does he have any suspects?"

"That's what I'm hoping to find out. There's the argument with Stephen hours before Margaret's death, which I'm assuming Jason's told Waverley about by now. Not that I can see Stephen being capable of the crime. I take it you'll be joining me for the meeting?"

"Try to keep me away." Marjorie had the mischievous glint in her eye that Rachel loved and feared in equal measure.

"For now, we assume that the person who killed her is one of the other nurses, or one of their patients," said Rachel.

"The woman was such a flirt, which complicates matters. There was hardly a single man she didn't fraternise with at the party, from what I could see, so maybe there's a spurned suitor out there who killed her when things got out of hand."

"Or a vengeful enemy among her company."

"Exactly," Marjorie agreed, taking a sip of tea. "Well," her face was etched with determination, "no-one is better suited to finding a killer than the two of us."

Rachel swallowed a lump in her throat. That was just the reaction she had been dreading.

***

The large ballroom was filled with the scent of fresh polish, a pleasant combination of lemon and wood. It was empty except for Rachel and Marjorie. Rachel remembered a cruise where she had danced with Carlos on the shiny floor, which was surrounded by lush carpet and tiers of table seating. A stage was at the far end and the room had four separate entrances.

After waiting and looking around for ten minutes, she was impatient to get this meeting over with.

"Here they are at last," Marjorie murmured.

Rachel spotted Waverley, Jason and Sarah weaving their way through the tables towards them. She tensed, having forgotten to mention to Marjorie Sarah's previous connection to the deceased's brother and how upset she had been. Rachel hoped Sarah was okay, feeling a knot tighten in her stomach.

"Rachel, Lady Marjorie," Waverley's greeting was gruff but respectful.

Jason gave Rachel a nod and leaned down to kiss Marjorie on the cheek. "Nice to see you, Lady Marjorie."

"Likewise, Jason," Marjorie said. "I'm pleased someone has remembered to bring their manners." She trained her piercing eyes on Waverley, who seemed uncomfortable at the scrutiny.

He coughed before speaking. "Erm, my apologies for being late. It's good to see you again, Lady Marjorie, even if the circumstances are far from ideal."

Marjorie shot Rachel a triumphant look, and Rachel hoped this wouldn't become a sparring match. Waverley and Marjorie didn't always hit it off.

"Let's get down to business, shall we?" Waverley suggested. He looked at Rachel expectantly. "Can you fill us in on what happened last night?"

"Throughout the evening, or just when I found the body?"

Waverley checked his watch. "I was hoping to keep this short."

Marjorie shifted in her seat. Waverley's haste sometimes led him down the wrong path and often riled her into being short with him.

"I'll give you a summary of the evening, as some of it might be relevant," said Rachel. "Marjorie and I attended the Hawaiian-themed sail-away party where we observed the now dead nurse, Margaret Green, flirting with several men, including some of the ship's officers."

Waverley glowered at Jason as if that fact were somehow his fault. "Yes, we've gathered that piece of information."

"Marjorie and I also picked up on some tension within her group. Sarah mentioned it too, as she'd given them a tour of the ship before they came to the party."

Waverley nodded. "Yes, Sarah's told us."

Rachel continued, "One of the other female nurses played along with the flirting, although she seemed less comfortable with it. The actress's nurse followed Margaret's example. We noticed two patients, or clients, I'm not sure what they call them, weren't at all happy with the behaviour."

"Neither should they be," Waverley snapped. "Could you move on to what you were doing in the Sky Bar?"

Marjorie let out a harrumph, causing Waverley to rub a hand through his thinning hair.

"I'd like to mention a rather smarmy-looking man I saw hanging around," Marjorie said, "but it might not be relevant."

"Hanging around in what way?" Jason asked.

"He seemed interested in Margaret, that's all. She flirted with him in the same way she had done with every other red-blooded male, but he left before she did."

Waverley cleared his throat again, trying not to look irritated that this new knowledge was unrelated to his question. "Thank you. Now, Rachel, perhaps you could take us through what happened later."

Rachel nodded, noticing Sarah's face was pale. "Right. After seeing Marjorie to her room, I went to the Sky Bar to see if Malia was on duty and to introduce myself. She's the sister of someone Carlos and I met in Waikiki. We had a chat, and then I left the bar and went outside. It was a lovely evening."

Waverley sighed. Patience wasn't his strong suit.

"Something white caught my eye. There was a nurse's hat in one of the drainage gulleys. It rang alarm bells."

"Why?" Waverley asked.

"Because the female nurses had all been wearing starched cotton hats, and it was made of the same material. They wouldn't just leave them lying around. The thought crossed my mind, of course, that one of the nurses could have been very drunk and dropped it while with a man."

Waverley's face flushed. He wasn't programmed to discuss such things with younger women, but he said, "Which could still be true."

"Yes, it could," said Rachel. "I'd sort of come to that conclusion, but had a mooch around anyway. That's when I saw the body."

"Did you move her?"

"You know me better than that, Chief. I checked for a pulse and asked Malia to call you and the medical team."

"Malia? I thought you said you left her in the bar."

"I did, but she must have seen me when she came outside."

"Follow that up, Goodridge," the chief commanded.

"I assume Dr Bentley has examined her?" Rachel said.

"He has, and Margaret Green's body has been transferred back to Honolulu for a postmortem," Sarah explained, her voice catching slightly. "But he's certain someone strangled her. Her next of kin have been informed." Sarah's eyes filled as they had done the night before. Marjorie opened her mouth to say something, but Rachel gave her a shake of the head. Jason placed a comforting arm around Sarah.

"So, it seems as soon as you're on board, Rachel, we have another murder on our hands," said Waverley.

"I hardly think the two are related, Chief," said Marjorie.

Waverley looked less convinced. "I suppose not."

"We need to find out more about Margaret's movements before her death. Her relationships on board and whether anyone in her travel party might have wanted her dead," said Marjorie.

"Unfortunately, the murder took place during a busy time on the ship," Waverley replied, frustration clear. "No-one saw anything definitive…" he hesitated, then snapped, "What do you mean, we? There will be no *we*. My team is working on it, Lady Marjorie."

"I know you're not keen on us poking our noses into your investigations, Chief, but you know we can help," Marjorie said, fixing him with a determined stare. "We will, of course, be discreet, I promise."

"I suppose if I forbid it, you'll ignore me and go ahead anyway," Waverley said, his eyes switching to Rachel.

During this exchange, she had kept her eyes on Sarah, who remained sad.

"We can get alongside people in ways you can't," she replied. "And I did find the body."

"Fine," Waverley snapped. Clearing his throat, he rubbed his forehead. "But remember to keep me informed. This ship is my jurisdiction, and I am responsible for the safety of everyone on board the *Coral Queen*. Including you two." His pitch rose a decibel or two.

Rachel smiled, a glint in her eye. "We could never forget that."

"Rachel, it might be better if you didn't get involved," Sarah said, her eyes motioning a warning look towards Marjorie. Sarah was rightly concerned; Marjorie shouldn't put herself in danger with her advancing years.

"I tell you what," said Rachel, her eyes sharpening as she refocussed on the task at hand. "I promise we'll be ultra-cautious and stay on the fringes. But we can start by talking to the people who knew the dead woman best – her colleagues and their patients."

"We need to find out who did this, not just for Margaret, but for her family." Sarah's voice cracked, making Rachel more determined than ever. Marjorie looked questioningly towards Sarah, but Rachel again shook her head, warning her to say nothing.

"If we find anything, we'll be in touch," said Rachel.

"In the meantime, Rachel and I need to go ashore and sample this beautiful island," said Marjorie.

With the meeting drawn to a close, the security team left. Sarah gave Rachel a brief hug, and they parted outside the ballroom.

"What have you got in mind?" Rachel turned her attention to Marjorie.

"I saw they were selling tickets for a glass-bottomed boat excursion. I might be a little old for scuba diving, but that should fit the bill. Unless, of course, you would like to go scuba diving or surfing?"

Rachel took Marjorie's arm in hers. "A glass-bottomed boat sounds perfect."

Chapter 8

Light flickered off the water as Rachel and Marjorie stepped onto the glass-bottomed boat: a canopied catamaran with seats all around a viewing window.

"How wonderful!" Marjorie exclaimed as they boarded the vessel, her eyes shining. Once they were on board and seated, she added, "Look at the kaleidoscope of colours."

Rachel grinned, finding her friend's enthusiasm contagious. "It's beautiful," she said, her eyes feasting on the clear turquoise waters beneath the glass. She was enjoying herself until a loud, complaining voice dragged her attention away.

"Hurry up, will you? Can't you see I'm unsteady?"

Rachel's eyes turned towards the hullabaloo. "It looks like we've got company."

"So it would appear," said Marjorie, frowning.

Preston and another of the private nurses, the one who had seemed uncomfortable with the flirting the previous night, were coming aboard with their charges, Victoria and Brad. The oldest nurse of the original quartet, who appeared to be around forty, was trying to push a wheelchair containing the angry woman up the ramp. Preston and Brad walked on behind them.

"Victoria Hayes is a retired politician, and the male nurse is called Preston. Sarah says he's new and was taken on after his charge, Brad, broke a wrist last week."

"He looks new, doesn't he? Not at all confident. I know a little about Victoria," said Marjorie.

Rachel looked at her in surprise.

"There has been little opportunity to tell you, but I couldn't sleep last night. I'm still suffering from jet lag, so I went downstairs hoping the walk and a nightcap would tire me out. Emma Johnson was sitting alone in a bar and we chatted for a while. A more bitter woman it would be hard to find, but I suppose she feels she's been dealt a bad hand in life."

"What time was that?"

"It must have been around half-past twelve by the time I got dressed and made it to the bar, perhaps later. I wasn't wearing a watch."

Rachel mulled the new information over. "And Emma mentioned Victoria?"

"She's an ex-senator. I started the conversation, asking how well Emma knew her travelling companions and whether they were famous like her. She was rather derisive about Stephen and not much kinder about Victoria. They met after sharing a physiotherapist – she called him a physical therapist, I assume that's an American term for the same thing."

"Why was she down on Stephen?"

"Probably not posh enough for her, although he's rich; they all are. Of course, I didn't realise then we had an investigation on our hands, otherwise I would have been more probing."

Rachel smiled. "Why is Emma so bitter?"

"I didn't pry, but I expect it's the accident. She mentioned back pain keeping her awake and being forced to give up acting. She's also divorced and doesn't see her children, so that might have something to do with it."

"You seem to have unveiled an awful lot in a short space of time, even without knowing you were involved in an investigation." Rachel threw her head back and laughed.

Marjorie tittered. "I was just being polite, but she wasn't the nicest person to spend time with and I missed out on my nightcap."

"How so?"

"Well, as you know, I'd read about her having a drink problem, and she was drinking hot chocolate, so I didn't want to cause her to stumble."

"That's kind of you, Marjorie. Not that her companions, or the nurses, had any such consideration," Rachel murmured, her thoughts returning to the dead Margaret Green.

"You haven't told me why Sarah seemed so upset."

"Margaret Green's the sister of someone who used to work on the ship. Sarah knew him. Apparently, he left on the day you and I first met, but he still works for the cruise line. You know how sensitive she is. She's feeling for him, that's all."

"Mm," said Marjorie. "From the way she looked, I take it he's an old flame."

"An almost, but not quite," said Rachel.

As the boat began its journey, she and Marjorie listened to the commentary from the captain as he pointed out turtles and other marine life along the way. After he cut the boat's engines to allow the passengers to photograph and observe the creatures swimming beneath them, Rachel was soon mesmerised by the turtles and brightly coloured tropical fish.

"The reef is spectacular. Oh look! Eels." Marjorie's joy matched Rachel's own. She had scuba-dived off Waikiki beach, but had been too busy concentrating on how to breathe underwater to take much notice of the marine life.

After spending fifteen minutes enjoying the spectacle beneath them, Rachel nudged Marjorie. She motioned to where Preston and the other nurse were standing near the railing at the bow of the ship.

"Let's stretch our legs," she said.

"Good afternoon," said Marjorie, smiling as they approached the pair.

Rachel, too, offered a warm smile. "We met briefly at the party last night. My friend Sarah's a nurse on board the *Coral Queen*. I'm Rachel and this is Marjorie."

Preston said hello, but seemed nervous, while the other nurse nodded a greeting.

"It's a lovely day for a smaller boat trip, isn't it?" Rachel persevered.

"Sure is," the woman said.

Marjorie held out her hand. The woman took it.

"I'm Amelia. This is Preston. We rarely get the chance for outings like this, so we're making the most of it."

"Where are your charges?" Marjorie enquired, her sharp eyes scanning the deck.

"Victoria's over there." Amelia motioned to the miserable-looking woman. Wearing a dowdy brown dress and hat, she was holding onto a rail. Her wheelchair must have been parked elsewhere. "And I think Brad went to take photos from the back of the boat."

"Such important work you do," Marjorie said, earning grateful nods from the two nurses. "I imagine it must be challenging, especially when you have to deal with unexpected situations."

Amelia looked confused.

"We heard about your friend's death," Rachel explained, watching their reactions closely. "It must have been a shock."

The nurses exchanged an uneasy glance, and Amelia's voice wavered as she spoke. "Yeah, it was. I still can't believe it. Margaret was such a friendly person."

"We noticed," Marjorie muttered under her breath. Rachel gave her a warning look.

"Did you know each other well?" Rachel asked, holding Amelia's eyes.

"Only professionally. Although we socialised sometimes, and we accompanied the clients on the odd outings together." Amelia looked out over the water, deep in thought before adding, "Preston's new, but I'm told he got to know Margaret fast enough."

Preston fidgeted with his collar, his forehead sweating slightly. Rachel wondered if there might have been something going on between him and Margaret.

"Not really," he shook his head. "She was like that with everybody."

"Like what?" Marjorie enquired.

Preston's hands shook as he looked down at them. "Margaret could be a flirt. We all like to have a good time, though. You're only young once, so why not?"

"Awful that she was murdered, though," said Rachel. "Who do you think would want to do something like that?"

"Beats me. Margaret was friendly with everyone." Amelia fidgeted with the hem of her blouse. "Maybe she got overfriendly with the wrong person. I still can't imagine why anyone would do something so terrible."

"A treacherous flirtation indeed if it got her killed," Marjorie suggested.

Amelia's eyes darted around. Perhaps she was worried about Victoria, Rachel thought. Preston continued to avoid eye contact with either her or Marjorie.

"Will her death affect your cruise?" Rachel asked, exchanging a glance with Marjorie.

"No. Victoria's asked me to help with Stephen – he was Margaret's patient. To be honest, neither of them needs a lot of caring for. Stephen just needs heart meds and regular blood pressure checks, and Victoria can look after herself, mostly. I just have to change the bandage around her eye once a day. The ship's medical team could handle it, but you know – when you're rich, you don't want to stand in line. She keeps me on the payroll for that reason." There was no hint of resentment in Amelia's tone, and her eyes displayed kindness. Rachel couldn't quite work her out.

Marjorie's eyes were alight with curiosity. Rachel knew they were both thinking the same thing: there was more to Margaret's story than Amelia was letting on.

The engines of the boat fired into life again. "We'd better get back to where we were sitting. Enjoy the rest of your day," Rachel said, offering another warm smile as they walked away.

When they returned to their seats, Marjorie leaned closer to Rachel, her voice low. "What do you think?"

Rachel scrunched her eyes. "It seems everyone witnessed her flirting, but something about Margaret isn't adding up. Why the argument with Stephen? And did she have a fling with the new guy, Preston?" Rachel's mind was processing what they had gathered so far. "We need to keep digging."

"I agree," said Marjorie. "It looks as though we're heading back into harbour. Such a shame we didn't get to speak to Victoria and Brad. We should try later."

"Discreetly, of course," Rachel said, acutely aware of Waverley's warning. "We don't want to attract too much attention or risk undermining the chief's investigation. And be careful, Marjorie, you're sounding like a detective."

"Maybe I've learned a thing or two from you," Marjorie retorted, her eyes twinkling.

"Or perhaps you've had a few adventures of your own," Rachel replied, laughing. She knew full well that Marjorie had solved a murder or two on her own, with a little help from three of her friends.

The boat bumped up against the dock, and Rachel watched the faces of the nurses and their two patients as they disembarked. Victoria walked up the steps before getting back into her wheelchair, which was guided off via a makeshift ramp. She had swapped the bulkier electric one from the previous day for a self-propelled, or rather push-along one.

"Rachel," Marjorie said, nudging her gently with her elbow. "You're miles away."

"Sorry, I was thinking."

"You needn't tell me what about, but it's time to leave."

They were the last two on the boat and more people were queuing up to board for the next trip.

Marjorie teetered to one side after stepping onto the dock. Fear shot through Rachel as she reached out and steadied her with a gentle hand at her elbow.

"What is it?"

"It's nothing, dear. I lost my footing, that's all. Now, I think it's time to plan our next move."

"And I think it's time to find a café and get some fluids inside you," said Rachel. Although Marjorie was sensibly wearing a hat which kept the afternoon sun off her face, her skin was clammy.

"You're right, I could do with a refreshing drink."

Rachel led the way, casting anxious sideways glances towards Marjorie, checking she had fully recovered from whatever had happened. Relief shot through her when it appeared that she had. She scanned the waterside. There was a plethora of places serving refreshments, and the smell of smoked meat wafted through the air. Soft music and the sound of clinking cups, laughter, and conversations lifted her mood.

"That place looks nice," she said. "And there's shade."

Leading her friend to available seats at a table beneath a canopy that covered an outdoor café with a bar, Rachel realised how hungry she was. Perhaps that was what was wrong with Marjorie. They had skipped lunch because they were late leaving the ship after the meeting with Waverley. Rachel was used to missing meals, but she doubted the same applied to her friend. She kicked herself inwardly, vowing not to let it happen again.

"Do you mind if we order food?" Marjorie asked.

"I was just thinking the same thing," Rachel replied. "It's later than I thought."

After perusing the menu, Marjorie opted for a Hawaiian pizza and Rachel chose a salad with organic spinach.

"I'd like to try a mango black iced tea, please," Marjorie added.

"Good choice," the waiter replied.

"Organic lemonade for me," said Rachel.

The two of them sat back, relaxing and enjoying the fresh breeze. Once they had eaten, Marjorie perked up.

"I needed that," she said. "But it's time to return to the matter at hand."

"There's no stopping you, is there?" Rachel grinned before taking a sip of her iced lemonade.

"Having spoken to Amelia and Preston, I think we can rule him out," Marjorie said.

Rachel nodded. "He's the newbie among them, so I guess you're right, but we don't know enough about her."

"And his patient is also a 'newbie'."

"Although, in retrospect, there's no guarantee the murderer isn't also new. Amelia implied Margaret had flirted with Preston, and I'd be surprised if she didn't make a play for Brad. I'm guessing her more serious flirtations were reserved for men with money."

"Does that mean we're excluding the women?"

"Nope. Until we know the motive, we can't rule any of them out. Our next step is to discover where each of them was around the time of the murder. Hopefully Waverley will be on that. Did you notice whether they were still at the party when we left?"

"I can't say I did. It was so crowded, I was feeling claustrophobic, if I'm honest. What about you?"

Rachel cast her mind back to the party. "I'd lost interest by then. There's only so much time you can waste watching attention seekers."

"Quite right. Let's hope His Lordship has got that information. Are we certain it was one of their party that did the deed?" Marjorie asked.

"We can't jump to conclusions, but it makes more sense than there being a random strangler on board the *Coral Queen*. That said, we need to remain open-minded."

It was late afternoon by the time they strolled back towards the *Coral Queen*.

"Will Sarah be joining us this evening?" Marjorie asked.

"Yes. She was on-call last night, so she and Jason – unless Waverley's cancelled his leave – are taking us out for dinner."

"I love it when a ship docks for an overnight stay," said Marjorie. "It's a wonderful opportunity to explore the nightlife."

As long as it doesn't end in murder, thought Rachel.

Chapter 9

Sarah stomped into the main atrium, red-faced. Her strides were long and determined as she headed towards Rachel and Marjorie. Rachel noticed her eyes were blazing.

"Uh-oh. No Jason," Rachel muttered to Marjorie.

"Good evening, dear," Marjorie said, smiling at Sarah.

"Hello, Marjorie. Waverley's cancelled Jason's night off. Can you believe it?" Sarah threw her handbag onto a chair and plonked herself down after it. Recalling how many times she was called in to attend murder scenes, Rachel could well believe it, but she wasn't going to try reasoning with her friend when she was in this state. Marjorie, however, didn't appear to have the same reservations.

"I suspect it's all hands on deck when there's a murder investigation, if you'll pardon the pun."

Sarah glared at Marjorie, biting her bottom lip – a stress habit she had exhibited ever since Rachel had known her.

"Would you rather cancel?" Rachel offered, hoping it would do the trick.

Sarah let out a heavy sigh. "No, of course not. I'm disappointed because Jason hardly ever gets any time off." Tears threatened.

"I'm sure a little fresh air will do you the world of good," said Marjorie.

"In that case, come on, you two. I'm starving," said Rachel.

A short walk later, the warmth of the tropical air enveloped them when they sat at a beachside table. The sun dipped low in the sky, casting a golden hue over the sand. The rhythmic tunes from the bar added to the pleasant atmosphere.

After enjoying a hearty meal, they sipped cocktails garnished with vibrant umbrellas and pineapple wedges. Sarah was more relaxed.

"I love Hawaii," she said, closing her eyes and breathing deeply.

"It's quite beautiful," Marjorie agreed.

Rachel loved that despite her age, Marjorie had lost none of her zest for life and adventure. She nodded, taking in the peaceful scene. It was a welcome respite, however brief, from the chaos of what had occurred the previous night.

"This is just what we needed," she said, her voice soft.

"You'd better find this murderer soon, Rachel, because I want my husband back."

"I didn't like to ask earlier, but are they getting anywhere?" Rachel asked.

Sarah gave a sheepish grin. "Jason says I can be pretty scary when I'm in a mood," she said, laughing. "I don't think they've got very far. Malia had just finished her shift when she saw you, Rachel, so at least she's in the clear. Other than their occupations and medical conditions, there's not a lot of information about the passengers travelling with Margaret or her nurse friends. Waverley's requested police checks on all of them, but these things take time. Stephen Williams was flagged, but I don't know what that means and Jason didn't have time to explain."

"It might mean he's been arrested him for something in the past," said Rachel. "Its relevance depends whether it was for a major or a minor felony, as they call crime in America. I know you mentioned there was some friction, but what else did you make of them when you showed them around the ship?"

Sarah's forehead wrinkled as she bit her lip. "I didn't like them if I'm honest. Apart from Preston, he's the odd one out."

"He does appear to be out of his depth," said Marjorie.

"I warmed to him because he's so new. He only qualified a couple of years ago. He's fresh, you know?"

"We met him and Amelia on our outing earlier and chatted a bit. Amelia suggested Margaret had been flirting with Preston last night."

"Along with everyone else," Sarah said. "Jason's got a long list of men she – and the other woman, Olga – were throwing themselves at."

"Just as we suspected," said Rachel. "We've got to find out more about Margaret as a person. I'm sure the security team will gather as much information as they can on that front. Meanwhile, we keep quizzing people in her party. We'll eventually uncover inconsistencies in their stories and unearth the killer."

"Unless it's someone from outside her party," said Sarah. "Waverley's leaning that way."

Rachel glared out to sea. "We've considered it, but that's a one in a million." Her angry gaze drifted along the shoreline. It was then that she noticed Brad, his tall figure silhouetted against the setting sun as he strolled at the water's edge. From where she was sitting, he appeared deep in thought, unaware of being observed.

"There's Brad," Rachel murmured. "Quick, Sarah, you know him best. Get him over here."

Sarah did as asked. "Good evening, Brad," she called, waving him over.

Brad lifted his head, turning it in their direction. "Hi there."

"Would you like to join us?" Sarah asked, her voice friendly yet insistent, leaving little room for refusal.

"Thanks, Sarah. Don't mind if I do." He came over but remained standing. "I didn't get the chance to thank you for the tour last night. You were called away."

"It was a pleasure. These are my friends, Rachel Jacobi-Prince, and Lady Marjorie Snellthorpe," she said.

Brad greeted them with a nod.

"It's just Marjorie," said Marjorie.

"What a lovely evening," Brad said.

"Are you out on your own?" Sarah asked.

"Yeah, I left the rest of 'em in a bar further down the beach."

"Sometimes it's good to have a little solitude," Marjorie said, her eyes scrutinising the younger man.

"Take a seat," Rachel gestured towards the empty chair beside her. Brad hesitated for a moment, his eyes flicking between the three women before finally settling on Rachel. He sat down.

"Thanks."

"Is your nurse Preston with the others?" Sarah asked.

"I guess so."

"What about your arm?" she persisted.

Brad's right hand moved to his left arm. He was wearing the sling again this evening. "I said I'd be careful." He grinned. "I like my space."

As the sun continued its descent on the horizon, it cast an ever-deepening shade of orange on the beach. Rachel found it hard to imagine that fewer than twenty-four hours ago, a vibrant young woman who was now dead was still so full of life.

Brad raised his hand to the bar and a young woman wearing a brightly coloured dress appeared. "Can I buy you ladies a drink?" he asked.

"What do you recommend?" Marjorie asked the young woman.

"Hawaiian Margarita is our speciality, but we also have the classic Mai Tai or Blue Hawaiian," she replied.

With Rachel, Marjorie, and Brad settling for the margaritas, Sarah opted for the Blue Hawaiian. Brad was handsome enough, but his manner was all too unnatural for Rachel's taste.

"Thanks for the drink." Rachel held hers up.

"Cheers," said Marjorie, holding hers up too, and they all joined in.

"The sea can be so calming, can't it?" Rachel mused, her eyes drawn to the horizon where the sky met the ocean. "There's something about its vastness and depth that makes problems seem insignificant."

"I suppose," said Brad, his eyes lingering on Rachel for a moment too long before he turned to the others. "So what do you think of the cruise so far?"

"Rachel and I went on the glass-bottomed boat tour you were on today. We had a brief chat with Preston," Marjorie replied, expertly steering the conversation towards more serious matters. "It was quite fascinating."

Brad laughed nervously. "The conversation with Preston?"

Marjorie grinned. "As interesting as the young man appears to be, I was referring to the life underwater."

"We were just discussing the nurse who died, Margaret Green," said Rachel. "Sarah was on-call last night. Such a tragedy."

Brad's hand reached for his plastered arm again. "Terrible," he said.

"You knew her, didn't you?" Rachel prompted.

"Not well," Brad said, his expression clouding. "We met the night before the cruise. She seemed... nice."

"Nice? You must have formed more of an impression than that, surely?" Marjorie interjected.

"Not really," he shrugged.

Marjorie continued her look of disbelief.

"All right... I suppose she struck me as ambitious, someone who knew what she wanted and how to get it," Brad conceded, casting a wary glance at Marjorie. "But we barely spoke."

"Ambition can be a double-edged sword," Marjorie said.

Rachel added, her eyes fixed on Brad, "Sometimes it can even lead to a person's demise."

Brad shifted uncomfortably in his seat, his eyes darting between the three women as if trying to gauge their intentions. "All a bit too deep for me, ladies," he said, taking a drink from his glass.

"Tell me, Brad," Marjorie continued, her voice casual, "what do you think of the rest of your party?"

"They seem okay. They're a lot older than me. Victoria and Stephen can be a handful," Brad said, seeming relieved to shift the focus away from Margaret. "Victoria is... well... she's quite a character. She used to be some bigwig politician in New York and she's got a bit of a temper, according to Preston. He got that from her nurse, Amelia and I saw a bit of it myself on the outing today."

"I admit to noticing a surly demeanour," said Rachel with a chuckle. "What about Stephen? Do you have much of an impression of him?"

"He seems like a decent enough fella," Brad said, hesitating slightly. "But there's something about his relationship with Victoria that feels a bit off. They have a tense dynamic. I don't know why."

"In what way?" Sarah asked.

The waves lapped at the shore, soothing Rachel's jumbled thoughts. Brad broke into her reverie, answering Sarah's question.

"I overheard a strange conversation between them."

Rachel's eyes snapped back his way.

He looked around the bar, lowering his voice. "I wasn't trying to eavesdrop or anything, but I was standing nearby when Stephen told Victoria that Margaret had been stealing from him. He was none too happy about it."

"Stealing?" Marjorie repeated, eyebrows raised.

"Did he say what or why?" Rachel asked.

Brad shook his head. "I didn't want to get caught listening, and I like to stay out of other people's business, so I didn't hang around."

"You're right not to," Rachel said, sensing a veiled warning. "But I guess now that one of your company has been murdered, you might pay a bit more attention to such things, if only to pass it on to the ship's security team."

"That's a good point. It might be relevant, I guess. I'll tell them what I heard if they ask."

"As my husband is one of the security team, I can assure you, they will ask," said Sarah.

For the first time since joining them, Brad seemed taken aback. His cheeks flushed slightly, and he glanced out to sea before saying, "Sorry, I didn't mean to sound flippant. It's upsetting what happened to Margaret, but I'm on vacation and I could really use the break. Business has been brutal of late."

"What is it you do?" Rachel asked.

"I work on Wall Street," Brad replied, still looking uncomfortable.

"Stressful and hard work, I should imagine. Perhaps we should ease up on the questions," Marjorie suggested. "After all, Rachel and I are on holiday, too."

"Of course. Sorry if it sounded like an interrogation," Rachel said, although her mind continued to whirl with theories. "It's not every day one hears about a murder. If we weren't Sarah's friends, we wouldn't have any idea what had happened. I expect the rest of the passengers are blissfully unaware." Rachel didn't want any of the Margaret Green party to know it was she who found the body, or what she did for a living. At least not until the time was right.

"No worries," Brad said, relaxing. "I suppose I'd better go find Preston before he sends a search party after me." Brad left the table, his figure receding until he was out of sight.

"What did you make of that?" Sarah asked.

"The thieving could provide Stephen with a motive and that might have been what he was meaning when he had a go at Margaret during the party. We need to speak to him." Rachel swirled the ice in her glass, deep in thought.

Sarah yawned. "Time for me to call it a night, if you don't mind?"

"Not at all," said Marjorie. "I've had quite enough excitement for one day. Rachel and I will resume our enquiries tomorrow."

Rachel admired Marjorie's determination, but felt responsible for keeping her safe because her enthusiasm could lead her into dangerous situations. As they stood up to leave, a cool breeze swept in from the beach, ruffling her hair. She watched Marjorie strolling ahead, holding Sarah's arm. The thought of harm coming to either of them sent chills down Rachel's spine. It was important she and Marjorie kept to their tourist roles, so the killer didn't see them as a threat.

Chapter 10

Rachel jogged around deck sixteen, her ear pod pumping a steady stream of music into her right ear. The ship had left in the early hours and was now heading towards their next stop. Even with the music, she could make out the distant hum of sound coming from the island they were heading towards.

Several other early-morning runners appeared, and Rachel smiled or waved as their paths crossed. There was a sense of camaraderie, being part of an unwritten society with others who got up and started the day early. The run was shaking away the exhaustion weighing on her eyelids from lack of sleep.

Rachel reached the end of her run and stopped to take in the morning's beauty. Looking out on the calm waters of the Pacific, she smiled to herself, feeling a swell of happiness. It was a privilege to be experiencing paradise.

As she moved down to the deck below, Rachel looked over the inner rail. In her mind was the grim reminder of a young woman's lost life, which shattered her euphoria. Rachel observed Stephen Williams steering his electric wheelchair towards the buffet. Inhaling a deep breath, she headed down the steps. Her shower would have to wait.

On entering the bustling buffet, already busy with people helping themselves from the many offerings on display, Rachel looked around. The smell of freshly baked bread and pastries permeated the air.

"Good morning," she called, approaching Stephen.

"Oh, hello. You were with that posh woman, Marjorie, the other night, weren't you? Sorry, I don't remember your name," Stephen replied, his face lighting up in recognition.

"Yes. Sarah, who gave you the tour, is a friend of ours. The name's Rachel."

"Stephen Williams at your service." Stephen looked rather flustered, attempting to balance a plate on a tray while manoeuvring his wheelchair.

"Can I give you a hand?" she asked, nodding toward his precarious tray.

"Would you? I'd appreciate it." His relief was palpable. "I was gonna call one of the staff, but they seem busy."

Rachel took the tray from him and piled an assortment of breakfast items onto a plate at his request. Scrambled eggs, sausages, bacon, and hash browns.

"Now all we need to do is find you a table," she said.

"Over there by the window," he instructed.

Rachel placed the laden tray down and moved a chair away to make room for his wheelchair.

"Nothing like starting the day with a hearty meal," he said, chuckling at the mountain of food before him. "It's one of the few pleasures I have left, considering my age and condition. Would you like to join me?"

"Thank you, I'll get some food and will be back in a minute," said Rachel. She returned to the buffet to gather a couple of slices of toast and a bowl of fruit before returning to join Stephen, who was tucking into his hot food.

"One of them waiters asked if I wanted a hot drink. I had you down as a coffee woman." He pointed to the mug of strong coffee opposite him. "Was I right?"

"Spot on," she replied, placing her bowl and plate on the table.

"That's good because my doctor told me to steer clear of the stuff. Bad for the heart."

Rachel watched him shovel a rasher of greasy bacon into his mouth, certain the breakfast wouldn't be on his doctor's prescription either.

"Have you been to Hawaii before?" she asked, casting an appreciative glance at the sparkling ocean beyond the glass.

"Can't say I have. I've been to the Caribbean many times, but not the Pacific. Funny how we tend to go to the same places. I've still got a place in Jamaica, but don't get there too often these days. I should sell it, but the sea has always had a certain allure for me."

"Me too," Rachel admitted. "There's something calming about it."

"And I'm a Pisces, the fish," Stephen murmured, his eyes locked on the endless expanse of blue. "I'm loving this part of the world now I'm here, though."

"I saw you admiring the views during the Hawaiian-themed party the other night," Rachel said.

"Ah, yes," Stephen replied, a nostalgic smile on his face. "Now I spend most of my time in this contraption, there's not much else to do other than admire. It was a pleasant party. I've always been a partygoer, though I'm not as spry as I once was."

"Marjorie was saying something similar, but she does well," Rachel said with a chuckle.

"I didn't like to ask how old she was, but I'm guessing she's older than me and a lot fitter."

Rachel smiled, feeling it would be impertinent to ask him how old he was.

Stephen paused in between mouthfuls to look at Rachel. "I'm guessing you heard what happened to my nurse?"

She nodded. "Sarah mentioned it. It must have been a dreadful shock."

"Silly girl just didn't know when to stop," Stephen said, resuming his breakfast and taking a mouthful of scrambled egg. "Though I must admit, I wasn't expecting anything like that to happen to the woman."

Rachel feigned surprise. "What makes you say she didn't know when to stop?"

Stephen hesitated for a moment, his eyes glancing around before settling back on Rachel. "Well," he began slowly, "to be honest, our relationship had become… strained. I told the security guy yesterday she was never around when I needed her."

"Where was she?" Rachel asked, although she suspected she knew the answer, having seen Margaret's behaviour over two nights.

"You see," Stephen continued, a look of distaste crossing his features, "I had my suspicions about her. She always seemed to be looking for ways to ingratiate herself with my friends, and with the opposite sex, particularly those who appeared well-off."

"Are you suggesting that's what she might have been doing the other night?"

"Maybe. I'd been thinking of giving her the sack, to be honest." Stephen dropped his voice to a whisper. "She'd been helping herself to stuff for a while, but on the day we boarded, I found her rummaging through my belongings while I was resting. When I confronted her, she brushed it off as a misunderstanding and claimed she was looking for my pills."

"You didn't believe her?" Rachel said.

"Initially I did," Stephen sighed. "But later, I discovered some money and a few of my valuables were missing. I never reported it because I'm not that type and I didn't have any concrete evidence. Besides, I didn't want to cause a scene on the cruise, but I warned her I knew what she was up to and figured she'd behave for a while."

"Understandable," Rachel nodded sympathetically. "Do you think she might have been planning something else? Perhaps trying to steal from your friends?"

"Maybe," Stephen conceded, a flash of anger flickering in his eyes. "She was up to no good. But alas, we will never know what she was truly after. My guess is she flirted once too often and chose the wrong guy to go with."

"Let's hope the security team gets to know the truth about what happened."

"I'm guessing the guy has cut and run by now," Stephen said. "That's what I'd have done in his shoes."

"What makes you so certain a man killed her?"

Stephen wiped his mouth with a napkin before making a start on a glass of water. "Now you mention it, I'm not, but it just seems the most likely scenario, and I think that's where the security chief's head is at."

Rachel hid her exasperation at Waverley's habit of not only jumping to conclusions, but also sharing them. Instead, she asked, "Is there anything else you can think of that might explain what happened?"

"There was something," Stephen said, a thoughtful expression crossing his face. "I heard Margaret on the phone the night of the party. She sounded agitated."

"Oh?" Rachel leaned in closer, her curiosity piqued.

"It was while I was watching the hula dancing. She was standing by the rail speaking to someone – a man, I assumed by the tone of her voice."

"Any idea who?" Rachel asked.

"No," Stephen admitted, his brow furrowing. "But I heard her tell this mysterious person to stop following her around and that he should move on. I assumed it was an old flame calling up."

This was an interesting development. Who could this man be? Was it mere coincidence she was having an argument with someone, or was this person involved in her murder?

"Did you see Margaret leave the party that night?"

He scrunched his eyes, causing bushy eyebrows to meet in the middle, while contemplating her question. "No, I didn't. When I looked around for her to tell her I'd had enough and was going to bed, she had already disappeared. I assumed she was off with some man." He scowled, clearly annoyed by the memory. "She should have waited to see if I needed help. I am... was... paying her, after all. I guess she was annoyed because I challenged her, plus she'd had a fair bit to drink that night."

"How are you coping without a nurse?"

"I've persuaded Vicky to share her nurse, Amelia, with me," Stephen replied with a touch of pride. "It's not ideal, but it'll do for the time being. I just need someone to remind me to take the darned heart pills, that's all. Vicky won't admit it, but she and I go back aways."

"At least you've got help. What was it you did for a living? I think you mentioned you were a successful businessman?"

Stephen's eyes lit up at the opportunity to boast about his accomplishments. "Why, yes, I was. I built my company from nothing, you know. Started with just a small loan and turned it into a multimillion-dollar empire. None of these Harvard business degrees for me. I got through using my wits."

Rachel listened, noting the way he carefully avoided mentioning any specifics about his business. She wondered what secrets might be hidden beneath his interpretation of 'wits' and whether they could have any bearing on Margaret's murder. The dead woman may have been more like him than he was prepared to admit, and also might have known things he would prefer to keep hidden. Particularly if she made a habit of rooting through his belongings.

"That's impressive," she said. "Success doesn't come easy. I'm guessing you make it sound easier than it was."

"You're bright, Rachel, and you're right; it wasn't simple," he agreed, puffing out his chest a little. "But I believe in hard work and determination. It served me well over the years."

"Is that how you know Victoria? From your work?" Rachel asked, her thoughts already racing ahead. If Stephen had been involved in any dubious business practices, could that have made him a target for Margaret's scheming? And if so, would he have had a motive to silence her permanently?

"Something like that," Stephen said, lowering his voice conspiratorially. "We crossed paths back when she was running for the senate. She wasn't above... bending the rules, shall we say, to get what she wanted back then, although you wouldn't believe it now she takes the moral high ground."

Rachel raised an eyebrow, filing each snippet of information away in her mind before finishing her breakfast and polishing off the coffee.

"I'd better find Marjorie before she gets worried about me. Can I get you anything else before I go?"

"No thanks, Rachel. It's been nice talking to you. But you've chosen the right time to disappear before the force that's Vicky Hayes comes along."

Rachel heard a motor heading their way and turned to see the angry woman driving like a maniac through the narrow gaps between the tables. A man leapt out of the way before she ran over his foot, cursing under his breath. Amelia trailed behind like a scolded puppy. The imbalance of power between the two women was painfully apparent, and Rachel felt a pang of sympathy for the kind-hearted nurse.

"Ah, here they are," Stephen said in a louder voice.

"I'll see you around," said Rachel, making a hasty retreat towards the exit.

Chapter 11

The *Coral Queen* docked at Hilo, the capital of the Big Island, at precisely 10am. Sarah glanced through her balcony doors while donning her day uniform, feeling the same excitement she always did when the ship was in port. She thought of the passengers who would be eager to get ashore to explore the island. She too wanted to enjoy the day, as it was usually quieter, with a lighter load in the medical centre, on land days. The nursing and medical staff took turns to take shore leave, and today it was Gwen's turn.

Checking her uniform, she looked in the mirror. She was ready to start her shift, but first she needed to find Jason. He wasn't in their room when she got back after her night out, and had phoned late to tell her he was working an impromptu night shift.

"Sometimes I think you love your job more than me," she had teased him. He had replied that she was the one who had been out painting the town red while he was working.

Sarah was still annoyed with Waverley, but recognised she was being unreasonable. Her heart clenched with worry when she recalled Jason's tired voice. He should have been back by now. On her way to the medical centre, Sarah stopped by the security hub to see if he was there.

"Morning, Sarah," called Ravanos, one of Jason's colleagues. His cheerful demeanour was in stark contrast to her growing concern.

"Good morning, Ravanos," she replied, forcing a smile. "Have you seen Jason? He hasn't been back to our room yet."

"Yes," Ravanos said, scratching his head. "He handed over to me at eight. Looked like he could use some sleep, but he mentioned he wanted to check in with the chief before finishing. I assume it was about the dead woman."

"Thanks," she said, feeling a mix of relief and frustration. Her shift would start soon, and she still hadn't spoken to her husband. What was taking him so long?

As she walked towards Waverley's office, Sarah thought about how much she hated violence – it seemed to follow Jason and Rachel wherever they went. And now, with yet another murder on board the ship, Sarah longed to spend a quiet day off together with her husband. She knew that wouldn't be possible until they solved this latest crime.

"Jason must be exhausted," she muttered as she stepped onto deck three. "I'll just make sure he's okay, then I can focus on my work."

Good luck with that, her inner voice chided, knowing all too well her tendency to worry about him. Sarah cared about those around her, and that was especially true for her stubborn workaholic husband.

Approaching Waverley's door, Sarah caught sight of the security chief through his window. He seemed engaged in a serious conversation on the phone. The tension in his expression was obvious, even at this distance. She hesitated for a moment, wondering whether to interrupt or wait for him to finish.

Sarah peered through the office window, but on seeing no sign of her husband, she decided against knocking on Waverley's door. Instead, she opted to head back up to their stateroom.

"Knowing our luck, we've just missed each other," she muttered under her breath. Sarah checked the time and realised she couldn't afford to dawdle; her shift would start soon, and she had to be on time.

The lifts were bustling with passengers eager to explore Hilo, with queues snaking around the corner. Sarah had little choice but to take the stairs. As she ascended, her thoughts drifted back to Jason and the recent events on board. It seemed like everyone around her was being drawn into the chaos. Even when they were out last night, she could sense Rachel and Marjorie's cogs turning, made even more evident by Rachel's enthusiasm to speak to Brad. It was all Sarah could do to keep her focus on her own work.

"Jason is all right," she whispered to herself, her heart pounding as much from worry as exertion. She reached deck six and gasped for breath, cursing her lack of fitness. The huge steak she'd consumed the night before weighed heavily on her stomach, but Rachel had encouraged her, knowing it would cheer her up. At the time, it had done the job.

Sarah paused to lean against a wall and closed her eyes, trying to regulate her breathing. *If only I were a fitness fanatic like Rachel,* she thought ruefully. As she stood there, catching her breath, contemplating her next move, an uneasy feeling crept over her. *What if Jason's in trouble? What if he needs my help?* Shaking the troublesome thoughts from her mind, Sarah straightened up and set off up the stairs again, determined to find her husband before starting work.

Sarah felt the muscles in her legs burning when she reached deck seven, so she took another moment to lean against the wall, panting. It was quiet around the lifts on this deck. Most passengers would either be having a late breakfast in the buffet or heading ashore.

"Right, Sarah," she told herself between breaths, "time to give up and wait for the lift. You can do this." She stood up straight and pressed the call button, hoping it would arrive soon.

While waiting, she heard frantic footsteps running down the corridor. Sarah turned to find out what the commotion was all about, and saw Michael, one of the stateroom attendants, racing towards the phone. He stopped when he saw her with a panicked expression on his face.

"Nurse Sarah! Thank God, the lady, she's losing consciousness!" He grabbed her arm. "Quickly," he said, pulling her back the way he'd come. He let go of her and raced ahead.

"Slow down, Michael," Sarah called, her legs feeling like lead as she tried to keep up with him. "What happened?"

"I don't know. I just found her like this," he replied, pushing open the door to reveal a woman slumped in a chair.

Without hesitation, Sarah stepped into the dimly lit stateroom, quickly taking in the scene. It was dark apart from a bedside lamp. She spotted diabetic equipment on the nearby table as she moved inside.

"Michael, open those curtains. I need more light!" she commanded, her voice firm and steady despite her racing heart.

As Michael did as requested, sunlight flooded the room, illuminating the woman's pale and clammy face. Sarah recognised her and saw the beads of sweat on her forehead. That and her pallor were telltale signs of dangerously high or low blood sugar.

"Blast," she muttered under her breath, trying to stay calm as adrenaline coursed through her veins. With a sinking feeling, she attended to Emma Johnson, the retired Hollywood actress, while glancing around the room. Empty whisky bottles were scattered across the floor, furniture was on its side and the contents of Emma's dressing table were everywhere – the remnants of what looked like quite a bender. The alcohol would only worsen Emma's diabetic condition, making it even more urgent to act quickly.

"Emma, can you hear me?" Sarah said, shaking the woman gently. No response. She grabbed the glucose monitor from its pouch on the dressing table and checked Emma's blood sugar level. As she suspected, it was dangerously low. Sarah wasted no time in removing the glucose gel from the equipment pouch and rubbing it vigorously into Emma's gums. "Hang in there, Emma," she whispered.

"Severe hypo attack, room 7360, send medical team!" Sarah spoke urgently into her radio, her fingers trembling slightly from the adrenaline surge.

Moments later, she heard the coded announcement, "Situation Alpha. Alpha team to 7360. Repeat: situation Alpha. Alpha team to 7360," being broadcast over the ship's internal loudspeakers.

Janet Plover, the Welsh junior doctor, arrived within minutes, panting from the sprint. "Blimey! What happened?" she quizzed, taking in the stateroom's disarray.

"This is Emma Johnson, a diabetic who's hypoglycaemic. I'm assuming an alcohol binge exacerbated it," Sarah replied tersely, her focus still on Emma. "I've given her some buccal glucose gel, but we should start an IV."

"Right," Janet nodded, grabbing supplies from her bag. "Let's open those balcony doors too, shall we? It reeks in here."

Michael did as requested. The two women were working together to set up the intravenous infusion and administer glucose when Bernard burst into the room.

"Got your message. How's our patient?"

"Stable for now, but I think it would be safer to move her to the infirmary until she's recovered," Janet said, wiping sweat from her brow.

"I'll get a stretcher," Bernard vanished for a while, returning with a mobile stretcher. Together, they transferred the now semi-conscious Emma onto the stretcher, securing her for the journey down to the infirmary.

"Do you mind taking things from here?" Sarah asked, her voice wavering slightly. "I need to speak to Jason before my shift starts."

"Of course," Janet replied, giving Sarah a reassuring pat on the shoulder. "Go on, love. We've got this."

"Thanks," Sarah said, managing a weak smile as she watched them go.

With the medical team gone, Sarah turned to Michael. His eyes were still wide and filled with concern, a reflection of how she herself felt.

"Thanks, Michael; your quick action prevented that passenger from going into a coma. How did you know I was on the floor?"

"I didn't, but I couldn't use the phone in here." He walked across the room and held up a severed phone cable. "Plus, she's cracked the sink."

"Oh, my goodness! I assume you'll let maintenance know," she said.

"My assistant has already done so."

"Have you seen Emma Johnson's nurse, Olga?"

"Olga?" He shook his head, glancing around the dishevelled room. "No, I haven't seen her. I've been too busy cleaning staterooms."

Sarah noticed his tired eyes lingering on the empty whisky bottles and the various items strewn about the room.

"I guess I'd better let you get on," she said, stepping out of the room so he could get to work. She had every sympathy for Michael having to clear up that mess. The state of the room was appalling, and cleaning it would be difficult. No doubt someone would have a firm word with Emma about the damage she'd caused, adding a threat of repercussions if it happened again. She hoped Michael would receive an extra-special tip at the end of the cruise to make up for it.

As much as Sarah wanted to find Jason, the clock was ticking, and morning surgery loomed ever closer. Her heart ached at the thought of not seeing him before starting her day, but duty called. She fired off another text to see if he would answer.

"Jason," she whispered to herself, "where are you?" As she made her way along the corridor, she felt the weight of what had just happened pressing on her shoulders.

Sarah's thoughts were interrupted when she caught sight of a familiar figure emerging from a stateroom further along the corridor. Emma's nurse was about to turn in the opposite direction.

Sarah quickened her pace, calling out, "Olga! I need to tell you something. It's about Emma."

Olga's head swivelled, her eyes startled. When Sarah reached her, she noticed Olga had come out of Margaret's room – the room Waverley hadn't wanted to tape off for fear of alarming the passengers. Warning bells rang in her mind, but she tried to keep her tone casual.

"Isn't that Margaret Green's room? What were you doing in there?"

"Hi, Sarah," Olga replied coolly, brushing back a strand of blonde hair. "I loaned Margaret a necklace for the party the other night. Now that she's... well... gone, I didn't see the harm in retrieving it."

Sarah eyed Olga sceptically, wondering if she was telling the truth. How had Olga got hold of a key card for the dead woman's room in the first place? But she didn't have time to cross-examine her. Besides, Olga's excuse was feasible.

"Right," she said, "but I don't think the security chief would be pleased about you going in there, so I wouldn't do it again. If you give me the key, I'll let my husband have it. I may have mentioned he works on the security team."

"Sure," Olga replied, an enigmatic smile playing at her lips, but she made no effort to hand over the key. Sarah held out her hand, forcing the woman to give it to her.

"Where did you get this?"

"Stephen had one," Olga said, shrugging her shoulders as if that explained everything. "You said you had something to tell me." Olga examined her manicured fingernails, as if doing so dismissed any further conversation about her intrusion into a murdered woman's room.

"Yes. Emma took ill this morning. From the looks of things, she had a lot to drink last night and her blood sugar dropped. We've admitted her to the infirmary until she's fully recovered."

Olga rolled her eyes. "It had to happen sooner or later, I suppose, but she's been doing so well. Preston and I are going ashore today. Brad's given him the day off and Emma said she wanted to stay on board. I guess she'll have to now anyway. I'd better get ready. If I get time, I'll pop down to the infirmary before I leave."

Don't strain yourself, thought Sarah. She was about to suggest that under the circumstances, the nurse should reconsider her outing, but she realised there would be no point. The woman standing in front of her hadn't an ounce of compassion or commitment, as far as she could tell. Emma was better off without her.

"See you down there then," she said, and walked away.

When Sarah got to the lift, the phone in her pocket buzzed. Her heart leapt when she read the text:

Sorry I missed you. Going to bed for a few hours. Let's catch up later. Love you.

A wave of relief washed over her, and she allowed herself a small smile while tapping out a reply. At least one worry could be put to rest.

Chapter 12

"Please sign this health declaration form, ma'am," the attendant at Hilo Airport said with a smile, handing Marjorie a clipboard. Marjorie's forehead creased when she read the form before looking up to give the woman a withering stare.

"I can assure you I will not keel over during the flight."

Rachel tried to suppress a giggle while Marjorie begrudgingly signed the form. It was a disclaimer and medical declaration, confirming she had no heart conditions that a helicopter ride might make worse.

After handing back the clipboard, Marjorie whispered to Rachel, "My doctor keeps prescribing me blood pressure tablets, but I rarely take them. I find the more one stays away from a doctor's surgery, the healthier one becomes."

Rachel chuckled. "You'd better not mention that to Sarah. Now, come on. Let's enjoy the tour." It wasn't long before they were climbing into a bright white helicopter. Once they were safely buckled in, the rotors began to spin and the aircraft lifted off the ground.

"Look at that!" Marjorie exclaimed, pointing out of the window as the aircraft gained altitude. A gorgeous landscape stretched below them: a breathtaking mixture of lush native forests and jagged black rock formations. Rachel's excitement grew, and for a short time, she could forget about Margaret Green's murder, putting aside the conundrum of who killed the nurse.

"Dad would love this. Wait until I tell him we flew over actual volcanoes," Rachel said.

Marjorie nodded, her face lit up with childlike wonder. "It's incredible, isn't it? To think of all that power lurking beneath the surface. People can be like volcanoes." Marjorie looked down at the red lava channels snaking through the terrain, adding, "Sometimes calm and unassuming, but then erupting with surprising ferocity."

"Wow! Poetic, Marjorie, but very true," Rachel agreed. She felt a twinge of sadness as her thoughts drifted back to her day job and the dark depths some people sank to.

"Sorry, I didn't mean to ruin the moment. We can worry about everything else later," Marjorie said, giving Rachel's hand a reassuring squeeze. Rachel nodded, and they continued to marvel at the awe-inspiring landscape below.

"Over there," Naomi, their pilot, broke through Rachel's thoughts, pointing to the right, "that's the Little Kilauea Crater. It's one of the youngest and most famous craters in the National Park. It last erupted in 1959, creating a massive lava lake. The main summit caldera of Kilauea, though, is the most active volcano in the world and is constantly erupting. There's no current activity."

"How remarkable," said Marjorie, her eyes scanning the vast expanse of blackened rock below them.

"Incredible," Rachel agreed. Her pulse quickened as she ran out of superlatives, imagining the destructive force that could be unleashed from the depths. She'd only ever seen erupting volcanoes on the news or in films.

Naomi continued with her commentary about the park's history, geology, and its unique flora and fauna. The beauty and terror below them fascinated Rachel. The lush forests and the vibrant colours of the endemic plants clinging to the volcanic mountainsides impressed her. It made her wonder how they grew in such harsh conditions.

"Thank you, Naomi, for sharing your impressive knowledge with us," Marjorie said as the helicopter began its descent. "This has been an extraordinary excursion, and one I'll remember for a long time."

"It's been a pleasure having you both on board," Naomi replied.

"And please tell that woman at the desk I'm still alive and kicking," Marjorie added. Rachel and Naomi laughed.

When they touched down at the landing pad, Rachel spotted the nurse, Olga, with Preston. They were deep in conversation, but the body language was tense.

"Look," Rachel whispered, nodding in their direction while helping Marjorie climb out of the helicopter.

"That's Emma Johnson's nurse, Olga, the one Sarah mentioned last night and the mild-mannered young Preston." Marjorie's eyes scrunched while she studied them. "They look rather serious."

"I can't hear what they're saying, but I can bet they're not discussing the views," said Rachel.

"Indeed, no."

Marjorie and Rachel thanked Naomi again and moved away to allow her to get ready for the next tour. Rachel shot another look towards Olga and Preston.

"Olga seems rather bossy," said Marjorie.

Rachel studied the nurse as her hand gestures grew more animated. "And Preston looks like he'd rather be somewhere else."

"Whatever she's saying to him, he doesn't like it."

Rachel agreed. Preston was clenching his jaw and turning away from Olga. The helicopter pilot called the pair over, bringing an end to the intense conversation. Rachel and Marjorie got into the car that would return them to where they had been picked up for the tour.

"Are you hungry?" Rachel asked.

"I am, actually. I only ate a light breakfast just in case I got airsick."

"In that case, when we get out, we'll find a café and get lunch."

"What a marvellous experience that was. I'm so pleased we did it," Marjorie said, her eyes twinkling.

"Despite you being on your last legs," said Rachel, grinning widely.

Marjorie threw her head back, laughing.

***

They quickly found a bustling café, its tables crowded with tourists, many of them cruise passengers eager to eat after a morning spent exploring. Rachel and Marjorie ordered sandwiches and iced teas after taking seats at the only remaining free table.

"That was quite a morning, wouldn't you say?" Marjorie mused again, taking a sip of her tea.

"It was wonderful, thank you, Marjorie."

"My pleasure. I was just thinking those private nurses seem to have an easy time of it, don't they?"

"I had breakfast with Stephen Williams this morning. He more or less admitted that none of them need much care. I wonder if it's more about having someone to call on if needed."

"Or companionship," said Marjorie, "although you wouldn't have thought young Brad needed either, would you? Surely a man his age can manage a plaster cast by himself?"

Rachel shrugged, grinning. "Perhaps he was hoping for a young woman."

"Someone like Margaret, perhaps?" Marjorie mused.

"Or maybe I'm being facetious and the accident knocked his confidence."

"Whatever his reason, he doesn't seem to want Preston around much. First there was last night, and now today he's put the poor young man out to pasture again."

"With Olga Stone. Her patient Emma Johnson looks older than sixty-seven. I did an internet search on her last night. You mentioned she had back pain when you saw her, from that awful car crash she had a few years ago. As you said, she's shied away from the media ever since."

"It hasn't stopped the gossip magazines calling her out on drugs and alcohol, though," said Marjorie. "Did you carry out a search on our miserable politician?"

Rachel didn't get to reply. As if on cue, Victoria Hayes entered the café with Amelia following close behind. The café had filled up even more since Rachel and Marjorie had arrived with every vacated table quickly nabbed. Rachel seized the opportunity and called to Amelia.

"Feel free to join us."

"Are you sure?" Victoria asked, her tone curt and dismissive. Amelia seemed relieved and shot Rachel a grateful look.

"Oh, please do," Marjorie offered, gesturing to the empty chairs. "There's plenty of room."

Rachel watched Victoria hesitate for a moment before accepting. Rachel was as curious as Marjorie to learn more about the cantankerous former politician who liked to run people over in her wheelchair or hit them with her stick. This was the perfect opportunity.

"Thank you," Victoria said icily as she moved to one of the vacant chairs, after parking her electric wheelchair in a nearby space. She gave Amelia a stinging glance with her one visible eye before turning her attention to the menu.

"This is such a charming little café," Marjorie said, trying to break the tension.

"A bit too cramped for my liking," Victoria muttered. She eyed the crowds before perusing the selection of sandwiches and salads on the menu without enthusiasm. The grumpy woman finally ordered a shrimp salad and Amelia chose a seafood sandwich.

While they waited for their orders to arrive, Rachel noticed Victoria's demeanour softening under Marjorie's relentless charm offensive. By the time the food arrived, Marjorie had got her onto the topic of politics. The woman regaled them with tales from her years as a senator, growing more animated by the minute.

"I was a Republican senator," she said. "Dedicated my life to politics, not that I got any thanks for it. All you get as a politician is criticism, and when the others get elected, you're out on your ear…"

And so she went on. Rachel's fascination with Victoria's single-minded view quickly waned, until the older woman's voice took on a dramatic edge.

"…reputation and integrity are everything in politics. One wrong move, and your career can be over just like that." She snapped her fingers for emphasis, causing Amelia, who had been looking out of the window, to jump. Rachel paid attention once more, though inwardly, she was cynical about the idea of integrity and politics going hand-in-hand.

"Were you ever tempted to cross the line?" Rachel asked casually, picking up her sandwich. "It must be difficult to maintain such high standards all the time."

Victoria's left eye narrowed, and for a moment, Rachel wondered if she'd pushed her too far. But then the former senator let out a sigh, her shoulders slumping ever so slightly.

"Crossing the line, as you put it, is inevitable in politics," Victoria admitted, her tone subdued. "No-one can stay squeaky clean forever, no matter how hard they try."

"Did anyone ever use it against you?" Marjorie asked.

Victoria hesitated before responding, her voice almost a whisper. "Not until recently. I've received letters threatening to expose some sensitive facts from my past."

"Why now?" Marjorie asked, concern etched on her face.

"I don't know," Victoria said, her voice trembling. "But I'll be darned if I let them ruin the life I've built."

Rachel's mind raced, considering the implications of Victoria's revelation. Was that why she was so miserable? Did this have anything to do with Margaret Green's murder?

"Maybe it's some sort of prank," she said.

"I doubt it," Victoria snapped, the fire returning to her visible eye. "People like that don't stop until they get what they want."

"Or until they're stopped," Rachel added quietly, her thoughts already forming a new theory about the killer's motive.

Victoria took a sharp intake of breath, moving on to recount the events surrounding the threatening letters. She stabbed at her shrimp as her voice wavered between anger and fear.

"And you don't have any idea where these letters came from?" Rachel asked.

"I can hazard a guess… Stephen told me his nurse was overly interested in my past. It had to be her," Victoria said. "She must have been intending to blackmail me."

"Why the nurse and not Stephen?" Rachel asked, trying to keep her tone neutral.

Victoria laughed. "Stephen?" she replied, her jaw setting stubbornly. "No. But that ambitious little flirt would've if she hadn't…" She slammed her cutlery down, pushing the empty plate away.

"Died," Marjorie finished.

Rachel exhaled before asking, "What were the letters threatening to expose?"

Victoria's eye narrowed again, her lips forming a tight line. "I have no intention of discussing the details," she said sharply. "It concerns events from long ago and, as I've said, respect and reputation are everything for a former politician."

"By not revealing the contents, you might be hindering a murder investigation." Rachel couldn't help herself. This woman epitomised self-interest.

"Of course I'm not!" Victoria exclaimed. "There's a difference between protecting one's good name and condoning criminal behaviour. The two are not connected."

"Perhaps not," Marjorie interjected. "If you don't feel comfortable discussing the specifics, perhaps you could at least give us an idea of the nature of the threats?"

Victoria picked up her drink, sighing. "Very well," she murmured. "The letters threatened to reveal some… indiscretions from my past. Things I did in the name of political expediency that would tarnish my reputation if they were made public now."

"Blackmail is a serious crime," Rachel said, hoping to coax more information from the guarded woman. "What if it wasn't Margaret? Wouldn't it be better to contact the police or speak to the ship's security team?"

"I'm certain it was her. The letters started arriving soon after Stephen and I met at a social group. I'm equally convinced the letters have nothing to do with her death," Victoria said, her voice bitter. "Revealing such facts now can do no good, but it could mean the end of everything I've worked for. I don't even know why I'm telling you about it. Except the girl's death has weighed on my mind."

"Understood," Rachel said, exchanging a glance with Marjorie. She could see the wheels turning in her friend's head, too, as they both struggled to piece together the puzzle Victoria had unwittingly presented.

"Sometimes sharing a problem with strangers helps because they have no vested interest," said Marjorie.

Victoria nodded, her gaze distant and troubled. Rachel knew how far some people would go to protect their reputation. Whether or not Victoria thought it relevant, the truth about Margaret Green's murder could be hidden somewhere in those long-held secrets.

Marjorie leaned forward, her blue eyes flashing with concern as she studied Victoria's tense expression. "My dear," she said, her voice soft, "in this day and age, people are often more forgiving than one might think. They might be more inclined to accept the choices one makes in difficult situations."

Victoria scoffed, shaking her head. "You don't know people like I do. When it comes to politics, the vultures are just waiting for an opportunity to tear us down. No-one forgives and no-one *ever* forgets."

There was something about Victoria's aggressive defence that suggested she'd had unpleasant experiences in the past.

"Perhaps you're right," Marjorie conceded, "but holding onto the fear of exposure isn't doing you any good. Wouldn't it be better to face the problem head-on and find a resolution?"

Victoria stared at her half-empty teacup, her fingers gripping the handle. "I'm not prepared to risk it."

"Very well, but if you change your mind, you know what to do."

Victoria shook herself out, as if regretting the entire conversation. She barked a command at Amelia. They were leaving.

Rachel watched them go, the wheelchair rolling through the door with a faint squeak until it closed behind them.

"What did you make of all that?" Marjorie asked.

"It's hard to say. Could she have killed Margaret if she suspected her of sending the letters? It seems whatever it is she's hiding, she would do anything to protect it."

"But murder? Is she strong enough? Margaret didn't strike me as a weakling that a septuagenarian could overpower easily. There are far too many suspects in this case."

"And none we can rule out yet," Rachel agreed, her brow furrowed in frustration. "Something's bothering me about her revelation."

"Why she mentioned the letters at all?" Marjorie said.

"Exactly. We either caught her at a vulnerable moment, or she knows we're working with the ship's crew to solve the crime and she's aiming to misdirect us."

"But how would she know?"

"Sarah introduced us the other night, and if she'd also mentioned her husband works for the security team, it wouldn't take much working out."

"I'm of the opinion the problem has been weighing her down, and she wanted to get it off her chest," said Marjorie.

Rachel wasn't convinced. "We'll find out soon enough. I'm betting Stephen knows what it is she's hiding and I believe I might be able to get him to talk."

Chapter 13

The Jazz Bar was dimly lit, and the familiar sultry notes from a saxophone wove through the conversations of passengers enjoying an evening out. Rachel, Marjorie, Sarah, and Jason huddled in a secluded corner booth. The rotating illuminations on the stage cast a mixture of light and shadows on their faces.

After fifteen minutes of banter and catchup, Rachel mentioned the breakfast with Stephen Williams.

"We had an interesting chat," she began, her voice low. "I didn't need to ask him about the argument I heard him have with Margaret on the night she died. He openly admitted confronting her because, he said, she was stealing from him. Stephen believes she was working up to taking from others in his party. He didn't go into details, but said that some money and some expensive items had gone missing on boarding day."

"How did she respond?" Sarah raised a quizzical eyebrow, concern etched on her face.

"She denied it and shrugged it off, telling him he was imagining things. I heard her say as much," Rachel replied. "The main thing is, he doesn't seem angry enough to want to kill her, and even if he was, I don't think he's strong enough. He'd need to leap out of his wheelchair and strangle a woman much younger and fitter than him, and leap back in again," she added.

"He could have paid someone to do it on his behalf," said Sarah.

Rachel mulled the thought over. "We can't rule him out, especially after what Victoria said today. We'll tell you about that in a bit. I suppose it depends on what she stole and how much it meant to him."

"Good point," said Jason.

"Did you find Margaret's mobile?" Rachel looked at Jason.

"It's missing. We suspect it went overboard; too risky to keep it in case it was tracked," Jason said, his face serious. "The chief's asked the Hawaiian PD to liaise with NYPD and see if they can pull her phone records. There might be another complication," he said, leaning in closer, "on the theft front. The chief thinks that Margaret may have been in cahoots with someone on board. When we interviewed Stephen today – we didn't get a chance yesterday as he was off ship most of the day – he told us about the valuables and money missing from his room. We searched Margaret's room on the morning after she died and found nothing of that kind. Which means whatever she'd stolen, she had it on her or had passed it on before she died."

"If Stephen's telling the truth," mused Rachel, swirling her drink thoughtfully.

"What reason would he have to lie?" Marjorie asked.

"Assuming he's not the killer, he might wish to take advantage of the situation and prepare for an insurance scam," she replied.

Sarah's eyes widened. "Surely not?"

Rachel shrugged. "It happens, although he seems pretty rich, so maybe I'm just being cynical and he's telling the truth. In which case, it gives us a different angle to pursue."

"If that lead goes anywhere, I'll let you know," said Jason.

Sarah took a sip of Pernod before looking at Jason. "Something odd happened this morning. When I couldn't find you, I ended up on deck seven and was called to Emma Johnson. You should have seen the state of her room. She'd been on a serious binge. I felt sorry for Michael when I left."

"Sorry, Sarah, I'm not following," said Rachel. "Why were you called rather than security?"

"Whoops, I'm not making myself clear, am I? Emma's an insulin-dependent diabetic. She took her insulin but didn't eat enough afterwards. The combination of that and a truckload of alcohol sent her into a severe hypoglycaemic episode. If it hadn't been for Michael finding her like that, she would have gone into a coma, but she's recovered enough to stay on board."

"My goodness, how is she now?" Marjorie enquired, her tone sympathetic.

"No real harm done, but we've kept her in the infirmary. Graham wants her to stay for twenty-four hours just to be on the safe side," Sarah answered. "I don't understand why she did it. She has a history of alcohol abuse, but according to Olga, she's been dry for over two years."

"Told you," said Marjorie gleefully, "these gossip magazines can be quite informative."

Sarah raised an eyebrow.

"Marjorie's housemaid likes to keep up with celebrity gossip," Rachel explained. She wondered whether Emma's falling off the wagon had anything to do with Margaret's death, but couldn't see a connection as Margaret wasn't her nurse. "Do we know if she and Margaret had any dealings?"

Jason shook his head. "None that we've picked up on. Emma only met Margaret Green a few nights ago before joining the cruise. Perhaps there was just too much alcohol floating around." He frowned as he took a drink of soda water. Rachel knew Jason was teetotal because both his parents had been heavy drinkers and his childhood had been rough. It was only through Sarah's compassion that he had met with them again and invited them to his and Sarah's wedding. Rachel wondered how they were doing on the drinking front, but didn't feel now was the time to ask.

"I must be getting confused in my old age because I'm sure Emma told me they met sporadically for nights out," said Marjorie.

"With their nurses?" Rachel asked.

"Perhaps not," said Marjorie. "At the time I spoke to her, I didn't know we had a body on our hands or I would have paid more attention. She was quite bitter about things."

"Whatever the reason for her binge," Rachel said, "we'll find it."

The others nodded in agreement.

"Another funny thing happened this morning," Sarah said, placing her hand over Jason's. "After Janet and Bernard took Emma to the infirmary, I met Olga Stone. I wanted to tell her what had happened to Emma, but when I caught up with her, she was coming out of Margaret's room."

Jason scowled.

"Now that is interesting," Rachel said. "Did she tell you what she was doing?"

Sarah rolled her eyes. "She claimed she was retrieving a necklace she'd lent to Margaret on the night of the party. On reflection, it seems a rather lame reason, especially as Margaret didn't get back to her room that night."

"Unless she decided not to wear it," said Marjorie.

"How did she get hold of the key card in the first place?" Rachel asked.

"Just what I was going to ask," said Jason.

"She said it belonged to Stephen. I can't remember whether she said he gave it to her or that she took it," Sarah replied, handing the card to Jason. "Sorry, I haven't had the chance to tell you any of this, but I insisted she give it to me and told her not to go in there again. I wanted you to get some sleep, and then I got busy. It slipped my mind."

Jason frowned. He examined the card as if it might tell him something. "I'll look into how many of these were issued and track their usage."

"Why isn't Margaret's room cordoned off?" Rachel asked.

Sarah and Jason exchanged a look before Jason said, "The boss didn't want to alarm passengers. I guess we forgot to ask reception to block any current cards. The stateroom attendants know not to go in there."

Rachel admired Jason's loyalty. They both knew the room should have been cordoned off, and that it was Waverley who forgot to inform the reception staff, but Jason would never say so.

"Going back to Olga," Marjorie chimed in. "After our helicopter ride, which was spectacular, by the way, Rachel and I saw her with Preston. She was giving him an earful before they boarded another helicopter for an excursion."

Sarah frowned. "That can't have been long after she deigned to stop by the infirmary to visit her employer. She seemed more focussed on going on her outing with Preston than checking on her patient. If it were me, I would have cancelled under such circumstances. They don't seem to care."

Rachel took a sip of her martini and lemonade, her thoughts trying to piece together the puzzle.

"Rachel and I said more or less the same thing, and they don't work much," said Marjorie. "Although mark my words, that poor Amelia has her work cut out with Victoria, and now she's helping with Stephen as well. She got the raw deal."

"The bunch of them seem to have secrets," Rachel groaned, leaning back in her chair. "We need to figure out what each of them is hiding and whether any of them had a strong enough motive to kill Margaret."

Marjorie cleared her throat. "On the topic of secrets, Rachel and I persuaded Victoria and Amelia to join us for lunch after our outing. They had little choice, as there were no spare tables in the café."

"Victoria, the brusque ex-senator who has a tendency to wave her stick at people," Rachel continued, her eyes narrowing. "That's when she's not trying to run people over with her wheelchair. She tried that one in the buffet this morning just as I was leaving."

"I can't say I warmed to her when I gave them the tour on embarkation day," said Sarah.

"Anyway, after a reluctant beginning, Marjorie won her round. Apparently, she's been receiving threatening letters about past indiscretions."

"What type of indiscretions?" asked Sarah, her eyebrows arching.

"She wouldn't say," Marjorie replied, "but Victoria believes it was Margaret who sent those letters. She was incensed at the idea of her reputation being tarnished, suggesting that Margaret had been planning to blackmail her."

"Yes, she went on and on about how important it was that one's reputation was maintained," said Rachel.

"Blackmail could be a motive for murder," Jason remarked, rubbing his chin thoughtfully. "But would Victoria go to such lengths to protect her reputation?"

"If you'd heard the way she went on about it, you might believe so. Desperate people do desperate things," Rachel said, remembering the fire in Victoria's eye. "We can't rule it out."

"Plus," Marjorie said, her expression darkening, "as Rachel has mentioned, she has a temper."

"Except I'd expect her to wallop someone with a stick rather than strangle them. It all boils down to strength. Our guess is she and Stephen wouldn't be strong enough to overwhelm Margaret Green," but Rachel had a nagging feeling they were only scratching the surface of a much more sinister mystery.

"We don't know much about Amelia yet. A quiet and seemingly downtrodden woman, she moves with a sense of purpose, tending to Victoria's every need with the utmost care. Why does she put up with her?" Marjorie asked.

"Amelia doesn't strike me as the murdering type," Sarah remarked.

"I concur. She's quite the caring soul. I've watched how she is with Victoria. If she was going to kill anybody, it would be her obnoxious employer." Marjorie laughed.

"There might be more to her than meets the eye," said Rachel.

Jason interjected, his voice tinged with frustration, "We've hit a bit of a wall with the police in New York. They won't cooperate on background checks unless we have solid reasons to suspect any of the nurses or their patients."

"Typical bureaucracy," Marjorie huffed, rolling her eyes.

"However," Jason continued, a hint of excitement in his voice, "I've got a friend in the NYPD who might help us out, if it doesn't get her in trouble. And if that doesn't pan out, there's always the option of an old pal from the army. He's an ex-marine and works as a private investigator."

"Like Carlos," said Rachel. "Good thinking, Jason. In the meantime, let's see what we can dig up on social media about our suspects, including Amelia. That might tell us more than police checks."

"Indeed," Marjorie said.

As they went back to enjoying their drinks, Rachel's thoughts wandered to Olga.

Almost as if reading her mind, Jason said, "I'll interview Olga about what she was doing in Margaret's room. It seems odd that she'd go looking for a necklace at such a time."

"And we need to find out what sparked Emma's drinking session," said Rachel.

Sarah shook her head. "It's hard to understand, but she has been taking powerful painkillers for chronic pain. I didn't get to ask her, as I wasn't working in the infirmary today. It was Brigitte. Bernard's offered to do the night shift." Brigitte was Sarah's French colleague who had a tetchy relationship with Bernard and hated the fact that Rachel was a murder magnet.

"I don't want to admit this, but I wonder if Waverley's theory has merit," said Marjorie. "Is it possible that Margaret could have been robbing vulnerable elderly patients and passing goods and money on to an accomplice? If so, perhaps something went awry, or she got greedy, and that's what led to her murder."

"It's possible," Jason conceded, rubbing his head. "And if that's what happened, it might well be someone on the outside of Margaret's party we need to find."

They fell silent, each lost in their thoughts. Rachel listened to the jazz rhythm picking up as they weighed up the possibilities. With so many motives and potential suspects, it was becoming more and more difficult to untangle the threads connecting everyone involved.

"Whatever the case," Rachel said, breaking the silence, "we'll get to the bottom of it."

"We just need to follow every lead, no matter how small, then we'll find the truth," said Jason.

"And we mustn't forget the likelihood that the killer or accomplice is within the group of nurses and patients," Rachel said, leaning forward in her chair. "When we uncover their secrets, it could lead us to the person or persons behind the killing."

"Quite right," said Marjorie, her expressive blue eyes gleaming.

"It's difficult to rule any of the chief suspects out because none of them has a strong alibi," Jason added, rubbing his temple.

Sarah yawned. Rachel cast a sympathetic glance her way. It was hard work being a cruise ship nurse, and Sarah had been working most of the day and into the evening.

Jason picked up the signal. "It's time for me and Sarah to get some rest." He rose from his seat. "We can talk again tomorrow. Do try to enjoy your day in Kona. Have you got anything planned?"

"We've got a full day planned for tomorrow, so you will have to make do without our help," said Marjorie. "Seeing green turtles up close is top of my agenda."

"And local coffee making is mine," said Rachel.

"I'm pleased you're taking some time out to be on holiday. Have a great day."

"We will," said Marjorie. "Goodnight, both of you."

Left alone, Rachel and Marjorie returned to discussing the case. Rachel's thoughts drifted back to Emma Johnson and the questions surrounding her recent alcohol binge.

"How would you feel about a visit to the infirmary?" she said.

Marjorie grinned. "I would be happy to accompany you. I haven't seen Bernard yet and I love his sense of humour. We can visit on the pretence of my hearing Emma was unwell. Bernard can keep me entertained while you quiz our actress friend."

"You're on."

Rachel and Marjorie left the Jazz Bar with resolve.

Chapter 14

Rachel pressed the bell on the outside of the medical centre and waited. After a few minutes, she could see Bernard's short frame opening a door in the distance.

"Here he is now," she told Marjorie.

The main door opened, and Bernard beamed at them. "Let me guess why you're here," he said, stroking his chin and laughing loudly.

"What a pleasure it is to see you again, Bernard," said Marjorie, grinning.

"And you too, Lady... erm... Marjorie." Bernard was often uncomfortable with not using Marjorie's title, but she insisted.

"May we come in?" Marjorie asked.

Bernard stood to one side, gesturing them through with his arm before locking the door after him. "As much as I am thrilled to see the two of you, I'm guessing you're here to interview... rather... visit my patient?"

Rachel nodded. "You've got it. Is she awake? I forgot how late it is."

"Oh, she's awake all right. She's very much awake. She's – how do you say it? A night owl. We've been playing gin rummy and she's slaughtering me. Before I ask her if it's okay for you to visit, does she know who you are?"

"Tell her it's Marjorie, and that we met in the small hours after the Hawaiian party the other night."

Bernard's broad grin spoke volumes. "You're amazing, Marjorie. Okay, wait there. I'll see if she's receiving visitors."

Rachel watched him walking through the doors leading to the infirmary, shaking his head and chuckling to himself. He returned soon afterwards.

"It appears my gin rummy skills aren't exciting enough; she will be happy to see you. She has ordered me to get hot chocolate."

Rachel giggled. "I like this woman already."

Rachel and Marjorie made their way into the infirmary, leaving Bernard to call down to the kitchens. Emma was propped up in bed with four pillows, which almost swallowed her thin frame up. One eyebrow rose on seeing Rachel.

"Hello, my dear," said Marjorie. "I hope you don't mind, but I brought along the friend I mentioned the other night. The idea of visiting came to me as we were leaving one of the facilities upstairs."

Rachel noted Marjorie's omission of the word 'bar', which she thought was considerate under the circumstances.

Emma shrugged.

"This is Rachel, my dear friend," Marjorie finished.

"Hello," said Emma, with a forced smile. Her frailty was so much clearer in a nightdress and shawl. "How did you know I was here?" Her eyebrows formed a V shape.

"We saw your nurse out and about earlier today and you weren't with her, so I asked Sarah and she told me you had taken ill." Marjorie always put on an Oscar-winning performance when circumstances demanded it, which once more reassured Rachel that her friend's mental capacity was fine.

Emma relaxed. "I'm diabetic," she said, adding no other detail.

Bernard returned. "Hot chocolate is on the way, Your Highness."

Rachel and Marjorie turned to Bernard, shocked that he might have gone too far with his joking, but Emma burst out laughing.

"I've been telling him of the time I acted in a spoof musical about Queen Elizabeth I on Broadway," she said, pulling herself back together. "That was mid-career before I moved into soaps and film. And before…" her voice trailed off.

"Before your accident," Marjorie said.

"I'm always surprised to hear my fame reaches as far as England, but you told me your housemaid follows the soap."

"Avidly," said Marjorie. "She's a huge fan."

"What about you?" Emma looked at Rachel. "Are you a fan?"

Rachel felt her face flush. "Sorry. I get little time for television or film, but I did recognise you."

"At least you're not here for an autograph. It's so tiresome when people walk up to me from nowhere, you know? Nowadays it just reminds me of what I've lost."

The doorbell rang and Bernard went to answer it, returning a few moments later with a tray of drinks. Emma took hers and placed it on the table in front of her. Bernard gathered up the cards.

"Don't play cards with her. She'll fleece you. She's an amazing player," he said, grinning.

"Officer Guinto has been keeping me entertained," Emma said.

"You call me Bernard and I'll call you Emma," he said, winking.

"Deal," she said, before adding, "It's such a drag being kept in overnight, but he's been great and it's my own fault."

Rachel seized the opportunity. "What makes you say that?"

Emma hesitated before saying, "I expect Marjorie's maid read about it." She shot a quizzical look towards Marjorie, who nodded.

"But one never knows how much of what one reads is true. I'd much rather hear it from you," she said tactfully.

"Three years ago, I had a car accident which nearly killed me. The person who hit me didn't stick around."

"How awful," said Marjorie.

"It was hours before anyone discovered me. I was trapped in the wreck and couldn't call for help. Lucky... or maybe unlucky... for me, someone came by and saw the car down a ditch." Rage filled Emma's blazing eyes as she continued. "I was in hospital for six months solid, and it was touch and go for a while. The doctors said that if I'd been attended to straight away, things wouldn't have been so bad. So you see, although I lived, that woman ended my career and ruined my life. As it is, I live in severe pain."

"You saw it was a woman driver?" Rachel checked.

"Sure did. Not just that, she got out of the car and checked her darn bumper while I was crying out for help. Can you believe that? It was dark, but I saw the side of her face in the car's headlights. She was drunk. She teetered around for a while, then got right back inside and sped off as if nothing had happened."

"Did the police ever catch this woman?" Rachel asked.

"No. There wasn't much for them to go on. I lost consciousness, and they put me in an induced coma. I woke up six weeks later in a hospital bed. It took a while for my memory to come back. The highways in the US run for hundreds of miles. She could have gone anywhere."

Rachel had attended several hit-and-run accidents in her time as a uniformed officer and one when she was off duty, which was no accident. Sometimes the perpetrator wasn't caught. It was satisfying when they were, but she could never understand the mentality of anyone leaving the scene of an accident when it was obvious they had injured and, sometimes, killed another person. Even making an anonymous phone call was better than leaving someone to fate.

"You haven't said why you think it's your fault you're here," she said.

"As I told you, the accident left me in constant pain and I live on painkillers. After I lost the biggest role of my career, and because of the pain, I threw alcohol into the mix and before you know it, I was a drunk addicted to painkillers. The other night, I got the shock of my life and couldn't get over it. Last night it came back to me again, and I hit the bottle. The anger can be overwhelming. I'm afraid I trashed my stateroom. Of course, I'll apologise to Michael, the attendant. He's been so welcoming since I came on board."

Emma stopped talking and sipped the hot chocolate. As Marjorie and Rachel also sipped theirs, Rachel motioned for Marjorie to ask the next question.

"And this shock? Did it have anything to do with your car accident?"

Emma's face darkened. A tight-lipped glare aimed at no-one in particular could have graced a death scene in one of her movies.

"I thought I saw the woman who had ruined my life carrying on as if nothing had happened."

Marjorie's jaw dropped open. "You should tell the security chief."

Emma shook her head. "There's no point. No-one can do anything about it. Besides, it's not the first time I've imagined seeing her; my doctor reckons it's the drugs. Sometimes they cloud my brain. She haunts my nights, and sometimes my days. I guess it was my imagination playing tricks again."

"But surely—" Marjorie tried, but was cut off.

"I'm just a bitter ex-actress past her sell-by date who sees a drunken woman around every bend, and there were a lot of them about the other night. There's nothing more to be said. But I am sorry for the damage I caused." Emma looked at Bernard.

"It's forgotten," he said.

"Not quite forgotten," said Emma. "I had a visit from a member of the security team this afternoon – an Officer Inglis, who I wouldn't want to mess with. She warned me that if it happened again, she would have to throw me off."

Rachel smiled. Rosemary Inglis was an ex-athlete who had a muscular upper body, but underneath her appearance she was kind, as well as being an intelligent member of the security team.

"That sounds drastic," said Marjorie.

"Not when you snap a telephone line and it takes people half a day to fix it, not to mention having to have the carpets scrubbed and a new sink put in."

Marjorie's eyes widened.

"Emma cracked the sink," Bernard explained.

"What on earth with?" Marjorie asked, aghast.

"My mother's Oscar," she replied. "I'm convinced I was heading for an Oscar with what was meant to be my next role and I was always the better actress. Still, she got one and I didn't. But don't worry, I won't be drinking again during the voyage. For a start, it's made my ulcer play up and I'm mortified by what happened. Underneath the actress, I'm a private person who just wants to be left alone. My sister and my agent thought the cruise would do me good."

"I'm surprised nobody heard you making that much racket," said Bernard.

"Stephen Williams is on one side and tells me he sleeps with earplugs in, and the young trader, Brad, is on the other side. He was probably out half the night."

"Well, I'm sure the cruise will be good for you once you've got over this minor hiccup," said Marjorie.

Rachel was still processing all they had heard and debated with herself whether to ask the next question. "This person you thought was the woman DUI…" noticing Marjorie's confusion, she clarified, "…driving under the influence. Was it someone in your party?"

"Of course not. What makes you say that?" Emma snapped.

Rachel shrugged. "Sorry, I didn't mean to pry."

"I've told you. It's happened before, and no doubt it will happen again, but hopefully without the repercussions," Emma said with a tight grin.

Marjorie finished her chocolate and placed the mug on the tray. "Has Olga been to see you today?"

"She popped in this morning and again before she went for dinner. I don't need her for much, but I like to have someone check my insulin dose before I take it. When I'm home, I have someone come in twice a day. Olga's only been with me for a couple of months, but if it works out, she can come with me on other vacations."

"And is it working out?" Marjorie asked.

"It seems to be. She's around when I want her, but it's only fair that she gets to let her hair down when I don't. As I said, I like my space."

"So you didn't know any of the others before the cruise?" Rachel quizzed.

"I told Marjorie the other night, I know Victoria and Stephen a little. Victoria Hayes was quite the force a decade or so ago, but like me, she's past her best. She and Stephen go back a bit, according to Olga, but I'm not sure they like each other. But then, who likes a politician?"

"What about the nurses?" Rachel asked. "Do they know each other?"

"I think Olga, Amelia, and the dead girl knew each other."

Did Rachel detect an edge at the mention of the dead girl? She and Marjorie had noticed Victoria and Brad's disapproval of the two women's behaviour on the night of the party, but not Emma's. Still, considering her story, it was hardly surprising if she also disapproved.

"It was such a tragedy what happened to young Margaret. Do you know if they all got on?" Marjorie asked.

"If you're asking me whether Olga or Amelia killed her, I wouldn't know, but as I told the security guy yesterday, I would be surprised if they had anything to do with it. They seemed like an ordinary trio to me, catty at times, and all over each other at others. It's a bit like that in the acting world, so I get it."

"Preston seems a bit out of his depth," said Bernard.

"Perhaps he needs to make more of an effort," said Emma.

"I feel sorry for him. You have no idea what it's like for us poor male nurses, working in a female-dominated profession."

"Get away with you," said Emma. "Most red-blooded males would chop off an arm to be in his position, surrounded by beautiful single women."

Bernard grinned a cheeky grin. "Perhaps he has a girlfriend already."

"He could just be dedicated to his job. He's younger than the others. Sarah said he's not long qualified, so I guess he's just a bit overwhelmed," Rachel said.

"Back to the other nurses," said Marjorie. "Did you see Margaret leave with anyone on the night of the party?"

Emma rubbed her right temple, avoiding eye contact. "Not that I can remember."

"It might be time to let you get some sleep. I hope you get out and about tomorrow. The islands are magnificent."

"Thanks for visiting," said Emma.

"Well?" Marjorie asked Rachel once they had left the medical centre.

"She was lying about some things, but which ones I don't know. I believe she knows more about the nurses than she's letting on." With every interview, Rachel felt the story unravelling. But, like a spring, it coiled back into position and they were no further forward. "We should ask Jason to find out about Emma's accident and whether there's more to it than she says."

"Do you think she might have been targeted?"

"That's what I'd like to find out, but right now, I'm clutching at straws. My head's frazzled."

After walking Marjorie to her room, Rachel returned to hers, feeling as though something important was just out of reach.

Chapter 15

It was always a novel experience, going ashore via a tender. Two crewmen helped Marjorie to board the small vessel, where she and Rachel found seats on a bench. Once it was full, the tender boat left the ship for the brief journey to the Kailua-Kona Pier. They climbed out and Rachel shielded her eyes from the sun while looking back at the magnificent *Coral Queen* anchored in deeper waters.

Rachel was pleased they had left early because they had a lot to pack into the day. She donned her sunglasses, breathing in the fresh sea air.

"Nothing beats the smell of sea in the morning."

"I quite agree, it's so cleansing," Marjorie replied. "I've been looking forward to our excursions today."

"Me too," said Rachel. She spied the stop for the bus that would take them to the Coffee Plantation Museum and they headed towards it. Marjorie wanted to sit in the centre in case the roads were twisty, so they found seats near to the central exit. Marjorie sat next to the window and Rachel took the aisle seat where she watched the other passengers boarding. She was pleasantly surprised to see Emma with Olga.

"It looks like Emma's been discharged, and she's looking a lot healthier than she did at the start of the cruise."

"I'm pleased," said Marjorie. "Clearly the *Coral Queen's* medics haven't lost their touch."

Rachel grinned, watching the two women taking seats a few rows in front of them. "Let's just hope she stays off the booze."

"The poor woman's been through a lot and although I wouldn't normally feel sorry for a celebrity, in her case I'll make an exception." Marjorie chuckled. Rachel laughed along with her friend. As much as Marjorie tried to hide it, Rachel knew her to be kind-hearted and sympathetic when she needed to be.

"Here come Brad and Preston," Rachel whispered.

"We might be in with a chance of doing a little sleuthing over coffee." Marjorie's eyes shone.

"If we get the chance, I vote you have another word with Emma. She likes you and I would be very interested to know who she saw the other night that sent her into a frenzy."

"Didn't she say it wasn't the first time she'd imagined seeing the woman who drove her off the road? The poor thing is so dosed up with painkillers; they can make people imagine all sorts of things."

Rachel sighed. "Maybe, but I'd still like to ask again. There's something she's not telling us."

"In that case, I'll see what I can do," said Marjorie as the doors closed and the bus pulled away from the pier. Before long they were climbing a volcanic mountain, and Marjorie turned her attention to the views through the window. Rachel watched Olga and Preston, noticing the tension from the day before still simmering between them. They were seated on opposite sides of the aisle, avoiding eye contact with each other, and speaking only when necessary.

Rachel joined Marjorie in admiring the views. The two women chatted cheerfully about their surroundings, taking in every inch of this Hawaiian paradise. The lush green foliage seemed to stretch endlessly, with bursts of colourful flowers dotting the landscape.

"Look at those lovely red blooms!" Marjorie exclaimed, pointing out of the window.

"The information leaflet said to look out for them," said Rachel. "They're lehua flowers." She smiled, remembering a film she'd watched with her father when she was a teenager. It had starred Elvis Presley and was set in Hawaii.

After around thirty minutes, the bus pulled up at the Mountain Thunder Coffee Plantation, coming to a stop with a hiss of brakes.

"Here we are!" the tour guide announced. "You have two hours to explore the plantation, see how the coffee is made and, the best bit, savour the deliciously roasted coffee."

Olga helped Emma down the steps of the bus just ahead of Rachel and Marjorie. Once they disembarked, they followed the rest of the group towards the entrance. As the tour guide began explaining the history of coffee making in Hawaii, Rachel's attention drifted. Her mind wandered to the mystery surrounding Margaret's death. There were still too many unanswered questions and loose ends.

A nudge from Marjorie pulled Rachel from her thoughts. "The coffee tasting is about to begin. We should join the others."

Rachel pushed her musings to the back of her mind. "Lead the way."

"It's so lovely seeing Emma out and about," Marjorie said with genuine warmth. "And you're right about her looking better."

"She seems more contented somehow," said Rachel, watching Emma joking with someone who was asking for her autograph.

"And happy to sign autographs, I see," said Marjorie.

Rachel recalled how derisory Emma had been about people asking for autographs only the night before. "She could be putting on a show," she said.

"She is… or was… an actress after all," said Marjorie, chuckling.

Rachel and Marjorie joined the rest of the group, who had already gathered around a large table laden with many types of coffee beans and brewing equipment. A knowledgeable staff member explained the different roasting processes and how each affected the flavour of the resulting coffee. As the group took turns sampling the brews, Rachel's attention drifted to what Sarah had told them about Olga coming out of Margaret Green's room.

"Try this one," Marjorie suggested, passing Rachel a small cup. "It's heavenly."

Rachel took a sip, allowing the smooth, rich flavour to divert her momentarily from her suspicions. She was annoyed with herself, an avid coffee drinker, for being distracted, having looked forward to this outing more than most.

"Gorgeous," she said, licking her lips.

Emma seemed to be enjoying the experience as much as Rachel should have been. The woman even managed a chuckle as she shared a story about her days on set with another two passengers.

Rachel leaned over to Marjorie and whispered, "Have you seen Brad and Preston?"

"No, I haven't. Perhaps they've gone to explore the plantation outside."

Before either of them could speculate further, they were handed another brew. Soon the intoxicating aroma of coffee beans and the fascinating detail of how each drink was made captivated Rachel's full attention. Marjorie was more of a tea drinker, but she sampled several coffees with enthusiasm, closing her eyes to focus on the complex tastes in each cup.

Once they left the tasting room, Marjorie nudged Rachel, motioning towards some tables and benches where Emma was sitting with a cup of coffee in front of her. She spoke loud enough for Emma to hear.

"Do you mind if I take the weight off my legs for a while?"

"Not at all." Rachel played along. "I'm going to take a walk around. I'll see you soon."

Smiling at her incorrigible friend, who Emma appeared delighted to see, Rachel turned away and walked around the complex. Taking a path further into the plantation, Rachel noticed Preston sitting alone on the ground. Most of the tour group was still with the guide, and there was no sign of Brad. Preston had his head in his hands and was mumbling to himself. She walked towards him and crouched down.

"Hello. Are you all right?"

He looked up, eyes rimmed with red, and sighed. "I think I'm in trouble and I don't know what to do."

"In trouble for what?" Rachel asked gently.

Preston examined his hands as if weighing up whether to tell her what was on his mind. He shook his head.

"It might be nothing."

Rachel sat down on the ground next to him, pleased she was wearing navy-blue shorts which wouldn't show the dirt so much. She removed her sunglasses to look into his eyes.

"Tell me about it."

He groaned before taking a deep breath. "On the first night of the cruise, when I was leaving the Hawaiian-themed party, Margaret cornered me. She was drunk and falling all over the place. I put a hand out to steady her and she just kissed me out of nowhere," he said. "Olga says she saw us and has assumed we were together. She thinks I killed her."

"And did you?"

Preston's eyes widened. "No! I wasn't even with her. In fact, I was shocked. When I told her never to do that again, she gave me a load of abuse about thinking I was too good for the rest of them. The truth is I'm shy around women. Laughable, isn't it? I worked with them throughout my training, but I've never had a serious girlfriend."

Rachel put a hand on his arm. "It's not laughable. You just haven't met the right one yet. So tell me what happened after the tirade?"

"To be honest, I didn't take too much notice. She was just ranting, you know? I walked away and didn't see her again. But Olga's threatening to report me to the security chief who's been interviewing us."

"If she thinks you killed her friend, why hasn't she done that already?"

"Because she believes I've got money and valuables that Margaret took from Stephen, and she wants a share of it." Preston's voice was strained with despair. "Hell, I didn't even know Margaret was a thief. If I'm honest, I think it's an abhorrent betrayal of trust. Why would I take the stuff myself?"

Rachel pondered what Preston was saying. It explained what Olga had been doing in Margaret's room when Sarah caught her coming out the day before. It also added weight to Waverley's theory that Margaret might have had an accomplice.

"Did you notice Margaret carrying anything that night?"

"That's just it. She wasn't even carrying a purse. Her room key was in her skirt pocket. I saw her put it there after we left our rooms."

"If what you're saying is true, have you considered telling the security chief yourself? You should explain what happened and tell him you had nothing to do with Margaret's murder."

"Oh, I've thought about it all right, but I'm scared," he admitted, rubbing his hands together nervously. "I grew up in Chicago, and I've dealt with racial prejudice my whole life. Growing up, I saw lots of black people arrested who weren't guilty. They'll see a young black man who was with a white woman shortly before she was killed and assume I'm guilty."

Rachel shook her head, but understood. Sometimes Waverley could jump to conclusions, but they wouldn't be based on Preston's skin colour, rather the fact he had withheld information and the chief had no other leads.

"Look, I know the world can be unjust, but you have to trust that truth will prevail. Hiding and doing nothing won't help your situation, but it could make it worse if you don't come forward."

"Maybe you're right," he conceded, his eyes downcast. "But I feel trapped."

"Listen," Rachel said, placing a comforting hand on his arm. "Olga's the one in the wrong here. She should have gone straight to the security team and told them what she saw, then let them investigate. Some friend she is." Rachel felt her anger rising.

"She and Margaret had gotten to know each other, but I'm not convinced they were friends. More like competitors if you ask me."

Or accomplices. Rachel needed to give this more thought.

"Why don't you let me talk to the chief of security? My friend Sarah is married to one of the security team. They're reasonable people, and I don't believe they're racist. They will need to corroborate that what you're telling me is true, but they will listen. I promise."

"Do you think so?" Preston asked, relief washing over his face.

She nodded. "I'm sure of it."

Before they could talk further, Olga appeared out of nowhere. Her eyes narrowed.

"Am I interrupting something?" she asked, her stony gaze fixed on Rachel, but clearly meant for both of them.

"Nope, we were just talking," Rachel replied.

"Brad's looking for you." Olga glared at Preston.

"I'd better go," Preston answered, getting up and walking away with a defeated look on his face.

Rachel watched him go, her heart aching for the young man she believed was caught in such a complex web. As much as she would have liked to give Olga a piece of her mind, Rachel didn't want to pre-warn her she knew what she was up to.

Rachel got up from the ground and replaced her sun specs. "I'd better get back to my friend Marjorie… see you around."

"Sure will," Olga replied with a tight smile.

Chapter 16

Marjorie moved leisurely towards the table where Emma and Olga sat sipping cups of coffee. She greeted them with a bright, "Good morning."

Emma welcomed her with a warm smile, but Olga grunted.

Marjorie focussed on Emma. "I'm so pleased to see you out and about today. It's beautiful here."

"I'm pleased to be out of the infirmary, although the staff in there are wonderful... so *caring*."

Marjorie sensed the emphasis was a pointed dig at Olga, who ignored it, nonchalantly cradling her coffee cup in both hands.

"Especially Bernard Guinto. He's a hoot."

"He is rather," agreed Marjorie. "I had a spell in the infirmary once and I couldn't agree more."

"Oh?" Emma raised a quizzical eyebrow.

"It's a long story. I toppled down some steps. I'll tell you about it sometime." Marjorie omitted to say she had been pushed and that Rachel had saved her.

"Where's your young friend Rachel this morning?" Emma asked.

"She's gone for a walk. I thought it would be nice to have a sit-down," Marjorie explained.

"I don't blame you. Why don't you join us? The coffee's delicious," said Emma.

Marjorie pulled out a chair and settled herself into it. One of the staff brought her a cup of coffee.

"It's pleasant up here, and a nice breeze too," said Marjorie. The conversation between her and Emma was stilted, with awkward pauses and the small talk felt forced to Marjorie. She couldn't get to the point while Olga remained, making neither comment nor contribution. The nurse appeared disinterested, her eyes everywhere except in their direction, as if searching for something or someone else.

"You were right, this coffee is just delightful," Marjorie ventured, breaking a silence that had fallen over the table.

"Real good," said Emma. "Why don't you get me a couple of packs of the coffee beans I liked in the tasting room, Olga?" It was a command rather than a question.

"Okay," Olga replied, her tone curt. But she continued to drink her coffee, not moving.

"What was your favourite acting role?" Marjorie asked Emma.

"There were so many amazing parts... it's hard to pick one out," she admitted.

"I'll go get your coffee," Olga interrupted, standing abruptly. "And I need to use the restroom." With a cursory nod towards Marjorie and Emma, she left them alone at the table.

"At last," Marjorie muttered under her breath, relieved to have the opportunity for a more private conversation with Emma.

"I don't know what's the matter with her today," said Emma. "She's usually quite bright, but she's hardly said a word since we left the ship."

"Perhaps she's got something on her mind." Marjorie thought about what Rachel had said about the tension between Olga and Preston.

"Well, she'd better pull herself out of it."

Marjorie placed her cup back in its saucer and leaned forward, her eyes locking onto Emma's. "I hate to bring it up again, but I wondered if I might ask you something?"

"Sure, go ahead," Emma replied. Marjorie noticed a slight tremor as the other woman's hands lifted her coffee cup.

"When we spoke last night, you mentioned seeing someone who you believed was responsible for the hit-and-run accident you were involved in."

"Did I?" The tremor became more pronounced.

"I wondered if you would like to talk about it," Marjorie said, her tone gentle.

Emma looked away, then into her coffee cup before she took a deep breath. Marjorie could see the internal struggle playing out across Emma's features as she debated whether to reveal anything.

Marjorie waited and, after a long pause, Emma spoke. "I saw someone that night and I was shocked because it looked like the driver that crashed into me." She paused again, glancing around. "But I couldn't be certain. The drugs give me blurred vision sometimes."

Marjorie reached out a hand, placing it comfortingly on Emma's arm. "Would you recognise them if you saw them again?"

Emma swallowed hard, her eyes glistening with unshed tears. "The woman's dead. The person I recognised was Margaret," she confessed. "I hadn't noticed it before, what with the medication and all that, but on the night of the party she got so drunk, she was all over the place. That's when the shape of her face, the hair, and the way she behaved brought back the memory of the woman who got out of the car on that fateful night. I felt pretty sure she was the same woman who ran me off the road." Emma looked away again, deep in thought.

"I see," Marjorie replied. The revelation was unexpected and provided a powerful motive for Margaret's murder. If Emma had recognised her as the hit-and-run driver, it's possible she killed her. Was that why she got so drunk? "Did you speak to Margaret about it? Confront her with your suspicions?"

"I was going to, but then…" she paused, looking at Marjorie, her expression troubled.

Marjorie leaned forward and patted Emma's hand. "Did you have anything to do with Margaret's death?"

Emma shook her head vigorously. "No, it's not that. After I realised it was her, I followed her. I wanted to tell her what she'd done, make her realise how it had affected me… make her confess. Emotions were running high, and they filled me with rage. The mixture of drugs and the revelation, I wasn't thinking straight."

Marjorie's eyes widened. "What happened?"

Emma shook her head again. "Nothing. I followed her, but then I saw her with Preston. They were arguing."

Marjorie's pulse quickened. "What else did you see? Did you hear what they were arguing about?"

Emma frowned, rubbing her temple. "I'm sorry. It's all a blur after that. I had taken so many painkillers, it was dark, and I was upset. In a way I was pleased, but also frustrated she was with someone. I don't know what I would have done if I'd got near her. Anyway, because of that, I only caught snatches of their conversation."

"Try to remember," Marjorie urged. "It might be important."

"Margaret seemed to be angry. She said something like, 'Who do you think you are?' I didn't really hear anything else. I chickened out and left them to it. Now I think about it, she might not have been the driver at all and I think that's the conclusion I came to. Either way, I didn't want to listen to her ranting, so I heard nothing else."

Marjorie's mind raced. If Margaret and Preston had a falling out on the night of her murder, was he the one who strangled her? She gave Emma's hands a comforting squeeze.

"Is there anything else you can tell me about the night of the party?"

Emma shook her head miserably. "No, I'm afraid not. I went back to my room and crashed for an hour until I woke again. That's when I met you. I was trying to gather my thoughts and piece together what had happened. My back was sore, and I was reliving the accident all over again. When you came along, I was feeling pretty miserable."

"You did seem unhappy," said Marjorie.

"Sorry if I came across negative. I try not to let things get me down, but sometimes it's overwhelming."

"There's no need to apologise. You have been through a lot," said Marjorie.

"The next morning, I heard Margaret was dead. Olga told me someone had strangled her."

"Do you know who told Olga?"

"Amelia, I think. Stephen had been on to Victoria about it and before long, everyone knew. I feel so bad about how I reacted. Can you believe I was overjoyed at the news? That's why I started drinking – to celebrate. A surge of vindictive joy came over me, but it didn't last long. Later, I felt guilty about feeling that way, so I drank some more and so it goes on. That must have been when I trashed my stateroom. The anger I felt towards Margaret twisted back to me."

Emma's eyes looked sad. "If it hadn't been for your friend Sarah, I might have died from a hypoglycaemic coma. In the sobering light of day, I was, and am, appalled by my actions. What kind of person celebrates another human being's death like that? No matter Margaret's wrongs, she didn't deserve such a terrible fate. I hope they find whoever's responsible."

Marjorie patted Emma's arm and smiled. "Forgiveness strengthens us in the long run, and you're quite right. Margaret's killer must be found for justice to prevail."

The courtyard where they were sitting suddenly buzzed with people returning from their tour of the facilities. Brad was standing by a wall when Marjorie saw Preston join him. Rachel arrived soon afterwards.

Marjorie stood, her mind buzzing with questions. "It looks like it's time for the next round of touring. I'm sorry to have opened old wounds, but I hope to see you again around the ship. Enjoy the rest of your day."

Emma's smile was genuine. "You too… and thank you. It was good to get that off my chest and out in the open."

Marjorie noticed Olga stomping behind Rachel and thought it best to move away.

"See you later," she said.

Chapter 17

After buying wrist bands on the pier, Rachel and Marjorie boarded the next hop on, hop off bus to explore more of Kona. They spent the first ten minutes enjoying the views before Rachel turned to Marjorie.

"What did you find out from your conversation with Emma?"

"Quite a lot, actually. You were right about her backtracking about the woman she recognised on the night of the party. The one she believed caused her accident." Marjorie's eyes appeared sad and her expression was solemn. "It was Margaret Green, but I suspect you already thought that was the case, didn't you?"

Rachel nodded. "Sort of. Either her or Amelia; it couldn't have been Olga or Emma would have already done something about it."

"Speaking of Olga... she was positively petulant," said Marjorie.

"I can explain that, but what else did Emma say? Do you think we have our killer?"

Marjorie looked pensive while Rachel waited for a reply, eventually saying, "No, I don't believe so. She admits that after recognising her that night, she followed Margaret to have it out with her, but returned to her room after seeing her arguing with... you'll never guess who?"

"Preston," said Rachel.

"What I love about you is how you're always one step ahead," said Marjorie.

"Not really. I'd say we are level pegging. I happened to come across Preston in a morose state while you were talking to Emma. He told me about it."

"My turn to ask you the question you just asked me. Is he our killer?"

Rachel blew out a breath. "Unlikely. According to him, Margaret made a pass at him sometime that night, and he reckons he was angry about it and told her not to do it again. Then she got into a rage and gave him a mouthful before he turned his back on her."

"He walked away from a beautiful woman. Do you believe him?"

"When you put it like that, I'm not sure. He seems inexperienced with women and, beautiful she might have been, but she was off her head with booze, so maybe not that appealing. What did Emma say about the argument?" Rachel asked.

"Not much. She said she heard Margaret asking him who he thought he was, or something like that."

"Which fits in with his version of events," said Rachel. "Apparently she let rip at him for daring to assume he was too good for her, so what Emma heard concurs with his story. I'd say he's telling the truth."

"Except he's now the last person to see Margaret alive," said Marjorie.

"If Emma's telling the truth, he is, apart from the killer, and he's terrified he's going to be arrested."

"I'm surprised His Lordship hasn't done that already."

"What worries me is he might. Once Waverley finds out what happened, he's likely to throw Preston in the brig."

"And we have a duty to tell the chief," said Marjorie.

"Yes, we do. The thing is, I assured Preston the security team would listen to his version of events and be reasonable."

Marjorie let out a huff. "This is Jack Waverley we're talking about," she said.

"I know," said Rachel. "Preston thinks they'll arrest him because he's black."

"Oh, I see," said Marjorie. "Well, Chief Waverley is often misguided, but young Preston's mistaken if he thinks his skin colour will form part of the equation."

"I agree, but the chief is likely to arrest him all the same." Hearing what Emma had told Marjorie gave Rachel hope for Preston, although it could go the opposite way. She sighed. "Something else Preston told me was that Olga also saw him with Margaret, but she witnessed them kissing, which he says was what occurred before the argument. He swears the kiss was uninvited and unwelcome."

"Oh dear. This doesn't bode well for Preston, does it?"

"Not on the surface, no."

"Is that what the tension between him and Olga is all about? She thinks he killed her friend?"

"Yes... maybe... but here's where it gets complicated, and what keeps me hoping we can unravel the case before long. Olga thinks Preston took money and valuables from Margaret that night and she's threatening to tell security unless he gives them to her."

"What a nasty minx that woman is. Does he have these items?"

"He says not. Margaret wasn't even carrying a purse on the night of the party. I'm sure any CCTV footage the security team has seen will confirm this, but it doesn't mean they, or she, didn't stash the loot somewhere to go back for it later."

"Unless she'd already given it to the accomplice Chief Waverley believes she had."

"Olga's looking to me like she might have been the accomplice and maybe Margaret branched out on her own, or cut her out of any deal they had. The trouble is, it's all supposition. I don't have any evidence whatsoever. Olga could just be an opportunist, looking to exploit a situation for what she can gain."

Marjorie nodded. "You're quite right. We need evidence. I think it might be time to take a closer look at what Margaret was up to the night she died. There were hundreds of people at that party. Surely somebody saw something."

"Waverley and Jason are still interviewing people. Perhaps they'll come up with something."

"We know now that at least two people saw her after she left the party."

"Three, if we count Olga," said Rachel.

"So we have three suspects, but judging by what we have gleaned so far, none of them killed Margaret."

"It depends where Olga fits in. What if she was the accomplice and my theory that Margaret planned to cut her out on this occasion is right?"

"Except she's trying to take advantage of a vulnerable young man who she believes has the goods," Marjorie countered.

Frustration at their lack of progress threatened to overwhelm Rachel until something clicked that had been eluding her.

"If Olga really believes Preston is a killer, why would she risk her own life by threatening him? Doesn't it make more sense that she was the one who flew into a rage, strangled her so-called friend, and later went to Margaret's room to look for the goods? Finding they weren't there and remembering the kiss she witnessed, she believes Preston must have them. But we're back where we started. We have no proof."

"I wonder if she knew the security team hadn't found any such items and wanted to check for herself."

"She's clever enough to have milked Waverley for information if he questioned her," said Rachel.

"And there's still Amelia, Victoria, and Stephen who Margaret stole from, and then there's young Brad who we can't rule out yet," added Marjorie.

"Unless she was unconscious from the amount of alcohol she drank that night, I doubt any of the frailer, older bunch would be strong enough to overwhelm the younger and fitter Margaret Green. Although Preston says she was falling about all over the place, so she might have conked out."

"Brad wouldn't be able to strangle anyone with his arm in plaster."

Rachel rubbed her head until it hurt. "If we assume Margaret passed out that night, apart from a one-armed man, any of them could have done it. If Olga is just an opportunist, so far, Stephen and, I'm afraid, Emma have the strongest motives."

Marjorie opened her mouth as if to protest, but decided against it.

Proving Preston innocent, if indeed he was, would be no simple task. Rachel suspected Margaret had been involved in criminal activity for some time before her death. It might be a case of her choosing the wrong person to steal from, or was it a fatal flirtation that cut her life short?

"If Jason's friend has come up with anything from her unofficial enquiries, it would help us," said Rachel.

The bus came to a stop at Kahalu'u Beach, and they rose from their seats.

"We'll find out more tonight and share what we know with Waverley. Now I suggest we concentrate on green turtles and snorkelling," said Marjorie.

Rachel's eyes widened. "You're not seriously suggesting we go snorkelling?"

"It says clearly in the brochure the activity is suitable for all ages."

"But—"

"But nothing, Rachel. I'm surprised at you. However, if you're not up to it…" said Marjorie, eyes flashing.

Rachel felt ashamed for coming across as ageist. Why shouldn't Marjorie go snorkelling? Her friend was right to be indignant.

"I apologise, Marjorie. Come on, let's get suited up."

"Now you're talking," said Marjorie with a wide grin on her face. "I've been locked away for far too long. I'm going to take full advantage of what time I have left."

Marjorie took Rachel's arm as they headed towards the equipment hire booth in search of masks and fins. They hired two suitable wetsuits that fitted them both. Then, once they were kitted up properly and equipped with whistles in case they got into trouble, they made their way to the beach's edge, where a group of professional instructors awaited them. They joined some other eager adventurers ready for a taste of heaven on earth in the clear waters.

The instructors were helpful and friendly, and soon enough Rachel and Marjorie were in the shallows alongside four other people, ready to explore the beautiful underwater world beneath them. The view was breathtaking: schools of tropical fish swam around them, and Rachel could see bright coral reefs teeming with life.

As she swam deeper, she saw something that took her breath away – green turtles gliding along the depths. Marjorie gripped her arm, motioning towards the same spectacle. The turtles came closer to the surface and swam alongside them in graceful unison, their flippers propelling them through the sea. As Rachel watched this display of nature's beauty, she felt connected with these majestic creatures. They were sharing an intimate moment together; one that would stay with her forever.

After a while, Rachel reluctantly left the turtles to swim on, and continued exploring the depths of this magical world. She saw colourful starfish clinging to rocks and different species of fish darting about in synchronised patterns. Although absorbed by what was going on in the water, she was also making sure Marjorie was close to her and safe. She needn't have worried; Marjorie was a natural. The experience was like being part of another world – one without cares or worries, just peace and tranquillity in an abundance of natural beauty.

As they made their way back towards shore, Rachel was grateful Marjorie had persuaded her to take the opportunity. They arrived back on the beach after around forty-five minutes. Judging by the glow on Marjorie's face, she felt the same way as Rachel about what they had seen.

"That was divine," said Marjorie.

Rachel opened her mouth to reply, but a scream rang out from the shower block. Handing her flippers, snorkel, and mask to Marjorie, she ran on instinct towards the sound. By the time Rachel arrived, there was a crowd of people standing around, murmuring about someone having collapsed in the shower. The lifeguards had taken control of the situation, motioning for people to stay back. As Rachel watched Amelia being led away in tears, a few beach attendants forced her to stay with the crowd when every instinct told her she should be on scene.

Marjorie caught up and stood by her side.

"What is it? What's happened?"

"Someone's collapsed in the showers. Amelia's over there with a lifeguard, so I'm assuming she found whoever it was, or it's Victoria or Stephen."

"It's Victoria."

Rachel swung her head around on hearing Preston's voice. *Where has he come from?*

"Has she taken ill?" Marjorie asked.

"We couldn't find a pulse. I was nearby when Brad called for help. We all were. We'd been on the beach and came up to the block to wash sand from our feet."

"Did you try to resuscitate?" Rachel snapped. Why was Preston close to another attack? Was he taking her for a fool?

"We started to, then someone screamed, but Brad had already fetched the lifeguards and they took over. Her face was purple and swollen. I think someone had strangled her, just like..."

"Margaret," Marjorie finished.

"Sir, I need you to come with me." A Hawaiian police officer appeared behind Preston, along with a colleague, and neither looked friendly.

"Why?" Preston asked.

"We need to ask you some questions, sir. You were seen close to where the lady was before they found her."

"Along with fifty others. Have you seen how busy this place is?" Preston snapped, his eyes wide with fear.

The other officer had a hand on his holster.

"Best go with them," said Rachel. "I'm sure they will soon clear it up."

"And you ask why I didn't contact security?" he mumbled before shouting, "THIS IS WHY!"

Rachel watched Preston being guided into a waiting police car.

"We need to speak to the others," she said, anger rising in her throat. "Amelia in particular." She was about to burst past one of the lifeguards when she felt a hand grip her upper arm.

"I know that look, Rachel. Don't you dare!"

Chapter 18

Sarah had a firm grip on Rachel's arm as she steered her away from the frantic scene to a row of sunbeds neatly arranged in a semicircle on the beach. Gwen, who was already seated on one, gave her a wave. Rachel sat on the edge of a sunbed, agitated at being dragged away.

"Calm down, Rachel," said Sarah. "Jason and Graham are over there."

"Why didn't you say so in the first place?"

"Because you were about to barge past a lifeguard."

"She's right. You were," said Marjorie with a giggle.

Rachel saw the funny side and felt herself relax. If Dr Bentley and Jason were there, she would soon find out what had happened.

"Okay, point taken."

"Sarah and I went to help, but the lifeguards had it under control, so we left Graham in charge until the ambulance arrived," said Gwen.

"Preston told me he thought someone had strangled Victoria," Rachel said.

Sarah and Gwen exchanged a glance. "We didn't get close enough to see anything like that, but I heard Graham say there was a pulse," said Sarah.

Rachel heaved a sigh of relief. "At least that's something. Why didn't you tell us you had the day off?"

"Because I didn't, but after morning surgery had finished, Jason called to say he had a few hours leave this afternoon, so Bernard offered to cover for me. He'd been in bed all morning and was happy to do it. Brigitte is taking a few days off later in the week so Gwen had an extra afternoon off. As Gwen and Graham were already coming ashore, we joined them."

Rachel smiled at Gwen. There had been rumours for a while that she and Dr Graham Bentley were an item. Bernard had been hinting for at least a couple of years but, apart from the odd sign, they had not given anything away until now. It appeared they were going public.

"What's that grin on your face, Rachel?" Gwen asked.

"Nothing. I'm pleased for you."

"Me too," said Marjorie. "It's a shame your afternoon off has been interrupted, though."

"We're used to it. The last time Graham and I went for a night out on one of the overnight stops, a passenger dislocated their ankle right in front of us."

"Ouch! That sounds painful," said Rachel.

"Graham had it back in position before the ambulance arrived, which was more painful in the short term, but relieved the pain afterwards."

"And the passenger carried on as if nothing had happened, no doubt?" Marjorie quipped.

"Not quite. They spent the rest of the cruise in a plaster cast, but it could have been worse. Anyway, it looks like Mrs Hayes is being moved."

They looked over to where an ambulance crew were wheeling Victoria on a stretcher to their vehicle. Her head wasn't covered, so she was obviously alive. Amelia followed the stretcher and climbed into the ambulance with her.

Rachel saw Brad chatting to Olga and Stephen. "Where's Emma?"

"We saw her earlier; I think she went for a walk along the beach," Sarah replied.

"At least we can rule her out," said Marjorie, looking pleased.

Sarah frowned. "This isn't a game, you two."

"You're quite right, it isn't—"

"You like Emma, don't you?" Rachel said to Marjorie, intervening before a heated exchange took place. Sarah hated how Marjorie enjoyed investigating murder, and she worried about them both.

"I feel sorry for her," said Marjorie. "Beneath that gruff exterior, she's quite unassuming. The car accident and chronic pain have left her miserable."

"Chronic pain can do that to a person," said Gwen.

"Here's Dr Bentley," said Rachel.

"How is she?" Sarah was the first to ask when Dr Bentley joined them. It was odd seeing him in khaki shorts and a polo shirt rather than his crisp white officer's uniform, thought Rachel.

"Good afternoon, Rachel. Good afternoon, Lady Marjorie," he said, giving them both nods. Dr Bentley was ever the professional. They acknowledged the greeting before he answered Sarah's question.

"She's alive for now, although unconscious. She'll need to be put into an induced coma, I'm afraid. There's a lot of swelling around the airway."

"Is it true she was strangled?" Rachel asked.

"It looks that way. Jason is still over there talking to the police."

Rachel checked whether they had released Preston from the police car. She couldn't see him, but the car was still there, which was a good sign.

"Did anyone see what happened?" Marjorie asked.

"You'd better ask Jason that when he comes back. I was busy establishing an airway and putting in a Guedel," Dr Bentley replied.

"What's a Guedel?" Marjorie asked.

"It's a plastic airway tube that slides into the oropharynx, allowing for easier resuscitation."

"I'm not sure I'm any the wiser."

"It stops the tongue getting in the way," said Gwen, laughing. "Take it as a compliment he's talking to you like a professional."

Dr Bentley's eyes twinkled when he looked at Gwen. "I thought that was a simple explanation."

"Yeah, you did," Gwen teased.

Rachel enjoyed the moment between them and thought what a lovely couple they made. Gwen had been hurt in the past and Graham was a widower. Everyone could see how well suited they were, but they had both been determined not to get hurt again. Watching them helped Rachel to forget what had happened for a little while and be happy for two people who were obviously in love.

"Rachel!"

"What?" she asked.

"I asked if you wanted a drink. You and Marjorie look hot," said Sarah. "Marjorie's going to have an ice cream."

"Oh, an ice cream would be lovely. We've been snorkelling."

Sarah's eyes widened, but Gwen just grinned.

"Don't you start, Sarah," said Marjorie. "Age is just a number, or haven't you heard?"

Sarah's cheeks flushed, and she bit her lip.

"Ignore her, Sarah, she's teasing," said Rachel. "She rebuked me earlier for having the same misgivings. Although I must admit that once she is in the water, Lady Marjorie Snellthorpe is like a fish!"

Marjorie's wide grin said it all, and a lightness came over their gathering. It was good to have a proper catchup with Gwen, Dr Bentley and Sarah, who was in excellent form despite the fact her half-day off had been interrupted. All the same, Rachel kept a close eye on the police car which still held Preston while they chatted and ate ice creams.

Jason finally joined them, looking serious.

"Do you know what happened?" Rachel asked.

"Hello to you too," he said.

Sarah thumped his arm playfully. "You know she won't be happy until you've told her everything. I had to stop her breaking past a lifeguard."

Jason relaxed. "There's not much to tell. Although the showers were busy, everyone denies seeing anything out of the ordinary. It's as though they had all switched off. According to Stephen Williams, there was a lot of pushing and shoving to get to the cubicles. Mrs Hayes was in a disabled one which he had already used earlier."

"If no-one saw anything, why have the police taken Preston for questioning?" Rachel felt anger rising in her chest once more.

"He was seen helping Victoria into the wheelchair cubicle."

Preston had failed to mention that part of the story, which made Rachel wonder whether he was being entirely honest with her. He had already held back facts from the night Margaret was murdered. Perhaps her instincts were wrong this time and he was guilty.

"Where was Amelia when it happened?" Marjorie asked.

"She said Victoria had told her to stay with her belongings. She didn't want anything stolen. Amelia offered to go with her to the shower cubicle, but she was adamant."

"I can imagine. And where were the others?" asked Rachel.

Jason shook his head. "It's like the night of the party. None of them were in each other's sight. They only realised what was happening when someone screamed after Brad found Victoria. Brad heard her calling for help and by the time he got there, she was on the floor. Preston was the closest to the cubicle and the calmest. He examined her before the lifeguards arrived."

"So Brad was nearby too? Was Preston with him?" Rachel said, hopeful he could provide Preston with an alibi.

"I'm afraid not. Brad had come straight from the shower, and was still wearing a towel around his midriff. He had a plastic cover over the plaster."

"Are the showers unisex then?" Sarah asked.

"No, but the disabled cubicle sits between the two blocks and the walls are thin. Brad was in the one on the end. It's thanks to his quick action she's still alive."

Rachel's heart sank when she saw the police car pull away with Preston still inside.

"Sorry, Sarah, but I'm going to have to get back to the ship and report what's happened," said Jason. "You stay if you like."

Sarah hesitated, the corners of her mouth dropping.

"Come with us, Sarah," said Marjorie. "We were going to take the hop on bus to Ali'i market to do some shopping. I have gifts to buy for people back home."

"You go with them," said Jason. "There's no point coming with me. I'll be in meetings with the boss and, most likely, with the captain."

Picking up on Sarah's dilemma, Marjorie added, "You shouldn't go back to the ship when you have time off, and you don't want to stay here playing gooseberry, do you?"

"You're welcome to stay with us. We could even go snorkelling." Gwen's sarcastic laughter broke through the sombre mood.

Sarah grinned. "I think not, but thanks for the offer. I'll go with Rachel and Marjorie. Thank you."

"Right, that's settled then. Come along, Rachel, there's nothing you can do," said Marjorie.

Rachel was torn between heading back to the ship with Jason, going to the hospital to see if Victoria was awake or checking on Preston. None of the options was sensible as Jason had already told her everything he knew. Dr Bentley had said Victoria would need to be ventilated and the police were unlikely to let her anywhere near Preston. But if she went to the hospital, Amelia might be able to tell her something.

She sighed, forcing herself to move. "I guess you're right."

Rachel returned the snorkelling equipment, then the trio gathered themselves together and walked to one of the brightly coloured buses that had just pulled in. Jason followed and kissed Sarah, then took the bus heading in the opposite direction back to the ship. With a heavy heart, Rachel climbed aboard with Sarah and Marjorie, who both appeared to have put the eventful hour behind them. Rachel admired them and wished she could do the same. She would have to try.

Chapter 19

Something was niggling at Rachel, but she couldn't work out what it was. She would be annoyed if Preston had deceived her, but what if he was telling the truth? It wasn't as if he'd had much time to tell her and Marjorie anything before the police took him away for questioning. If he had just been in the wrong place at the wrong time on both occasions, it was bad luck.

But there was also the possibility somebody was playing a sick game with him as the pawn. The attack on Victoria called into question the idea that the motive for Margaret's death was some sort of ill-advised liaison or flirtation. It was time to find out what was going on behind the scenes and why Margaret's killer would try to kill Victoria, unless the two crimes were unrelated.

Rachel's head ached by the time she got to Waverley's office. Hoping he would be there, she knocked on the door.

"Come in," Waverley bellowed from inside.

She opened the door and walked in. Waverley was sitting behind his desk and Jason was leaning over his shoulder. They were both staring at his computer screen.

"Oh, it's you, Rachel. I thought it was Inglis."

"I'm here, sir." Rosemary arrived behind Rachel.

Rachel liked Rosemary Inglis, who was a competent addition to Waverley's security team. She smiled at the broad-shouldered former Olympian, remembering what Emma had said about not wanting to mess with her. Rosemary had competed in white-water slalom events before taking up her post as security officer.

"Let's all sit down, shall we?" Waverley got up from behind his desk and strolled over to the informal seating arranged around a coffee table in his office. He motioned for Rachel to join them. "Did you get him?" Waverley looked at Rosemary once they were all sitting down.

"Yes, sir. The police didn't have enough evidence to hold him. They've insisted he doesn't leave the ship until they have DNA results, which are being fast tracked."

"I take it you're talking about Preston?" Rachel said.

"Yes. The Hawaiian police department requested we escort him back to the ship," said Jason.

"Goodridge and I have just been looking at a report sent over from New York." Waverley appeared in no mood for chitchat.

"And?" Rachel asked. She and Rosemary waited for him to answer, but he sat back in his chair, a smug grin on his face.

"First, you need to share what you've found out, because if you're holding back on us, I'll ask you to leave."

Waverley was clearly in one of his belligerent frames of mind, which didn't bring out the best in him. Rachel was pleased Marjorie wasn't with her, or the security chief would have come off worse.

"I'm not holding back, I just haven't had time to tell you anything, that's all. We shared everything we had so far with Jason last night."

"Not everything," said Waverley. "I bet you knew Smith was the last person to see Margaret Green alive." It was more of an accusation than a question.

Rachel shifted uncomfortably in her seat. "Other than her killer, you mean?"

"Don't play games with me, Rachel. Our agreement was that we share information and that I'm in overall charge of this investigation."

"You're right, I know that now, but I didn't until this morning," said Rachel. "I was going to tell you, but I must warn you that Preston believes he won't get a fair hearing."

"Whyever not?" Waverley's eyes popped out on stalks.

Rachel cleared her throat. "Because he's experienced racism in the past."

"You know as well as I do, Rachel, that there's no place for that sort of thing on board this ship!" Waverley's voice had risen several decibels. "We've got over seventy nationalities working on board, for Pete's sake."

"I know," said Rachel.

"But I hate it when would-be criminals pull out the race card. Have you considered the man might be guilty of murder?"

"Of course I've considered it. In fact, it's looking very much like he is. But I'm not convinced."

Waverley huffed in exasperation. "I believe you when you say you would have given us this information, whether you're convinced or not. It would have given us more clout with the NYPD authorities instead of having to get in via the back door."

"Preston Smith has a record of violence, Rachel," Jason said.

Rachel felt as though someone had slapped her. Rosemary shot her a sympathetic look.

Waverley got up and moved to the printer, sifting through a pile of papers. He handed her one relating to Preston. She skimmed it. The record was from Chicago PD.

"But this was years ago and he got off with a warning."

"He got off because the judge took into account his otherwise unblemished record," said Waverley. "I bet he didn't tell you about that, though, did he? Or about the kindness of a white judge."

"You know, Chief Waverley, that racism exists within police forces in America and, I'm ashamed to say, in England. No matter whether we would like it to be otherwise, a black person's — especially a black male's — experience is very different to a white person's. But let's get back to the point. Surely you're not linking a minor felony committed years ago…" she looked at the sheet again, "…against a man, to the murder and attempted murder of women?"

"Whilst we can't dismiss it, I won't condemn him on that basis. However, you cannot deny he was the last person to see Margaret on the night she died – a fact he's held back from us – and the last person to see Mrs Hayes before her attack."

"I assume the attack on Victoria wasn't a robbery?" Rachel quizzed.

"You assume right. All her belongings were with her nurse Amelia, and the jewellery she was wearing was still with Mrs Hayes," said Waverley. "Did Smith tell you anything, Inglis?"

Rosemary shook her head. "No, sir, other than he didn't attack Mrs Hayes."

"Who would attack a harmless old woman?" Waverley snapped.

Rachel thought of the stick-wielding, wheelchair-racing harridan, but didn't bring it up.

"Why are you grinning?"

"Sorry. It's just that Victoria Hayes can be quite aggressive when she wants to be, and she treats her nurse like a slave. Have you considered Amelia might have attacked her employer? Perhaps she waved her stick once too often."

Waverley looked at Jason and gave him a nod.

"Amelia told us she was left in charge of their belongings. If she'd been close, she could have had time to enter the cubicle and attack her employer unawares. The thing is, she says she was well away from the crowds trying to take showers."

"Can anyone confirm that?"

"Not yet. And something else has cropped up. According to my mate in New York, Amelia's records are suspect."

"In what way?" Rosemary asked.

Jason answered. "The woman didn't exist until she graduated from high school."

"So you think she's living with a new identity?" Rachel turned to Rosemary. "It means she's either a criminal who did a deal with the prosecution services, or she's in witness protection for innocent reasons. I suspect the latter because she's working as a nurse."

"We have to be careful not to put her at risk," said Waverley.

"But we don't know whether she committed a crime in another state where the laws are different and took advantage of a new start in New York. She could be working as a nurse using false documents and could still be our killer," said Rachel.

"You're right," said Jason, "and I've asked my friend Celia to look into her previous background just in case there's a mistake, but without raising any alerts."

"What about the others?" Rachel asked.

"Nothing on Olga Stone has come through yet. Stephen Williams has been investigated for money laundering and industrial bribery. Nothing's ever stuck, and they have never linked him to violence." Waverley handed Rachel the rest of the papers. "I hate to say it, but Preston Smith seems to be our man. Olga told us he was all over Margaret on the night of the party."

Rachel slapped herself on the head. "Idiot! I forgot to mention. Did Olga also tell you she threatened Preston? She told him she would report seeing him with Margaret on the night of the party if he didn't hand over the money and valuables stolen from Stephen Williams."

Waverley rubbed a hand through his thinning hair and cleared his throat loudly. "You'd better start from the beginning."

Rachel explained how she had found Preston that morning, and what he had told her. "If it hadn't been for Victoria's attack, I'd have said you were on the right track with the thefts and the accomplice line of thinking. Olga Stone's a ruthless woman who's not above blackmail. I was almost convinced she was the accomplice, and that she had murdered Margaret, either out of jealousy or because she had backtracked on their deal. The other thing Marjorie and I thought was that she is just an opportunistic vulture."

"Where is your sidekick, by the way?" asked Waverley.

"She was tired after our day out and a late night last night. She's more inclined to believe Preston is the criminal than I am and has accepted the case might be closed. On that basis, I persuaded her to eat in her room and have an early night."

Waverley considered what Rachel had said. He rubbed his eyes. "It appears we're not much further on than before. Could Olga Stone have been trying to rob Victoria Hayes and something went wrong? Perhaps she panicked and ran away when Mrs Hayes cried out."

"But wouldn't she have known that Amelia was guarding her things?" Rosemary quizzed.

"I suppose she could have been going for the jewellery. Victoria wears some expensive jewellery which she might have left to one side. There was a shelf for such things and the cubicle wasn't locked," said Jason. "Maybe Mrs Hayes caught her sneaking inside."

"Had she removed her jewellery?" Waverley snapped.

"No, she'd only gone inside to wash sand off her feet, according to Amelia Hastings."

Waverley cursed under his breath. "So it could be her, but I still say Smith's the prime suspect. If he wasn't working for one of the passengers, I'd put him under house arrest, but without evidence… well… we'll keep an eye on him. See to it, Goodridge.

"Inglis, you follow up on Olga Stone. Reinterview her and challenge her on what Rachel has told us. Tomorrow morning, we'll contact the agency they all work for and ask if there have been any reports of stolen property. I'll speak to Stephen Williams about the theft again… see if he can tell us exactly what he thinks she stole and get Ravanos to search Smith's room. You search the dead girl's room again, Goodridge, and the other two rooms while they're not on board."

"By the other two, I assume you mean Victoria and Amelia?" Rachel quizzed. "Would you like me to help?"

Waverley gave her a look that could have melted snow, but then his expression mellowed. "We are pushed. I can't let you enter the passenger rooms by yourself, but you could help Goodridge. Is that all right with you?" Waverley looked at Jason.

"Very all right," he replied. "I suggest we start with Amelia's before she comes back from the hospital."

"Right. Get to it," Waverley commanded.

Rachel leapt up and followed Jason out of Waverley's office, happy to be doing something that might lead to finding the killer.

Chapter 20

Their search of Amelia's room led nowhere. Jason didn't feel they could check her safe without permission or a good enough reason, so it was a waste of time. There was nothing in Victoria's room to suggest any reason for the attack at the beach either. And no sign of the letters she said she'd been receiving. Rachel wondered if she had destroyed them.

"Sorry, Rachel. This isn't getting us anywhere. I think I'll join Ravanos with Preston," said Jason.

"Good idea," she replied. "If you're going to speak to Preston and look around his room, you'd best do it without me. It will work better if he doesn't suspect me of being formally involved in investigating him. I'd like to keep him onside for now because, if he isn't the killer, he could know more than he thinks."

"What do you mean?"

Rachel sighed. "I wish I knew, but something tells me he might have witnessed something that hasn't registered with him yet. Something that could lead us to the killer. Both times he's been close to the scene and my feeling is, if I can get him to feel less defensive, he might think a little clearer and remember something significant."

"That makes sense," said Jason. "Catch you later."

When they went their separate ways, Rachel headed upstairs to the buffet. It was getting late, and she hadn't eaten since stopping for an afternoon snack with Marjorie and Sarah in the marketplace. The buffet was relatively quiet when she filled her tray and went to find a seat.

No sooner had she sat down than Sarah joined her.

"Hello, you. Has surgery finished already?"

"An hour ago. You lose all sense of time and place when tracking down criminals, don't you?" Sarah put a tray of food on the table. "I thought I'd find you up here, knowing how much you like junk food."

Sarah laughed. Rachel grinned in good humour. She was a health food fanatic, something Sarah would never be. Sarah loved fast-food. They were opposites in so many ways, but their friendship was much deeper than their lifestyle habits. Having grown up together in a small village and attended the same university in Leeds, where Rachel had studied history and Sarah nursing, they had remained best friends into their married years. They had been bridesmaids at each other's weddings, and Jason and Carlos were now good friends too. Their husbands shared experiences of being in the army, although Carlos's service had been more clandestine than Jason's. Still, they carried similar scars, things that only men and women who had served in war zones would ever understand.

It was the same in Rachel and Sarah's jobs. They experienced things only their professional colleagues could understand, but it didn't mean they couldn't relax in each other's company.

"Funny how you, the health professional, prefer the junk, and me, the copper, runs every day and lives on salad."

"Interspersed with the odd steak," Sarah teased. "Is it true most detectives eat junk food and have messy cars?"

"You watch too much television," said Rachel.

"If you say so. Anyway, my bad food habits come from too many skipped meals and meetings in the pub after work," Sarah replied. "And as long as I stay busy, the rushing about keeps the weight to slightly above healthy. I'm looking forward to being an obese retired nurse one day."

Rachel giggled. "I might join you. But for now, I want to stay fit enough to chase bad guys. By the way, I didn't say too much earlier, but Marjorie and I are thrilled about Gwen and Dr Bentley."

"You've known him long enough to call him Graham now," said Sarah.

Rachel sipped her coffee. "It wouldn't feel right. Remember, in the force, we still use sir and ma'am mostly."

Sarah finished a mouthful of burger before speaking again. "This isn't a random meeting. The reason I'm not having a slap-up meal in the officers' mess is that I thought you might like to know that Victoria Hayes is stable."

"Awake?" Rachel's heartbeat quickened.

"No. Graham was right on that front. She's in an induced coma and is being ventilated by tracheotomy until her airway recovers. However, the attacker may have met their match. There's blood and DNA on her walking stick. She must have got a hit on target."

"Ooh. Good for her. Hopefully, they'll get a match."

"That might be more difficult. Amelia said her employer got into an altercation with a dog owner earlier in the day and hit out, so the blood could be from that poor soul."

"Someone should tell that lady, if she recovers, she can't go around walloping people with her walking stick."

"She'll most likely say she couldn't see what she was doing. Her eyesight isn't the best in the non-patched eye, according to what Amelia told Graham over the phone."

"Is Amelia coming back to the ship?" Rachel asked.

"Only to pack up their belongings. She plans to take them to the hospital and if it looks like a long stay for Victoria, she'll fly back to New York the minute the Hawaiian police give her permission."

"They won't unless someone verifies where she was at the time of the crime. I'm surprised Waverley's letting her leave the ship."

"He doesn't have any reason to suspect she killed Margaret Green and even if he did, without evidence, he couldn't hold her."

"What about Stephen? Doesn't he still need a nurse?"

"Not really. We can remind him to take his medication."

"I'd like to talk to her before she leaves the ship," said Rachel.

"We're about to set sail again. I can let you have her room number as long as you don't tell anyone I gave it to you."

"No problem. I've already been in her room with your husband."

Sarah's jaw dropped, and her eyes widened. "Seriously? You're as bad as each other. I don't suppose you know whether my husband will come back to our room tonight?"

"Sorry, he didn't say. Waverley's on a mission, but I'm sure Jason will be in touch. When I left him, he was going to interview Preston again with Ravanos and search his room."

"Poor Preston. He seems such a nice young man. Totally out of his depth... and so innocent."

Rachel didn't want to burst the bubble and mention Preston's criminal record, so she just shrugged. "We don't know for certain he's not involved in this."

"In my humble opinion, he's innocent."

"I won't argue with you on that point, but he was close to both people just before their attacks."

"Are we certain the crimes are linked? We do get passengers being mugged occasionally when they go ashore."

"Both victims were strangled, or attempted in the second case, but it gives us what we call in the force an MO, or modus operandi."

"I've watched enough television to know that means a way of doing things. Is strangling an unusual way to kill people? I mean, surely there are easier ways to murder people, like bashing them over the head, poisoning, even stabbing them."

Rachel stopped eating for a moment. "You make a good point there, Sarah. Maybe this really is the killer's MO." Rachel thought back to the report of Preston's previous crime. It had involved attacking a man with a baseball bat. She smiled before patting her friend on the shoulder. "Good detective work."

"What?" Sarah looked confused.

"We're looking for someone who likes to choke the life out of their victims and I'd stake my reputation on the fact they have used this method long before now."

Sarah's eyes widened. "Please don't tell me we have a serial killer on board."

Rachel shook her head. "I don't think so, in the usual sense, but we have someone whose fury makes them use their hands to shut people up."

"Does that mean you know who it is?" Sarah looked hopeful.

"Unfortunately not. But there's something telling about the method. It's like they want the victim to see the power they have over them before they die."

"That's horrible," said Sarah. "You'd better catch them before they do it again."

"I intend to," said Rachel, trying to formulate a plan as to how to go about it.

"Can you narrow it down at all?"

"I've been wracking my brains over that one. The perpetrator doesn't have to be excessively strong because Margaret was drunk that night. She might have passed out or fallen asleep before they strangled her. And Victoria might be a strong biddy, but she's not so fit she wouldn't be easy to overcome. We can rule out Emma because, although she could have been in the frame for Margaret's killing, she was walking along the beach this afternoon."

"And Amelia was watching Victoria's belongings while she was being attacked," said Sarah.

"Nobody has confirmed that yet, but I think Amelia has every reason to want to stay out of the public eye, so I don't think it's her."

"Brad found Victoria," said Sarah. "But his arm is in plaster, so it's not him."

"Right," said Rachel. "That's two, possibly three in the clear, along with Victoria now. And Stephen is highly unlikely."

"Which leaves Preston and Olga. I hate to admit it, but it's looking more and more like Preston, as much as I don't want to believe it was him," said Sarah.

"My money's now on Olga, with Preston as a possible. Amelia is the least likely, but still on the list."

"What will you do now?" Sarah asked.

"My priority is to speak to Amelia. If she's in the clear, we'll have narrowed it down to two."

"Rachel, please be careful, and whatever you do, make sure Marjorie doesn't put herself at risk. You know how she thinks these investigations are a game."

"Trust me, Sarah. And don't worry about Marjorie. That lady's as astute as she ever was, but I promise I'll be watching her back every minute."

"So where is she now?" asked Sarah.

"Having an early night," said Rachel.

Chapter 21

Marjorie dabbed at the corners of her mouth with a napkin, having finished the last of her dinner. She glanced around the suite, decorated in rich tones of teal and gold, and sighed. Now she'd eaten, the prospect of an early night seemed unappealing. She didn't need rest; she needed excitement.

"I wonder if Rachel would like company," she murmured to herself, reaching for the telephone on the bedside table. She dialled Rachel's room and waited, drumming her fingers on the polished wood. The phone went to voicemail.

"Rachel, I've got a second wind and I'm not tired. I expect you're out investigating or meeting Sarah. I'll look for you in the usual places," Marjorie said, disappointed to have missed her friend. But, determined, she got up.

"There's only one way to find her and that's to get moving."

She picked up a shawl and left the suite. Marjorie concluded Rachel would most likely be in the Jazz Bar. It was one of their favourite meeting places and seemed like a good place to start her search, but she wanted to pick up an information leaflet about their next port first. The leaflets were in the main atrium.

The ship's corridors were filled with the sound of laughter and chatter, but it faded as Marjorie entered the main atrium, where her ears were treated to the soothing tones of classical music. Her eyes scanned the area, taking in the grand staircase adorned with flowering plants, which led to the upper decks. A string quartet played an elegant waltz on the marble floor, casting a spell of enchantment over the entire scene.

Marjorie picked up her leaflet, and then spotted the familiar figure of Stephen Williams, sitting in his electric wheelchair on the edge of the dance floor. His head and shoulders swayed gently in time with the music. The elderly gentleman seemed remarkably relaxed, considering what had happened to his old friend. Or perhaps old sparring partner might be a better description.

"Good evening," she said, approaching him.

"Hello, Marjorie," Stephen replied when he caught sight of her, his face brightening. "Would you like to join me?"

"Thank you, I will for a moment," she said, taking a seat next to his chair. "I was looking for Rachel, but this beautiful music is worth pausing for."

"They are quite talented," Stephen agreed, his eyes following the graceful movements of the violinist's bow. "I've just had news of Vicky. She's on a ventilator, but is stable for now."

That explained why he appeared at ease. "Do the doctors think she'll survive?" Marjorie asked.

"Amelia's back on board ship. She tells me it's touch and go, but there's a good fifty-fifty chance. The darnedest thing is Amelia's leaving in the morning, so I've got no nurse."

"If you don't mind me saying so, I'm not convinced you need one."

He grinned. "We'll see, won't we? The way things are going around here, I might need a bodyguard. Could be whoever attacked Margaret and Vicky's gonna come after us one by one."

"I don't think you should joke about such things. Do you know they arrested Preston?"

"Yeah, but word is, the police have released him."

Marjorie blinked in surprise, but was pleased the police had let him go. "I suppose no-one has a clue about who might be responsible at this point. But I doubt they have ruled him out entirely."

As they continued to discuss the attack and various other happenings since they'd boarded the ship, Marjorie was eager to discover more about the relationships between each member of Stephen's party.

"Do you believe Preston could have had anything to do with Victoria's attack?" she asked, watching for his reaction.

"Hard to say," Stephen said, his gaze drifting to the string quartet. "I don't know him well enough. But if you ask me, there's more going on with that young man, and some others in our group, than what we see. Mind you, anyone could have attacked her after the way she was behaving today. She almost ran into a kid she was in such a mood. If I'd been one of the parents, I'd have wanted to strangle her myself. Then she had an altercation with a guy whose dog was off the lead and approached her wheelchair. Smacked the dog and the guy away with that stick of hers."

"Had something upset her?"

"Who knows?" Stephen shrugged. "She was ranting at me about stuff from years ago, accusing me of telling Margaret what had happened. And then going on about receiving threatening letters from someone – she assumes Margaret – trying to extort money from her."

"And did you tell Margaret?"

"Nah, it's all in her imagination. If anything, Margaret overheard me and Vicky talking about it."

"Victoria mentioned receiving letters to Rachel and me, and you're right, she seemed convinced Margaret had sent them. What was it she was so frightened of coming into the light?"

Stephen sighed, his fingers tapping to the rhythm of the waltz on the armrest of his wheelchair.

"A little bribery, that's all. It happened years ago when Vicky was running for the senate. I needed her support for one of my building projects and she needed votes. It was a fair exchange, votes for contracts. But I never told Margaret about it, or anyone else. It doesn't do to discuss private business dealings with strangers, although I don't know why Vicky was making such a big deal about it. Who cares?"

"I tried to tell her that much when she told us," said Marjorie.

"As for the letters, I have no idea who's behind them, but if Margaret heard something, it wouldn't surprise me if it was her."

It surprised Marjorie how Stephen spoke so matter-of-factly about such serious matters. "Interesting," she murmured. "I can't imagine there being a lot of fallout if word got out, but I wouldn't know, not being American."

"Most people wouldn't care. I guess it would damage both our reputations for a while, but there are bigger scandals for the newshounds to be following right now. Our former president divides opinion for one. Mind you,

Victoria opposed him back in the day, so he might like to take advantage of a minor diversion."

"Politics is such a murky world, isn't it?"

"Life is murky, Marjorie, but I'm sure you know that already. I wonder…" he paused before continuing, "…maybe Margaret wasn't the blackmailer and Vicky received another letter."

"Did she mention anything like that?" Marjorie asked.

Stephen raised an eyebrow, intrigued. "Nope, but what if she worked out it was someone else and threatened to report them?"

"Alternatively," said Marjorie, "Victoria could have discovered something about Margaret's death, something crucial, and the killer couldn't risk her exposing them. In which case, they would try to silence her before she could say anything."

"By strangling her in a shower cubicle?" Stephen asked sceptically, though his expression betrayed that he considered the idea plausible.

"Why not?" Marjorie nodded, her eyes glinting with determination. "If we can uncover the connection, we'll be one step closer to solving Margaret's murder. I wonder what Victoria will have to say when she regains consciousness."

"Assuming she ever does wake up from her coma, and even if she does, she might not remember anything,"

Stephen muttered, his fingers twitching with restless energy.

"People have come back from worse."

As Marjorie and Stephen continued their conversation, the string quartet played on, its soothing melodies creating calm in the grand atrium.

"You're quite the sleuth, aren't you, Lady Marjorie? Why are you so interested?"

"I hate to see injustice, and I especially hate the thought of a murderer walking freely among us. As you said, we never know who might be next."

"That's quite the argument."

Marjorie felt her lips tighten. "Does Victoria have any next of kin?"

"Yeah, she's got a squeaky-clean daughter who's looking to make a name for herself."

Marjorie wondered if Victoria was worried her past might affect her daughter's ambitions. It would explain why she was so angry about the possibility of her secret coming out. And she hadn't seemed concerned on hearing Margaret was dead.

"I assume someone has contacted her daughter?"

"Amelia phoned her earlier, as did the doctor at the hospital, but she's too busy to fly out and visit." Stephen's voice dripped cynicism. "It doesn't matter what you do for kids, sometimes they just grow up bad."

Not wanting to get into a philosophical discussion with Stephen on the subject of child-rearing, Marjorie was pleased when she noticed Brad and Preston walking through the atrium. The two men were engaged in a heated discussion.

"If you'll excuse me, Stephen, I'd better find Rachel. Enjoy the rest of your evening. I'm sure the ship's nurses will take good care of your needs should you have any." Marjorie rose from her seat.

Stephen giggled. "I'm sure they will. I'll keep you posted on that." He turned his attention back to the string quartet as Marjorie scurried after the two men.

"Excuse me, gentlemen," she said, approaching Brad and Preston. They stopped their conversation and turned to her.

Preston greeted her with a nod. "How can we help you?"

"I was wondering how you're feeling?" Marjorie said.

Brad didn't appear in the mood to chat. Excusing himself, he walked away, leaving Marjorie alone with Preston.

"Truth be told, I'm annoyed," Preston replied, his tone edged with frustration. "I'm free, but I can't leave the ship until they have DNA results, and now Brad's saying he doesn't want my help until I'm in the clear. It's not fair. I have done nothing wrong." He looked and sounded like a petulant teenager.

"The police have to carry out their enquiries. I'm sure it won't be long before you're in the clear. Did you see anything suspicious after you took Victoria into the shower cubicle?"

"There might have been something, but I'm not certain of it, and I'm not saying anything until I've looked into it myself." Preston glanced around as if worried someone might overhear them.

"Shouldn't you let the security team or the police do that?" Marjorie asked.

Preston shook his head. "Not yet, because if I'm wrong, they'll just twist it around and put the blame right back on me again. You and your friend Rachel should be careful too. Word's getting round that you're unofficially investigating what happened to Margaret."

"I see," said Marjorie, wondering if this was a veiled threat. "Who exactly is spreading this word?"

Preston's eyes focussed on something behind Marjorie. "I'd better go."

When Marjorie turned to check who or what he had seen, there was nothing other than a group of teenagers heading for a night out. She watched Preston walk away, deciding to go back to her suite after all. Rather than go straight upstairs, though, she took a stroll on the outside deck, wanting to process everything she had learned so far. The brisk ocean breeze filled her lungs, invigorating her senses.

As she walked along the deck, Marjorie couldn't shake the feeling that someone was following her. But every time she spun around, all she could spot were deep, mysterious shadows.

"Get a grip, Marjorie Snellthorpe," she muttered under her breath. "You're turning into a paranoid old woman." Nevertheless, she hastened her steps along the deck, expecting something sinister to emerge from the darkness. Her heart raced, and adrenaline surged through her veins.

Just as she reached an entrance back into the main ship, panic gripped her. She felt hands lock around her neck from behind and a rush of breath on the side of her face. Ignoring the intense burning pain in her throat, Marjorie scrabbled for the door handle, trying to escape, but the grip just tightened. She felt tears streaming down her cheeks as she realised that this could be the end.

Chapter 22

The grip on Marjorie's throat tightened, and she gasped for air. She clawed at the hands, desperate to break free.

"Who are you? What do you want?" she choked out between raspy breaths, hoping that a nearby passenger might hear her struggle.

The attacker didn't respond, but loosened their grip when the sound of running footsteps echoed across the deck.

"Stop!" a familiar voice shouted from behind them.

The attacker released Marjorie and pushed her out of the way before disappearing through the door. Marjorie flopped against it after it closed, coughing, and gasping for air. She tried to focus, wanting to identify her assailant, but she hadn't seen who it was. Nobody else was around who could have seen what had happened.

"Marjorie, are you all right?" Rachel rushed towards her, concern etched on her face.

"Someone…" Marjorie wheezed, rubbing her sore throat, "…tried to strangle me." Her pulse was still racing, and anger mixed with fear in her gut. "I think my shawl saved me. I'd pulled it tight around my neck to prevent a draught."

"Did you see who it was?" Rachel asked urgently, scanning the area for any sign of the attacker.

Before Marjorie could answer, her vision blurred, and darkness threatened to overtake her. The last thing she heard before passing out was Rachel calling for help, her voice fading as if carried away by the ocean breeze.

***

Marjorie opened her eyes to find Rachel still leaning over her, cradling her head in her lap.

"Stay with me, Marjorie," Rachel pleaded, gripping her hand. "Help's on the way."

"I'm sorry, Rachel," Marjorie whispered, trying to stop the swimming in her head.

"Marjorie… it's okay, don't try to talk."

"Let me help… I'm a nurse!" Amelia's voice rang out, sounding more assertive than usual, and Marjorie saw her pushing through a small crowd that was gathering. She dropped to her knees next to Marjorie and felt her pulse.

"Someone attacked her," said Rachel.

"She'll be okay, but we need to get her downstairs to the medical centre."

Two crew members arrived with a stretcher at the same time as Janet Plover. The doctor quickly checked Marjorie over before instructing the crew to lift her onto the stretcher. Rachel held Marjorie's hand as they moved her. She felt the warmth of safety once inside the ship's interior. The medical team wasted no time in getting her to the infirmary. She heard Amelia offering to help, and Janet agreed she could accompany them.

"Do we know what happened?" Janet asked when they were in the lift.

"Just that someone tried to strangle her," Marjorie heard Rachel say. Her voice sounded angry and determined.

"What's happening around here?" Amelia sounded slightly hysterical. "First Margaret, then Victoria, and now your friend."

"I don't know, but believe me when I say I'm going to find out." Marjorie recognised the edge in Rachel's voice before it softened. "Will she be okay?"

"She'll be fine after some rest," Janet replied.

The lift arrived at its destination on deck two, and the medics wheeled Marjorie into the infirmary. Sarah was there waiting for them.

"I heard the call on my radio. How is she?"

Marjorie felt an immediate surge of energy as she replied, "Will everyone stop speaking as if I'm dying? It was a slight shock, that's all. I shall be fine if somebody can bring me a cup of Earl Grey tea."

Rachel burst into hysterical laughter before squeezing Marjorie's hand. "You scared the life out of me."

During the next fifteen minutes, the medical team helped Marjorie transfer into a bed. Janet Plover insisted she stay in for the night, and Rachel and Sarah clucked around like mother hens. Marjorie tolerated the fuss because she knew how much they cared for her, but she was all too aware that Rachel would be more resolved now than ever to find whoever was responsible.

Once she was sitting up in bed, supported by pillows, with a cup of tea in her hand, Marjorie tried to recall what had happened. Amelia was crying in a corner while speaking to Sarah, and Dr Janet Plover had been called to attend a crew member who had gone down with a temperature. Rachel was in the chair next to the bed.

"How did you know where I was?" Marjorie asked.

"I didn't. When I got back to the suite after a late dinner, I heard your message, and when you didn't answer the phone in your room, I checked with Mario. We looked inside in case you were sleeping, and then I checked the Jazz Bar. I saw Stephen in the atrium and when I asked him if he'd seen you, he told me you had said you were looking for me, but that he saw you speaking to Brad and

Preston. After running around for a bit, I took to the outer decks, knowing how you like to stroll in the fresh evening air. At first, I was pleased to hear your voice, but when I heard the panic, I called out and ran."

"I fear if you hadn't turned up when you did, I might have been this killer's third victim."

Rachel's voice was solemn. "What do you remember?"

"Not much. Stephen's partly right. I had been speaking to Preston – not Brad – he was in a mood and left us. Preston was angry about the police insisting he stay on board the ship and said Brad wanted nothing to do with him until the DNA results were in. After talking to him, I was going to give up and go back to bed, but decided to take in the fresh air first. That's when I felt as though someone was following me in the shadows. Every time I turned to look, there was nothing there. I hurried towards a door, but just as I got there, I felt someone's hands gripping my throat. They couldn't get a firm grip through my shawl and my wriggling, but it wouldn't have taken them much longer.

"Just when I thought it was the end, I heard someone running – you – and they let go and disappeared inside. Alas, I didn't see who it was."

"Do you have any idea whether it was a man or a woman?"

Marjorie shook her head. "They were wearing leather gloves. I know that much because I tried to grab their hands."

"That narrows it down," said Rachel, sounding hopeless.

"Sorry I can't be more help."

"Funny how Preston was the last person you were speaking to. That puts him at three scenes," Rachel said. "I'm thinking this isn't a coincidence."

"You believe he's the one doing this?"

"Either that or someone's doing a pretty good job of setting him up."

"Which reminds me," said Marjorie. "When I asked him, Preston implied he might have seen something this afternoon, but said he wanted to do some investigating himself."

Rachel looked thoughtful. "It could be a ruse to divert attention away from him."

"Yes, it could, and he suggested people would think that unless he had more information. I think that's why he wanted to do something about it. Anyway, I'm feeling much better, Rachel, and Amelia is leaving. Your time would be better spent speaking to her about what happened this afternoon, I feel. She might know something."

"Are you sure?"

"Quite sure. Sarah will take good care of me."

Sarah appeared as if on cue. "I've volunteered to take the night shift."

"There you are then. Now go. I'm in excellent hands. You track down this killer before someone else is attacked."

Rachel leaned in and kissed Marjorie on the cheek. "I'll do my best," she said before hurrying after Amelia.

Chapter 23

Rachel found Amelia at the lifts. The woman was a couple of inches shorter than Rachel, around 5 foot 8. She had wavy shoulder-length red hair and looked to be in her mid-forties. Her face had a few lines on the forehead and bags under her eyes, suggesting she hadn't been sleeping well. She wore a long-sleeved shirt, a pair of trousers, and open-toed black shoes.

Amelia's green eyes were full of emotion, anxiety and apprehension when Rachel looked at her. They were wide and deep as if she was bracing herself for bad news.

"I'm glad I caught you. Thanks for what you did for Marjorie. She means a lot to me."

Amelia blinked rapidly before answering, "No problem. Glad it turned out okay."

"How's Victoria?" Rachel asked.

"In a coma. She might recover, she might not. The doctors say it depends on how quickly the swelling around her airway goes down."

"She strikes me as a fighter, so let's hope she lives. I picked up a late edition of the local paper when I got back to the ship; she's made the news."

"Oh." When Amelia's eyes widened and the blinking became rapid again, Rachel knew it was time to delve into her past.

"Look, back in the UK, I'm a detective. I think it's time we had a serious conversation about what's going on. Do you fancy going for a drink?"

Amelia hesitated, still blinking rapidly. She eyed Rachel. "How do I know you're telling the truth?"

Rachel reached into her handbag and brought out her purse. She showed her ID, pleased she'd kept it on her person rather than leaving it at home.

"About that drink?"

"I don't drink," said Amelia.

"The cocktail bar in the Sky Lounge is quiet at this time of night, and they do great mocktails which are non-alcoholic."

The lift dinged, and the doors swung open. Both women got inside.

"Okay, but I'm not sure I can help."

As the lift climbed, Rachel detected a heavy scent of perfume mixed with the sweat of anxiety. She would need to tread carefully, she thought, sensing Amelia could bolt at any minute. The woman's nerves appeared to be getting the better of her as she twisted the long handle of her handbag around her index finger and avoided eye contact.

Once in the Sky Lounge, Rachel ordered a Sunrise Mocktail and Amelia asked for a Club Soda and Lime. After Rachel had a brief conversation with Malia at the bar, they found a table out of the way of the other passengers. Amelia remained tense, her hands shaking when she picked up her drink.

"Please believe me," said Rachel. "Whatever you tell me that isn't relevant to this case stays between us. I'm asking you to trust me."

"It's difficult to trust people when there's a target on your back," Amelia murmured. Her breathing was staggered, as if she was trying to regain her composure.

"If it helps, I've already sussed that you're not who you say you are... and that you're most likely in a witness protection programme. How am I doing so far?"

Startled, Amelia focussed her eyes on Rachel, defiantly holding her gaze. "How did you know? Who else knows?"

"As far as I'm aware, only one or two in the security team, and they don't know for certain. Whatever's gone on in your past, I'm not prying for the sake of it. Just tell me if you think it has anything to do with these attacks."

"That's the problem, I don't know. When Margaret was murdered, I thought it might be a hit to frighten me, or a case of mistaken identity. I used to dye my hair black. But then..." Amelia took out a tissue and blew her nose.

"Victoria was attacked, and she's the wrong age."

Amelia nodded. "Then I got to thinking at the hospital, what if they're making me suffer first? It's what these people do..." Amelia's lips quivered as she tried to contain her emotions. Her eyes reddened from the tears she had been holding back, and her hands shook as she rummaged in her bag to find a tissue. Her shoulders trembled as gentle sobs overtook her, and tears made rivulets down her cheeks.

Rachel moved closer, placing a hand over hers. "I didn't want to bring back painful memories for you, but we need to track down whoever is doing this."

"I know," said Amelia, wiping tears from her eyes.

"And now, do you still believe this is about you?"

"I'm so sorry," she blubbered. More tears trickled down her cheeks and pooled on the table in front of her, each shuddering sob echoing in the air like a soft hiccup. She took a deep breath, composing herself again. "Don't be angry with me, but when your friend Marjorie was attacked, I was almost relieved."

Rachel tensed, not trusting herself to say anything. She waited.

Amelia continued, "You see, unless she's worked out who is responsible, there would be no reason to attack her. She's not connected with me." She swiped at the tears still falling and looked at Rachel. "It's still terrifying to think there's a killer in our group and I can't afford to attract attention to myself. I'm leaving tomorrow."

"I heard," said Rachel.

"The Hawaiian police are satisfied about my whereabouts when Victoria was attacked. Someone vouched for me, so I'm going to fly straight back to New York. Please, could you make sure Victoria's belongings get to the hospital? I can't go there now. If the press are involved and my photo gets out – it's been years, but these people don't forget."

"What happened?" Rachel asked, taking a sip of her mocktail.

"Years ago, I was involved with some... what you would call unsavoury people," Amelia confessed, her voice barely above a whisper. "I did and saw things I'm not proud of, but I left it all behind and escaped that life. You guessed right. In exchange for giving evidence, I changed my name and started over as a private nurse."

"It can't have been easy. Who are these people?" Rachel wanted to be certain Amelia wasn't mistaken about whoever she was running from not being involved.

"My husband was in a gang. The gang leader, Jay Cowley, killed my brother after he came to my home to persuade me to get out. I refused to go with him, but on his way back to his car, Jay just shot him in cold blood. Frankie – my husband – told me to get over it. Fearing for my life, I complied for a while, waiting until they stopped watching me. But I swore to myself on the day my brother died, I'd get them back.

"Finally, the chance came. I feigned an illness when they were going out on a job. I escaped in the middle of the night and went straight to the out-of-state police. After that I did a deal and turned evidence for a new life.

"Soon after I got away, Jay killed Frankie, but I was past caring about him. I would never forgive him for what he let Jay do. It doesn't matter that Jay's locked up; if the other gang members find me, they'll kill me without a second thought. As much as I'd like to help you find out who attacked your friend, I can't get mixed up in anything that would bring me into the public eye. Working as a private nurse has kept me hidden, and I'd like it to stay that way."

"I understand," said Rachel.

"Believe me, I'm not that person anymore, and these attacks have nothing to do with me. Victoria can be a pain, but I've grown to like her. I hope she lives and I wish you every success in finding out who attacked her and killed Margaret."

Rachel did believe her. "What you did was exceptionally brave. Most people would have been too terrified."

Amelia blinked further tears away. "My brother was my rock. It was the least I could do, but it will never bring him back. He tried so hard to keep me out of trouble, but when I met Frankie, the excitement sucked me in, and back then I loved him. I was blind. If I could turn back the clock, I would, but I hope that putting one piece of scum behind bars for the rest of his life has gone a little way towards making amends."

"You did the right thing. And you've saved someone else from losing their brother or husband," said Rachel.

"As I said, it didn't bring Patrick back, and being in witness protection means I can never see the aunt who brought me up."

Rachel tried to imagine how hard it would be not to see her family again. She loved her parents and her brother, and couldn't bear to think of the wrench if she ever had to do what Amelia had done.

"Thank you for telling me all this. I'll speak to the security chief and ask him not to do any more digging into your past."

"Thank you. There are always cops on the payroll of these gangs, and it only takes one to put out an alert."

"Will you go back to the agency?"

Amelia shook her head. "No. If news of what's happened gets back to New York, I don't want to be around. It's time to move to a different state, California maybe. One reason I trained as a nurse after all this happened was so as I could pick up work anywhere in the US if a situation like this arose. I avoid working in major hospitals, but I could work in a clinic or do private work for another agency."

"Will you ever put down roots again?"

Amelia opened out her palms. "I doubt it, but you can never say never. You might not believe this, but although I started nursing for all the wrong reasons, I love the job.

Working as a nurse gives me a sense of purpose, despite my past. It's almost like I'm making atonement for my sins."

They finished their drinks and after they stood, Rachel moved around the table and pulled Amelia into a hug. "I wish you as much happiness as you can get in this life. You've paid a heavy price for your past and whatever you think of yourself, believe me when I say that none of us is blameless. We all need forgiveness. I know God has forgiven you. I just hope you find it within you to forgive yourself."

"Thanks." Amelia pulled away, looking again at Rachel. "The police in England are lucky to have someone like you." With that, Amelia turned on her heels, leaving Rachel staring after her.

"I mean it," she called into the gap left by Amelia, before turning her thoughts to the murderer. "So who the heck are you? Whoever you are, you'd better believe I'm coming after you."

Chapter 24

Waverley's office was empty, and the lights were out when Rachel got there. It wasn't surprising, as the time was well after midnight. Instead of making her way to the security hub, she texted Jason a message.

"Have spoken to Amelia Hastings. Please don't do any further checks. Will explain when I see you. R. x"

No-one from the outside would have known there was anyone in the medical centre as it was locked up. Rachel pressed the bell. Sarah answered the call after a couple of minutes. When Rachel saw her checking through the glass, she stood back and waved.

Sarah unlocked the door, and Rachel stepped inside. "I couldn't go to bed until I was sure Marjorie was okay," she explained.

"Relax, she's sleeping like a baby. Waverley and Jason stopped by to check up on her and to interview her. There's no CCTV footage available from where she was walking, so they're no wiser as to who attacked her. It could have been anyone."

"How did Waverley seem?"

"How do you think?"

"Stressed out of his head."

"Understatement," said Sarah. "Do you want to come in for a coffee? There's a quiet room off the infirmary, from where I can monitor the patient." Rachel heard the exhaustion in Sarah's voice, a solemn whisper of fatigue. She also noticed the distinct dark circles underneath Sarah's eyes, a stark sign of long, sleepless nights. They reminded her of her own battle to stay awake in the face of exhaustion.

"Yes, a coffee would be good. It's kind of you to put in the extra shift. I appreciate it."

"She's my friend as well, Rachel. Besides, it was the least I could do after being given an extra afternoon off. Bernard phoned down to offer, of course, Marjorie being his favourite aristocrat and all that."

Rachel grinned as she followed Sarah into the infirmary. She checked Marjorie was still sleeping before entering a small nurse's station-cum-office.

"I haven't been in this room before."

"That's because it used to be a storeroom, but Gwen had it made into a nurses' station for us when we're on duty in the infirmary. Not every patient enjoys being stared at the whole time. Turns out it's been quite a hit. We can catch up on notes while keeping an eye on the monitors."

Rachel studied a screen displaying what she assumed was a replica of Marjorie's heart monitor.

"You stay here while I nip into Gwen's office and get us some hot drinks."

Rachel sat upright in the chair, her eyes fixated on the pulsating lines and numbers displaying Marjorie's heart and respiratory rate while she slept. Her friend appeared to be in a deep sleep. For that, she was thankful.

Sarah returned carrying two steaming cups of hot liquid. Coffee for Rachel and tea for herself.

"Is that normal?" Rachel pointed to an out-of-the-ordinary squiggle on the screen.

"Yes. It's just an ectopic beat," Sarah replied. "Lots of people have them, and as long as they're occasional, they're fine. I bet you get them from drinking too much coffee."

Rachel nodded, reassured by the words. "How would I know?"

"They feel like missed or extra beats."

"Hm, not sure I'd notice."

"At the pace you live life, you probably wouldn't." Sarah lowered herself into the chair and blew into the mug before taking a careful sip. Then she peered up at Rachel. "You have to work out who's doing this, Rachel."

Rachel heaved an extended and tired sigh as she ran her fingers through her long hair. "I wish I could, but all I have so far is who *isn't* doing it."

"At least that's progress," said Sarah.

"I suppose so. I've just ruled Amelia out for reasons I can't go into."

"Fair enough. She was really upset about Marjorie and Victoria."

Having spoken to Amelia, Rachel guessed the upset was most likely guilt at being relieved the attacks had nothing to do with her past. She didn't mention it, having promised Amelia she wouldn't reveal any details.

"Amelia's leaving tomorrow and taking some things to Victoria on her way home," said Sarah.

"A slight change of plan: she's in the clear as far as Victoria's concerned and is going straight home. She's asked me to make sure Victoria's bags get to her, so I'll take them to the hospital tomorrow myself."

Sarah raised an eyebrow before tittering. "I take it Hawaiian geography isn't a strong point?"

"What do you mean?"

"You haven't switched on the television in your room to check the map." Sarah's amusement caused her face to light up.

"When have I had time to do that?"

"Just saying."

"Are you going to tell me, or what?"

"Hold on a minute; I'm savouring the moment. It's so rare I get to know something you don't."

"You've savoured it long enough, now tell me."

"We're already on our way to Kauai – I did mention we were about to set sail earlier tonight, but I guess your thoughts were elsewhere – and the journey back to Kona is 284 miles. The only way to get between the two is to fly."

"I wonder if Amelia knew that when she asked me to get the bags to Victoria."

Sarah grinned. "You've been had. Either that or she assumed you knew you'd have to get them sent by some other means."

Rachel nodded. "Whatever, she had her reasons for changing her plans. Is there any other way we can get the belongings to Victoria?"

"There's freight, but she's got money and her credit cards with her, so she can buy anything she needs from the hospital when, or if, she wakes up," said Sarah. "The cruise line will forward the rest of her belongings on our return to Honolulu."

"Shame, I was hoping she would have woken up and been able to tell me who attacked her."

"Wishful thinking, Rachel."

"You know me. Forever the optimist."

"Well, Mrs Optimist, you've said you know who it isn't. That must mean you have more idea about suspects."

"I think I've narrowed it down to two."

"The two we discussed over dinner?"

"Yes. Olga Stone and, as much as I hate to say it, Preston Smith."

"Marjorie told me she spoke to Stephen before the attack, and he admitted to bribing Victoria when she was running for office. He wondered if there had been another blackmail letter. If he's right, maybe Olga sent it."

"Taking over from where her friend left off, you mean?"

"That's what Marjorie thinks he implied," said Sarah.

"But why would Olga attack her?" Rachel massaged her temples. "Unless Victoria found out it was her and threatened to tell the police."

"Good point, Rachel. But even if that were the case, I don't know why she'd attack Marjorie."

"Not without good reason anyway. She's definitely up to something if Preston's telling the truth about her. And if he isn't, it puts the blame fair and square back at his door," said Rachel. "I wish I could see him as a murderer and a person who would be happy to attack old women, because everything points to him."

"Perhaps it's one of those rare occasions where your instinct is wrong and Preston is a ruthless psychopath who has been lying to you and everyone else since coming on board. Have you considered it might have been him who made the pass at Margaret rather than the other way round, and she rejected his advances? You only have his word for it that she kissed him. And, from what I hear, she went for men with money, not poor fresh-faced nurses."

"You've changed your tune!" teased Rachel, remembering Sarah being convinced of Preston's innocence. "But you make a good point. You're suggesting he didn't enjoy being rejected and it turned nasty, so he strangled her? Yes, I have considered it. He's certainly strong enough to have done the deed."

"But you still don't believe it's him?"

"I'll follow the evidence, and if it is him, he'll get what he deserves. Trust me on that. If Preston attacked Marjorie, I'd be happy to see Waverley lock him in the brig. But first I want to dive a little deeper into the enigma that is Olga."

"I'd still like to know what she was doing in Margaret's room," said Sarah.

"Me too."

"There's also Brad."

Rachel leaned closer. "Would you be able to strangle someone while wearing a plaster cast?"

Sarah shook her head. "No. There would be limited movement in the fingers, but not enough to get a grip on someone's throat, unless the assailant only used one hand."

Rachel took a drink of her coffee before looking up. "They didn't," she said. "I read Dr Bentley's report. Two hands were used to strangle Margaret, and Marjorie said she felt two hands around her throat. Also, Brad didn't know any of them before the holiday. Which leads us back to Preston or Olga."

"Could the two of them be working together?"

Rachel considered for a moment, remembering the tension between them. It hadn't appeared to be put on and Preston wouldn't have known she would stumble upon him when he was upset. That was when he told her about Olga threatening him. Unless, of course, he was distressed about killing someone. She had to admit it was a possibility.

Rachel drained her coffee cup. "I'll give that some thought, but for now I need to get some sleep. Maybe it will all make more sense in the morning. Most of my inspiration comes during a run. Try to get some rest. Are you allowed to sleep?"

"No, but sometimes one of the others comes down in the middle of the night and gives those of us on the shift a couple of hours' break. We all do it for each other, although it's usually Gwen or the doctor on call."

"Wow! You've got great colleagues, Sarah. I'll be down to check on Marjorie after my run in the morning."

"Goodnight, Rachel. Sleep well and don't do anything silly during the night."

Rachel smirked. "What, me?"

The two of them laughed quietly so as not to wake Marjorie from her peaceful slumber. Then Rachel headed back to her room, her mind whirring with possibilities. So many people seemed to harbour secrets, so many had things they were desperate to keep hidden. She slid her card into her door, turning the handle at the green light.

"That's what's going on here. I just need to find the relevant secret."

Chapter 25

Rachel stood on the balcony of her suite, her eyes heavy and her head foggy from lack of sleep. She was up and dressed, watching the ship navigating a stream that led into a channel to Nawiliwili port on the island of Kauai. She had read the literature placed on her bed by Mario the night before, and could see why, from the vibrant landscape in the distance, it was known as the Garden Island.

The warm sea breeze mixed with saltwater felt refreshing on her face, bringing her eyes back to life. Soft trills rang in her ears. Seabirds followed the ship's path, looking for fish disturbed by the magnificent vessel separating the water as it glided along.

Marjorie would be disappointed not to be going ashore today. With that thought in mind, Rachel decided to skip her morning run and go straight to the infirmary. When she stepped inside her suite and closed the balcony doors, she heard a thud-thudding at her door. She hurried across the room, fearing something had happened to Marjorie.

As soon as she opened the door, an exasperated Sarah burst inside. "Where were you?"

"On the balcony. What's happened?" Rachel's throat went dry.

Sarah was panting from exertion, her face was red, and she looked close to tears. "It wasn't my fault. I couldn't stop her, Rachel. I tried."

"Slow down… what are you talking about, Sarah?"

Sarah stopped her tirade, open-mouthed. "She hasn't told you, has she?"

Rachel saw the fatigue on Sarah's face and stepped closer, wrapping her arms around her friend's shoulders in a comforting embrace before pulling back to look into her anxious brown eyes. "I assume you're talking about Marjorie?" She couldn't help grinning with relief that Marjorie was obviously all right.

"Humph! Who else?" Sarah flopped onto the bed settee.

"Let me get you a coffee or something." Rachel didn't have to call Mario to get drinks because there was a knock at the door. "I swear that man's psychic," she muttered, opening the door for the second time in minutes. Mario stood on the threshold, carrying a tray of tea and coffee.

"I saw Nurse Sarah run past my room and thought she might need something to drink," he said as Rachel stood aside to let him in. "I've taken the liberty of ordering Nurse Sarah a fried breakfast, and croissants for you, ma'am Rachel."

Sarah cheered up immediately. "Thank you, Mario. Just what the doctor ordered."

"And may I say, Lady Marjorie is in remarkable spirits this morning." The Salvadorian steward winked.

Rachel sighed. "Thanks, Mario, I owe you. Tell her I'll be with her soon."

"No problem. She's asked for a fry-up herself." Mario left the room, chuckling.

Sarah let out a loud harrumph.

"Tea or coffee?" Rachel asked, taking a seat next to Sarah.

"Strong coffee, please."

Rachel poured them both coffee from the jug and added milk. "I take it from your distress that she discharged herself?"

Sarah bit her lip. "You take it right. At six o'clock this morning, she got dressed, thanked me for looking after her, and left."

"And you couldn't stop her?"

"I tried, Rachel, but she wouldn't listen to reason, and whilst it would have given me great pleasure to put her in handcuffs, it's not allowed."

Rachel smirked at the imagery. "I guess not."

"You're taking it all very well."

Shrugging her shoulders, Rachel replied, "Marjorie's Marjorie. Besides, if she's being belligerent, it means she's fit and well."

"Pffft. If you say so. Although she owes me a night's sleep."

"I'm not sure it goes like that, but if it had been left to her, she wouldn't have stayed in the first place." Rachel sipped the coffee, happy that Marjorie was fit enough to be awkward, but concerned she might be in one of those unstoppable moods.

"I suppose not."

Mario arrived as soon as they had finished their first mug of coffee and Rachel was pouring a second. He laid breakfast for the two of them on the table and after he left, Sarah tucked in hungrily.

"I hope they've given you the day off after your night shift," Rachel said.

Still eating, Sarah mumbled, "I'm on call tonight, but I have all day off. Gwen's covering morning surgery while Brigitte and Bernard take shore leave."

Rachel watched her friend devouring the meal as if she was starving. "You should get some sleep. I'll keep Marjorie under close supervision."

"Perhaps you should hire one of those private nurses to follow her around," Sarah retorted.

"Can you believe that's what Jeremy would like? But we've seen how that goes," Rachel giggled.

"Whoops! You're right... not thinking straight... brain addled." Sarah polished off the remains of a fried egg, which she always kept until last, before looking up. "Jason said to tell you he got your message about Amelia. What's with all this secrecy?"

"All I can tell you is the same as last night. She isn't a murderer, and hers is not my secret to tell."

"Okay, I won't ask again," said Sarah. If anyone understood the importance of confidentiality, it would be a nurse, so Rachel was satisfied the subject was over.

"Sorry about what happened to Marjorie last night. When we met in the buffet, I really thought she was tired and having an early night."

"She said she got a second wind after dinner," said Sarah, before rubbing a hand around her abdomen. "And after eating that breakfast, I can understand why. The food on this ship is wonderful. I'm never going to get to sleep now."

"If I know you, you'll be out as soon as your head hits the pillow. You could sleep on a washing line." Rachel envied Sarah's ability to fall asleep anywhere when she needed to and was sure the dark lines would soon be gone. It was something she hadn't mastered herself.

Grinning, Sarah replied, "You should try it sometime."

"And you should try running," Rachel quipped and they both laughed.

Mario returned to clear away their trays. "An update from the suite across the corridor," he said. "Lady Marjorie says she's ready to go ashore whenever you are."

Now it was Rachel's turn to frown as Sarah's face broke into a wide grin. "Have a nice day," she said, getting up and walking out, still tittering.

Rachel's plan to visit Marjorie and then track down Olga Stone was well and truly scuppered. She got up, grabbed her handbag, and headed towards the door. The shrill ringing of the phone in her room stopped her in her tracks. She turned back and picked it up.

"Hello?"

"I've been trying to get you on your mobile before you leave the ship—"

"Oh, I think it's still on vibrate and in my handbag, sorry. Sarah's not long left. She told me you got my message. We were right about Amelia and witness protection. She's not involved, and I think it would be in her best interest for us to let it go where she's concerned."

"Yeah, I figured, but that's not what I'm calling about. In the light of last night's events, the boss has put Preston Smith in the brig. I thought you might like to know."

"Makes sense," said Rachel. "He needs some cooling off time either way. Marjorie said he was angry last night when she spoke to him." Rachel felt it best not to mention

Preston had told Marjorie he was keen to do some investigating of his own. His being under arrest in the brig would put a stop to any of that nonsense. If he was telling the truth.

"Another thing, Amelia said to tell you thanks for the ear. Does that mean anything to you?"

Rachel smiled. "Yes. Did you hear Marjorie's discharged herself?"

"You could say I heard," said Jason. "Sarah's furious with her – she's not that happy with me either. I hope you sent her to bed."

"Mario fed and watered her, and I've sent her on her way. She was much happier when she left because Mario told me Marjorie wants to go ashore, so now it's down to me to keep an eye on her." Rachel sighed.

"Work's been tough on us both since we got back to sailing. I'm sure we'll find a happy medium soon. Sometimes I think Sarah's had enough of the cruise ship life, so I guess I'll have to give it up one day."

"It's been a tough couple of years. Give her time," said Rachel.

"Will do."

"While I've got you, are there any new leads?"

"Nope. The boss is convinced Preston's our man, even though he didn't want him to be, but we'll keep an open mind. Olga Stone's been cosying up to Stephen since he's lost another nurse."

"Hm," said Rachel. "Watch her closely. If she's not the murderer, she's certainly after something. I reckon she was in cahoots with Margaret on the thieving front, or she's a vulture waiting for the pickings."

"Point taken. I'll keep watching her. For now, she's gone ashore with Emma and Stephen."

"I don't suppose your NYPD friend has come up with anything about her?"

"It's still only Preston who has a record and Stephen who has a question mark over his past. She'll be doing a bit more digging when she gets the time."

"Stephen's just a rich man who bends the rules like so many others," said Rachel. "Quite a likeable rogue, my dad would say."

"Maybe," said Jason.

"He told Marjorie he bribed Victoria when she was running for senate. Sarah knows more about it because I haven't spoken to Marjorie yet this morning."

"After Sarah's had some sleep, I'll ask her."

"Okay, I should get across the corridor and see what Marjorie's got in store for me today. Knowing her, it'll be something like scaling a mountain."

Jason guffawed at the other end of the line. "Whatever it is, enjoy your day, Rachel."

"Thanks, I'm sure it will be eventful," she said, smiling at the image of Marjorie strapped up with climbing rope and, more importantly, with relief that her friend was not suffering any ill effects from her close call the night before. Rachel was certain she would find the true murderer, as she still didn't believe it was Preston.

Chapter 26

"Shall we stop for a drink? I'm sure you're thirsty," Marjorie said.

After the initial excitement and determination Marjorie had showed, Rachel realised the previous night's attack had taken its toll, which was hardly surprising. Even when she herself was involved in skirmishes through work, it took her time to reflect and weigh up what happened afterwards.

"There are plenty of places to choose from. Would you like to be inside or out?"

"Oh, outside, please." Marjorie rubbed her neck. "I need the air."

They chose a table in a café protected from the sun by a canopy and ordered iced teas. It was hot, but not stifling, and a refreshing breeze made its way through. Rachel and Marjorie sat in companionable silence for a while, watching shoppers going in and out of a busy shopping centre.

"It would have been nice to explore the island in more detail," said Marjorie. "I'm sorry we haven't been able to. I hope you don't feel you've missed out."

"We've done plenty of exploring over the past few days. I'm happy to take it easy for a day," Rachel said, taking a drink of her tea. "This is lovely."

Marjorie gazed into the distance. "You mustn't worry about me, Rachel. It was a nasty shock, but I'm quite all right."

There was no getting away from the fact that Rachel was worried. Worried the attacker might try again, having failed. What she couldn't fathom was why Marjorie had been attacked at all… unless it was Preston.

"I know you'll be fine, but we have to be careful until we're certain they've locked the right person up." Rachel had told Marjorie when they left the ship that Waverley had confined Preston to the ship's brig.

"You're quite right, of course, because I find it hard to believe it was Preston. He warned me you and I should be careful. That word has got out we are investigating Margaret's murder."

Rachel felt her jaw drop open. "When?"

"Last night."

"Why didn't you mention this before?" Rachel asked.

"It slipped my mind until now. What with all that's gone on, plus, I took little notice at the time. I was too busy trying to work out what he thought he knew, and then… the attack."

"Of course," said Rachel. "What I can't work out is whether Preston's taking us all for idiots, or whether someone else is trying to make it look as though he is."

"But why?" Marjorie asked. "He's new, so he can't have made any enemies in such a short space of time."

"That's what I've been mulling over. The only one who has targeted him, whether by design or accident, is Olga. The tension between the two of them was palpable yesterday. She's obviously convinced he has the stuff Margaret is alleged to have taken from Stephen's room."

"She's also another flirt, that's for sure. But is she a killer? Perhaps we have to accept Preston's more devious than he makes out."

Rachel stared into her drink. In some ways, she wished it were true; that they could wrap the case in a neat bow, relax, and enjoy the rest of their holiday with Preston in the brig.

"You know, I almost hope it is him so we can forget about it," said Marjorie.

"I was just thinking the same thing," said Rachel glumly.

Marjorie's bright blue eyes filled with empathy when she looked at her. "Stop blaming yourself, Rachel. It was I who wanted to get involved in the first place and I who spoke to Preston and Brad last night. What happened to me isn't your fault. And if anything else should happen to me, that won't be your fault either."

Swallowing a lump in her throat, Rachel acknowledged Marjorie was right about her blaming herself. Sarah had warned her last night she had to protect her friend, and she had failed. The weight of what might have happened to Marjorie had she not arrived when she did was almost too much to bear.

She took a deep breath. "Nothing's going to happen to you because I will not let you out of my sight unless you're sleeping."

Marjorie sighed before grinning. "That's what I was afraid of."

They finished their drinks in silence, each deep in thought. Rachel was about to suggest they have another when she spotted Olga, Emma, Stephen, and Brad coming out of the shopping centre. Emma was having what looked to be an amicable conversation with Stephen while keeping pace with his wheelchair. It was good to see her looking happier.

Marjorie pointed them out, having seen them as well. "You don't think it could be Emma, do you?" she asked.

Shaking her head, Rachel replied, "Highly unlikely. Remember, she had gone for a walk along the beach when Victoria was assaulted."

"Oh, that's good. I'd hate it to be her."

"You and your soft spots," said Rachel, grinning.

"Pot and kettle," Marjorie retorted.

The smile was wiped from both of their faces when they saw the irresponsible Olga flirting with Brad. Rachel felt her eyes narrow and saw Marjorie's lips tighten.

"After all that's happened, you would think she'd be a little more circumspect, wouldn't you?" Marjorie said.

"I don't believe circumspection is in that woman's vocabulary."

"Well, I'm surprised at Brad. I imagined he had a little more about him."

Rachel watched the couple trailing behind Emma and Stephen, heading towards the stop where shuttle buses picked up cruise passengers regularly. Olga whispered something in Brad's ear, and the pair giggled. Rachel noticed Brad's hand touch the small of Olga's back while they waited.

A shuttle bus arrived and Olga reluctantly stopped flirting when Emma called her to help Stephen onto the vehicle. Brad used his good hand to help Olga lift the chair on board after Stephen had climbed inside.

"I really don't like her," Rachel said, but wondered if Preston had deliberately manipulated her opinion with his version of events. She didn't enjoy feeling this way. Could she have been so easily moulded?

"Olga's not the best nurse in the world, but perhaps we shouldn't deny young people their fun, and Brad admitted he's been dealing with a lot of stress at work. If he's finding himself able to unwind despite everything that's happened, we should be pleased for him. He looked furious last night when he was talking to Preston. I'm sure he believes Preston is the murderer. He told him he wants nothing to do with him until the DNA evidence comes back."

"Good point, Marjorie. Maybe Brad's uncovered something that would help us put this to bed. I'll try to speak to him later."

"Or you could ask His Lordship to do so, and we could get on with our holiday," Marjorie suggested.

"Really? You want me to give up when we're so close to finding the truth?"

Marjorie's eyes watched the shuttle leave with its full load. "Yes, I think I do. We must accept we are probably wrong about Preston. Olga's a silly and immature young woman, but I doubt she's a murderer."

Rachel wasn't convinced. "She gives the impression of being a dumb blonde, but I think there's a ruthless sociopath underneath the facade."

"Aren't sociopaths antisocial?" Marjorie asked.

"Yes, they are, but they're also manipulative and can use charm – or, in her case, flirtation – to get their way. I'm betting she tried that with Preston before turning on him – another sociopathic trait. Now she's using the charm on Brad, no doubt for her own reasons."

"To rob him, you mean?"

"It wouldn't surprise me. Whereas it would surprise me if she was genuinely interested in him."

"Why? He's not that bad looking."

"Because he's socially inept. Haven't you noticed how he never looks comfortable?"

"That might be because he's in pain from that arm. Although if he wants to attract a good woman, he should change his shirt once in a while," Marjorie chortled.

"It might be the only one he has that fits over the plaster," said Rachel.

"Then why not wear a short-sleeved shirt, or a t-shirt? He's got the physique to get away with a vest even."

"Like I said... socially inept. I doubt they take fashion lessons on Wall Street."

"What a couple they will make. A sociopath and a socially inept man."

Rachel felt sorry for Brad. "An ideal match from her perspective," she murmured.

"We should warn him," said Marjorie.

Rachel would warn him, but she didn't want to involve Marjorie and put her in danger from Olga Stone, so she said, "No. They're grown adults – leave them to it."

Chapter 27

Rachel's heart dropped when she opened the door to her suite. Right away, a large piece of paper on the floor caught her attention. She reached down and picked it up, reading the bold letters: "*IF YOU WANT THE OLD LADY TO STAY ALIVE MIND YOUR OWN BUSINESS*". Her stomach twisted with anxiety.

Fear soon turned to anger. This time the killer had made a big mistake. Rachel about-turned and headed across the corridor to Mario's working room. She knocked.

Mario opened the door straight away. "Hello, ma'am Rachel. I was just arranging tea for Lady Marjorie. Would you like some coffee?"

"Not right now, Mario. I need to see someone. Please, could you keep an eye on her and make sure she doesn't leave her room under any circumstances? I'll be back soon."

Mario was used to Rachel and Marjorie's tendency to attract trouble, so he didn't seem surprised. "You can trust me."

"Thanks, Mario," she called over her shoulder while marching down the long corridor, the folded note gripped tight in her hand.

Waverley looked up from his desk when Rachel stomped in without knocking. "What's wrong? Is Lady Marjorie all right?"

"Yes, she's fine, but I found this under my door when I got back just now." Rachel threw the note down on Waverley's desk.

He frowned as he read it, rubbing his forehead. "I don't understand. We—"

"You have Preston Smith in the brig. Who knows about that other than your team?"

"No-one. The passengers in his party had all left the ship when I moved him to where he couldn't do any harm."

"Good. That means they've overplayed their hand."

"I'm not sure I follow," said Waverley, still staring at the note.

"If the killer had known Preston was in the brig, they wouldn't have stooped to this. My guess is the perpetrator assumes this note will send you – or me – in Preston's direction again. I need to speak to him."

"Hang on a minute, Rachel. I understand your concern for Lady Marjorie, but he could still be involved."

Rachel shook her head. "That's just it. I was beginning to think so myself, but not anymore. Not after this." She picked the note up.

Waverley groaned. "Do you have an idea who's behind it then?"

"I have a theory, but we're going to need Preston's help to cast our net."

"Mr Smith might not be in the mood to help us. He's been ranting all day at Inglis about his rights and how wrong we are."

"In which case, I'm banking on his desire to prove his innocence being stronger than his fury. Let me speak to him. I've got to know him a little. He's more likely to trust me than you. He's got a thing about officials."

Waverley rubbed his head again, the tremor from his overuse of caffeine a thing of the past; his hand was steady. He stared at the note once more.

"We must keep Lady Marjorie safe. What you ask is highly irregular, but if it brings this case to a close, I'm willing to try it."

It won't be the first time I've interviewed one of your suspects in the brig, she thought, but said, "Thank you. Marjorie's having tea in her room, so I'd like to do it now, if you don't mind?"

"I'll call down and tell Inglis to expect you. But she has to be there with you, Rachel."

Even better, Rachel thought as she hurried towards the door. Rosemary Inglis was sensible and wouldn't interrupt except to help.

Rosemary was waiting for her when she arrived. "Good to see you, Rachel, but what's this about? The chief said we might have the wrong man."

"Almost certainly," Rachel replied. "All will become clear when I speak to him."

"Go in there. I'll bring him through."

Rachel entered the office where brig guards stayed when a passenger or crew member was under ship arrest. They carried out regular checks to make sure no harm came to the suspect, just like the police custody team did on land.

Preston appeared surprised to see her and almost smiled, but the look was quickly replaced as anger hardened his features. His mouth set in a tight line, his jaw clenched, and the muscle in his neck twitched. Rosemary suggested he sit down and Rachel did the same.

"What's this about? Are you some sort of undercover security?" He shot the question at Rachel like a bullet loaded with venom.

"No, but I am a detective back in England. I'm here to help you."

Preston's fists unclenched and he relaxed a little. Rosemary was behind him, standing by the door.

"How?"

"First of all, I don't believe you killed Margaret Green and I don't think you attacked Victoria, or my friend Marjorie."

Preston shifted in the seat opposite Rachel, his brow furrowed. "Amelia told me about your friend before she left this morning. I'm sorry about that, but you need to tell these guys I didn't do any of this, because they're not listening to me." He jerked his head back in Rosemary's direction.

"That's because someone is trying to frame you. Are you willing to answer some questions?"

"Sure, if it's gonna help," he said, relief washing over his face.

"Let's start by being honest. Tell me about your criminal record." A cloud appeared over Preston's face once more, but Rachel gave him an encouraging smile. "I just want to understand."

"Fine," he snapped. "I suppose it doesn't matter now, and you might not believe me anyway. I never touched that man."

"Then tell me what happened."

"What's this got to do with me being in here?"

"Probably nothing, but a violent past can influence how those in authority see you."

Preston opened his mouth to speak, but she put a palm up to stop him.

"I know it's not fair, but that's how it is, so it will help me understand if you tell me how you got that record."

"It was years ago," Preston muttered before going quiet. Rachel wondered whether he was going to refuse to cooperate and was debating whether to move on, but then he started to explain.

"My brother was just thirteen. Some boys had been picking on him at school and one night they beat him real bad. My mom complained to the principal, but these boys had contacts, so he told my mom and Jerome to let it go."

"But he didn't?"

"He did, but that wasn't enough for them. They got one of their older brothers to wait for Jerome, who was on his way home from baseball training. The guy started pushing and shoving and threatening him. Jerome had a baseball bat in his hand, and he'd just had enough." Preston paused for breath, eyes pleading for her to understand, before going on. "Jerome was... is... one of the good guys. He wouldn't hurt anyone under normal circumstances. But everyone has their limits."

Rachel empathised. She hated bullies and had always done everything she could at school to stop them in their tracks. Who knows what she might have done if she had suffered like Preston's brother had?

"So you took the blame?"

"Jerome called me. He was in pieces. I had just finished senior high and was about to go to college, but I would do anything for my brother. That incident could have finished his education; he'd have been kicked out. It would have also finished my mom."

"How come the guy Jerome attacked didn't tell the police the truth? That it was your brother?" Rosemary chipped in.

Preston grinned. "And let people know he'd been taken down by a thirteen-year-old? No. His street cred was more important, and it worked out for the best. I got off lightly.

But the record hindered my job applications, even though I got through college. That's why I moved to New York."

"How's Jerome now?"

"He's doing just fine, soon to be finishing senior high and heading for college to study law. Mom moved him from that school; worked night and day to put him through a better school. I send money whenever I can. As I said, it was for the best," Preston frowned again, "until now."

"Thank you for sharing that. Believe it or not, it helps us. But we need to talk about now," said Rachel. "I need you to tell me everything you have seen and heard before and during this cruise. Miss nothing out."

Preston more or less repeated all he had already told her about Margaret on the night of the party and about Olga threatening him. Now Rachel knew about his past, it helped her to understand why he was so reluctant to get involved with the security team and why he'd used racial prejudice as his excuse. He hadn't wanted to mention the real reason.

"Any other time, this would have been a great job. An all-expenses-paid cruise looking after a guy who don't need looking after at all. But even without poor Margaret's murder, it's not for me. If I get through this, I'm going back to working in a hospital."

"There's one thing you haven't mentioned. Marjorie told me you thought you knew something, and that you were going to investigate it yourself."

Preston shook his head. "Having seen how the police and – no offence to you, mam…" he turned to look at

Rosemary, "…and the security team jump to conclusions, I'm not pointing the finger at no-one unless I'm certain."

Rachel let out a deep sigh. "It would really help me if you told me what you suspected. Whoever has been doing this is purposely putting you in the frame to take the fall. The security team has done exactly what I would have done in their position."

"That may be, but—"

"Preston, this isn't about protecting a thirteen-year-old boy. It's about catching a ruthless murderer who not only preys on young women, but is not above trying to kill defenceless old women, and probably you if you get in their way."

Rachel could see him weighing up what she had just said and waited patiently for him to decide.

"I need to be sure."

"In that case, let's work together," she said.

After a pause that appeared to last an eternity, Preston nodded. "Okay," he said. "How?"

Chapter 28

Everything Preston had told her confirmed what Rachel believed, that Olga Stone had been in collusion with Margaret Green when she stole from Stephen, and from other rich clients. So why did she now have her doubts?

Marjorie answered the door as soon as Rachel knocked.

"Perhaps you can explain why Mario has kept me prisoner for the past two hours!"

Rachel doubted Mario would dare do such a thing. "You mean he asked you to wait for me?" she challenged.

"Perhaps I exaggerated. You've been off warning Brad about Olga Stone without telling me." Marjorie wrapped a shawl around her shoulders.

"No, I haven't. Sorry, Marjorie, but when I got back to my room, I received a note threatening you harm if I didn't mind my own business. I went to see Waverley, and then Preston."

"Oh," said Marjorie. "In that case, tell me more over dinner. I haven't eaten enough today."

Rachel followed her determined friend along the corridor, admiring how coolly she had taken the news that someone had once more threatened her. "There's not much to say except it proves Preston's innocent. He's convinced Olga is the one. I've concocted a plan which might catch her out."

They had reached the lifts when Marjorie looked at her. "That's what you thought all along, wasn't it? So why do you look so glum?"

They moved inside the lift, which was empty. "Something still doesn't add up. Preston says he's been watching Olga, who has been watching another passenger. He also saw Olga in Amelia's room last night before she got back to the ship."

The lift stopped on deck four and Marjorie headed towards the main restaurant. "Which goes to show she's a thief and not to be trusted and your instincts were right."

Rachel shook her head. "No, there's more to it. Why Amelia's room? There would be nothing to steal."

"You have a point there," said Marjorie, pausing. "What do you think she's up to then?"

"She's snooping."

"Snooping?"

"Yes. It's the sort of thing Carlos would do."

"Oh, I see. You think she's an undercover police officer or something like that?"

Rachel slapped her head. "That's it! She's a PI. My guess is someone hired her to follow Margaret to gather evidence, and it all got out of hand."

"Well, well," said Marjorie. "I suppose this calls for a detour. We can eat later."

"Are you sure? I'd suggest you eat, but I don't want you out of my sight until I know who sent that note."

Marjorie bristled. "I'm not a child, and I don't need a babysitter, but I want to know what is going on and whether you're right."

Rachel put her arm around Marjorie and kissed the top of her head. "Sorry, but you'd rather I was honest. And I'm sticking to you like glue, whether you like it or not."

"Pah! Come along then. Time to see His Lordship with your new theory."

Rachel knocked on the chief's door, which was ajar. They walked into a busy room.

"Ah, Rachel and Lady Marjorie," said Waverley. "Just in time. May I introduce you to Olga Stone, Private Investigator?"

"Uncanny," said Marjorie. "That's just what we were on our way to tell you."

"Really?" said Rosemary. "You worked it out?"

Rachel nodded. "It was when Preston said Olga had been in Amelia's room. The only reason she would do that would be if she thought Amelia might be part of the theft ring. Preston assumed it was because she was the killer."

"But he wanted to be sure," said Rosemary.

"We concocted a plan to catch you in the act." Rachel looked at Olga.

Olga gave a sheepish smile. "Sorry if I've been rude. You seemed to hang around a lot, and at first, I thought you might be the accomplices."

Marjorie chuckled. "Oh my. It appears our halos have slipped," she said.

"Have a seat, ladies, I've just ordered a drinks tray," said Waverley. "Ms Stone is about to tell us what she's been doing on board the *Coral Queen*."

Once drinks had been delivered and they were all sitting comfortably, Jason arrived. "I've just got the—" he stopped in his tracks when he saw Olga. "Ah, you already know." He poured himself a glass of water, but remained standing. "I was just about to say I've got the background on Olga Stone and it turns out she's a private investigator."

"Better late than never," Waverley muttered. "Well, Ms Stone?"

"I'm sorry for deceiving you all, especially after what happened to Margaret, and then Victoria, but I had a job to do."

"Which is?" Waverley asked.

"There've been several thefts from clients of the Consummate Care Nursing Agency, so they asked me to carry out a discreet investigation. When I crosschecked the timelines relating to the thefts with the nurses and clients, I narrowed it down to a handful of potential suspects. The agency agreed to let me infiltrate the group – I trained as a nurse years ago. Emma doesn't actually need any modern medicine or healthcare, apart from being diabetic, so after I'd done a short course on insulin management, we got her permission."

"She's known about your role all along?" Marjorie's eyes were wide.

"Yes, she's had things go missing, like many people who joined the physical therapy group since they started socialising together. I ruled out the physical therapist early on and eventually narrowed it down to Margaret Green or Amelia Hastings. The cruise seemed the ideal opportunity to bait the thief."

"By putting them in a position where they couldn't resist taking some high-value objects," said Rachel.

"Precisely. Ever since coming on board, I've been more convinced than ever there's an accomplice and I've been trying to prove it."

"Which is why you put young Preston under pressure," said Marjorie.

"Yes. He was new to the group, and I thought he might have joined the cruise to take and hide the stolen goods, but it's not him."

"So who is it?" Waverley snapped.

"Patience was never your strong point, was it, chief?" said Marjorie.

"I assume you've ruled out Amelia, and so have we, so now you think it could be Brad," said Rachel.

"I did. He was the other newcomer to the group, but I've gotten close to him and got an invitation into his room. I had a quick look inside his safe while he was using the bathroom. There was nothing."

Waverley's neck reddened, followed by his face. "How did you get the PIN to his safe?"

"That was easy. Most people use their birth dates. I pretended I was interested in astrology and asked him for his."

"I don't approve of your methods," said Waverley, looking apoplectic. "I could have you put under house arrest."

Olga shot him a bright-eyed, innocent look. "It won't happen again, I promise. Anyway, I didn't think it was him from the start, which is why I left him alone. I've looked him up. He's got a rich daddy who could buy him out of trouble, so he doesn't need to steal, plus, he has a lot of his own wealth. I just needed to cross him off my list."

"Some people steal for the thrill," said Rachel.

"Which is why I've gone to the trouble of crossing him off my list."

Rachel suspected she might also enjoy Brad's company. "Is there anyone else on your suspect list?"

"That's why I'm here." Olga turned her attention to Waverley. "There's a passenger called Devon Myerscough. I noticed on the first night when Margaret was doing a lot of her flirting – that's how she trapped her victims, by the way – that he and she met at regular intervals."

"Oh, I noticed him hanging around on the night of the Hawaiian party," said Marjorie, looking smug. "If you remember, Chief, I told you about the smarmy man who was interested in Margaret. She spoke to him a few times, but in the end, I just assumed he was another man she was flirting with."

Rachel was shocked and proud at the same time.

"He looked rich, so I thought at first he might be one of her targets, and didn't take too much notice. Like you." Olga looked at Marjorie. "He wasn't a client of Consummate Care, so wasn't my concern."

"That's ruthless," said Rosemary, echoing Rachel and, most likely, Marjorie's thoughts.

Olga shrugged. "Like I said, I had a job to do, and my prime concern has been to protect Consummate Care's clients."

"And how's that going?" Rachel couldn't resist a bit of sarcasm. Although Olga was not their murderer and had a bona fide reason for doing what she'd done, Rachel still couldn't warm to her.

"If you're referring to what happened to Victoria, I say she most likely brought that on herself. She was forever jabbing at people with that cane of hers or running them over." When everybody in the room looked at her in astonishment, Olga qualified her remark. "Not that I think she deserved what happened, but it wasn't something I could prevent. But back to this Myerscough; he's been popping up quite a bit during my investigation. When I searched Margaret's room a couple days after she was killed... your wife caught me." Olga looked at Jason, who gave her a hard stare.

"Go on," said Waverley.

"I found a photograph in her belongings. It was taken a few years ago, but I've concluded it's the same guy. Since then I've been watching him while excluding the others. I wasn't sure how many people were involved."

"Devon Myerscough must be the person Preston mentioned, the one he thought Olga was colluding with but refused to point the finger at without proof," said Rachel to Rosemary.

Olga looked slightly confused, but went on. "He's been cosying up to a lot of wealthy older women travelling alone. I'm surprised you've had no reports of theft, Chief Waverley."

Waverley and Jason's quick exchange of glances suggested they had, but he was too professional to comment. "Do you have any proof he's been stealing?" Waverley asked.

"That's where you come in. I can't get ahold of his room key and if I try to talk to him, he'll know we're on to him."

"This is hard to believe. Surely if this man was involved with Margaret, he would have left the ship the morning after her death."

"Any normal man would, but this guy's arrogant. Think about it – he's happy to steal from old people – that in my book is the lowest of the low."

"You have some moral compass then," Marjorie muttered, but only Rachel heard what she said.

"Do you think he could have killed Margaret?" Waverley asked.

"I don't investigate murder, but I'd say if it wasn't Preston, and I'm guessing you don't think it was, then he might have."

"This Devon Myerscough," said Rachel. "Have you noticed him anywhere near Marjorie?"

"No, but since I crossed you two off my list, I haven't been following you."

"Please tell me you didn't go into our suites and check our safes," said Marjorie. "Not that I use my date of birth anymore since Rachel warned me not to."

Olga grinned. "No, I confirmed you were Brits, so there was no need. Margaret's contacts didn't stretch that far. Besides, Emma told me you weren't involved, and that you were friends with staff on board."

"Surely you knew that from the night of the tour?" Marjorie sounded aghast.

"Sarah introduced us," Rachel said.

"My eyes were on Margaret. I wasn't paying much attention to the tour."

Rachel decided it was time to intervene before Marjorie got dragged into a war of words with the rather laissez-faire private investigator. "I expect it's time to pay Mr Myerscough a visit, Chief."

"Indeed. Thank you for your help, Ms Stone. We'll take it from here."

"If you find proof, I'd appreciate it if I could have it for my report."

"We owe you that much," said Waverley, looking more chipper than he had in days.

"Can I release Preston?" Rosemary asked.

"Yes" said Waverley.

"And tell him we don't need to go through with our plan," said Rachel.

"And the next time you concoct a plan with a prisoner in my brig, I'd appreciate you telling me about it," said Waverley.

"We'll leave you to get on then. Rachel and I are going for dinner," said Marjorie.

Rachel was pleased the investigation appeared to be nearing its conclusion and was happy to leave the arrest to the security team.

As they were walking away, Olga caught up with them.

"No hard feelings," she said.

"None at all," said Rachel.

"Tell Emma from me, she hasn't lost her acting skills," said Marjorie.

"I will. She'll be pleased to hear it," Olga said as she marched ahead.

"Will you be seeing young Bradley now that you're off duty?" Marjorie called.

"No. To be honest, he's not my type. Gives me the creeps," Olga replied. They watched her turn the corner and heard her footsteps running up the stairs.

"Emma's not the only actress," said Marjorie, "she gave a good impression of being infatuated with the poor man earlier. Still, that's another investigation concluded."

"What about the attack on Victoria?" Rachel muttered. "And you?"

"The same man, of course. You heard Olga. She wasn't interested in us. He must have thought we were getting close to catching him." Marjorie took Rachel's arm. "Now, come along. Let's eat."

Chapter 29

The *Coral Queen* restaurant was bustling with a cheerful dinner crowd as Rachel and Marjorie sat down at their cosy window table. The tempting aroma of a shrimp dish wafted through the air, so they ordered it for themselves. Rachel was happy with the choice, savouring every bite. The succulent texture of shrimp melted in her mouth.

"This is the best shrimp I've ever tasted," she said between bites.

Marjorie smiled, her own plate nearly empty. "It's a delightful meal. Although knowing who killed Margaret and no longer being the target of a madman might be making it taste better. We can enjoy our food without having to worry about it. I've noticed when you're on a case you shovel your food down."

Rachel nodded, but her brow furrowed as she continued to mull over the facts in her head. Something about the case still wasn't adding up.

"Rachel," Marjorie chided. "We've done our job and done it well. The security team is handling the arrest, and justice will be served. You must let it go. Please try to relax now. I don't want Carlos telling me off if you go home stressed."

Rachel sighed, pushing the last stray shrimp around her plate. "I know, I know. It's just there's still something bothering me about the whole situation. You're right, though, Marjorie. I should try to forget it."

As Rachel attempted to take Marjorie's advice, her mind kept circling back to the recent conversations and the latest news delivered by Olga. They had apparently put together the puzzle, but somehow, it didn't fit as neatly as she would have liked. She felt there was a stray piece waiting to be put in place.

"I mean it, Rachel. It's over," Marjorie reassured her, reaching across the table to pat her hand. Rachel managed a weak smile, hoping her friend was right.

After finishing their meal, Rachel and Marjorie left the restaurant and strolled towards the Jazz Bar. The atmosphere was as lively as ever, with laughter and conversation filling the air.

Rachel smiled. "The jazz might help."

"It has its charms, although I prefer classical myself. The string quartet last night was exceptional," Marjorie said, her eyes darkening before her hands moved to her neck. "Before that beast tried to switch my lights out, that is."

They made their way through the crowd to the booths and spotted Jason and Sarah. Sarah waved, and they joined the couple in the booth.

"Good news," Jason announced as they sat down. "Following Olga Stone's revelations, we've arrested Devon Myerscough."

"That's wonderful," said Marjorie, "isn't it, Rachel?"

Rachel nodded, trying hard to bury her doubts. "Yep, glad to hear it. Has he confessed?"

"It appears we've got our man," but Jason's voice didn't sound as certain as his words.

"Good," said Marjorie, nudging Rachel's arm.

Rachel forced a smile, but the nagging feeling inside her refused to dissipate. She looked around the Jazz Bar, taking in the cheerful faces and lively atmosphere, wishing she could let go of her concerns and enjoy the evening.

"He's admitted to being a thief and a scam artist," Jason continued. "Apparently, he and Margaret had been working together for some time."

"Were they in a relationship?" Marjorie asked.

"No. But she's been stealing bits and pieces from clients for about a year and passing them on to him to sell. More recently, she gave him the addresses of clients from the agency. He cold-called them, getting some of them to invest in a cryptocurrency scam. The reason neither was caught was because he targeted other nurses' clients primarily."

"How cruel," said Marjorie. "Did these people lose a lot of money?"

Jason's lips tightened. "I guess so. He's a scumbag all right, but he denies killing Margaret. His story is that, on the night of her death, she had handed him some money and other items, but warned him that Stephen Williams was suspicious. She told him she'd have to stop stealing for a while and they should avoid being seen together. He says she advised him to enjoy the cruise, which is what he's been doing."

"Dreadful. If the woman hadn't been killed, I'd say more, but I refuse to speak ill of the dead," Marjorie declared.

"Yeah, and this is where his story gets confusing. According to him, he didn't know Margaret was dead."

"I find that hard to believe," said Sarah.

"Me too," said Jason, "but that's what he's saying and he gave a good impression of being shocked when we told him. It was only when he realised he was going to be charged with murder that he became more talkative about his crimes and owned up."

"So he reckons since Margaret last spoke to him, he's just been enjoying the cruise?" Rachel quizzed.

"It's partly like Olga said. Myerscough's been targeting women travelling alone, but not just the elderly like she thought," Jason explained. "He chooses his victims carefully, looking for those who appear vulnerable. Then he sweet-talks his way into their rooms before robbing them of their jewellery and a bit of money. He takes the stuff after plying them with drink so they don't realise what he's done until later. We've had a couple of reports from women, but the descriptions were sketchy. Now we have him, I'm sure they'll be able to identify him."

"Disgusting," Sarah muttered with a grimace.

"I hope you have enough evidence to hand him over to the authorities," said Marjorie.

"We have, and the good news is we've recovered most of their belongings, plus some belonging to women who haven't come forward."

"But if Devon Myerscough isn't the killer," said Marjorie, "then who is?"

"Good question," Rachel said, her mind racing.

"Let's not jump to conclusions," cautioned Jason. "We still need to gather more evidence and find out if Devon is only telling us part of the truth to save himself. The boss thinks he's guilty on all counts. And we don't believe some random stranger who she annoyed attacked Victoria."

"I'm with you on that one," said Rachel.

"The boss is convinced Devon killed Margaret, attacked Victoria for reasons yet unknown, and then twigged you and Marjorie were investigating. He then attacked you," Jason looked at Marjorie before continuing. "The only evidence we've got so far in relation to the murder, though, is the fact that Olga saw Devon and Margaret together before her death."

"But she also saw Preston with Margaret, and so did Emma. The timeline suggests to me that unless Devon and Margaret met again later that evening, Preston is still the last person to have seen her before her killer," said Rachel.

"True," Jason admitted, "but Devon had a sizeable amount of cash hidden away in his cabin, which we believe has come from his activities on board. It's still possible that he met with Margaret again after she was with Preston and they argued. He's a smarmy good-for-nothing who I don't think would be averse to murder if his lucrative business was under threat." Jason rubbed his bristly chin thoughtfully. "I suppose if it wasn't him and it clearly wasn't Olga, it has to be Stephen. Rachel overheard Stephen Williams having a go at Margaret on the night of the murder and Devon confirms he accused her of stealing. Maybe Stephen's the killer after all."

"But he's an old man in a wheelchair," said Marjorie, eyebrows raised.

"An old man who has a history of bribing politicians, including Victoria," Jason pointed out. "He's not an innocent victim."

"Stephen confronted Margaret about robbing him, but he admitted that to me, not knowing I'd seen them arguing," said Rachel, considering the possibility. "Even if he had taken matters into his own hands because he felt threatened, I don't think he could have done it himself. I've seen him out of his chair and he can barely breathe. If, by some feat of strength, he killed Margaret – which is a stretch of the imagination – he couldn't have dashed in and out of a shower cubicle to attack Victoria, or raced after Marjorie last night. Besides, he was still listening to the string quartet when I was looking for her, exactly where Marjorie left him."

"Precisely," Marjorie agreed. "It's absurd to think he could have committed the two latter crimes. You're the nurse, Sarah. What do you think?"

Sarah looked tenderly at Jason, holding his hand before answering. "Stephen has heart failure and takes medication to curb the symptoms, but he wouldn't have the strength to do what you describe."

"So we're back to Devon," said Jason, not in the slightest bit offended. One of the reasons Rachel liked him so much, apart from the fact her best friend loved him, was his humility.

"If it hadn't been for the note warning me to back off, I'd be leaning towards Preston, but we know it wasn't him because you had him locked up in the brig. I'm sure I'd have noticed this Devon person if he'd been linking us to the investigation. And let's face it, he hadn't even realised Olga was following him, so I doubt very much he would have known about us. Let's not discount other possibilities yet."

"Just when we think we've got it all figured out, it turns out we haven't." Jason took a large gulp of water.

"Don't be despondent. You've solved half of the crime," said Marjorie.

"Well, I'd better leave you guys and get back to work." Jason finished his water and left the Jazz Bar.

"Me too, I'm on call tonight." Sarah hugged Rachel before she left. "Let it go, Rachel. It will be one and the same man."

Rachel watched her friend leave the Jazz Bar before exhaling a large breath, far from convinced.

Chapter 30

Rachel and Marjorie made their way through the bustling corridors of the *Coral Queen* after leaving the Jazz Bar. Marjorie stopped suddenly.

"Are you okay?" Rachel asked.

"There's Emma in the coffee bar. Do you mind if we stop by? I'd like to tell her what a superb actress she still is."

Rachel was tired and her head was spinning, but she too admired Emma, as neither of them had suspected Olga of being anything other than her nurse. Albeit a rather uncaring one.

"Not at all," she said.

Emma looked up from her mug of hot chocolate, smiling warmly. "I hear you know about Olga now," she said. "Sorry for the deception, but I was sworn to secrecy."

"Don't apologise," said Marjorie as she and Rachel took seats at the table. "We're in awe of your acting skills. We would never have guessed."

Emma's eyes sparkled with life. "Actually, it's got me thinking I could still do the job. My agent has been on at me to take on other roles for a while, but I was too short sighted to consider them. I wonder if that's why he suggested this holiday."

"How exciting," said Marjorie. "If I were you, I would carry on. You're too talented to sideline yourself."

"You're right, Marjorie. It's time I put the whole blasted accident behind me. Margaret Green's dead now, and I need to stop imagining every young drunk I see is the woman who drove into me. I'm going to bury the past with her."

"Where's Olga tonight?" Rachel asked. "Celebrating her victory?"

"More than likely. We had dinner, and I think she was going to play the tables in the casino. I hope her winning streak doesn't end there. I think the agency will pay her well for her services, and now that she's caught the robber and killer in one go, her PI business should skyrocket. That's what she's hoping for, at least."

Marjorie and Rachel exchanged a glance. "I'm pleased it's all turned out for the best. This Devon Myerscough sounds dreadful."

"Seems so. Although Olga blames Margaret for everything, she gave him the idea. She reckons he took advantage of what she told him was possible. At least Olga's got justice, poor girl."

Rachel had been ready for bed, and although pleased for Emma, she couldn't be overjoyed for Olga. Now she was jolted awake.

"Sorry, I don't understand. If Olga's business is about to launch into the big time, why would she be a poor girl and why would she need justice?"

"Because Margaret was responsible for her having to work night and day to make ends meet."

Marjorie's eyes widened. "In what way?"

"If I'm honest, Olga has struck me as the type who would rather spend her life living it up than working, so I've been impressed with how determined she's been to find the culprit responsible for the robberies." Emma took a sip of her hot chocolate while a waitress brought two of the same for Rachel and Marjorie.

"We know what you mean," said Marjorie. "She certainly isn't a dedicated nurse."

Emma chuckled. "No. But nonetheless, she has been obsessional about finding evidence to prove Margaret a thief. Almost too much so, seeing as the woman is dead."

Rachel leaned forward in her chair. "And yet uninterested in finding her killer," she murmured.

"Right. Anyway, I was putting my makeup on before dinner and she was as high as an eagle in its nest. When the security chap called her to tell her this Devon fella had confessed that he and Margaret were in cahoots, she was ecstatic. Going on about how Margaret got what was coming to her and rejoicing about going to the newspapers once she got back to New York."

"I'm not sure the company she did the work for would be happy for the press to get hold of the story," said Rachel.

Emma shrugged. "She might be exaggerating. I guess she felt I was still bitter, and would join in her celebrations, but I couldn't. Margaret deserved to be punished for what she did, but despite my initial reaction, I can't celebrate the way she died."

"What makes you think Margaret was responsible for Olga's circumstances?" asked Rachel.

"While she was celebrating, Olga got a call from the agency and left it on speakerphone because she was filing her nails. The woman on the other end was pleased that she had tracked down the thief and scammer who had been targeting their clients. I was only half listening, having already heard enough crowing from Olga, but my ears pricked up when the woman said she hoped it would go some way to making reparations for what had happened to her nan."

Rachel and Marjorie exchanged glances before Marjorie asked, "What *did* happen to her nan?"

"It appears the thief – Margaret – had a hand in her losing her life savings. Crazy woman didn't believe in banks. Margaret got her accomplice to visit and offer the old girl a guaranteed way to triple her money."

"By investing cryptocurrency," said Rachel.

Emma nodded. "Margaret did the groundwork, telling the poor woman she shouldn't keep cash in the house like that, and how she would be a target for thieves. And then her accomplice – Devon – followed that up with a very convincing argument for trusting him with the money. He gave her certificates of ownership and everything, telling her she could spend it whenever she liked. All she had to do was contact him."

"When did she find out she had been swindled?" Marjorie asked.

"Not long after. The old lady had forgotten she was going to put down a deposit on a small condo for Olga, and when she rang the number this shark had given her, it didn't exist. Of course, Margaret didn't come under suspicion then because she hadn't taken anything. Until tonight, I didn't realise how personal this was to Olga or what was driving her. No wonder she worked so hard. I can understand why she's celebrating. Although if she's got any conscience, she'll regret it later."

"It explains why she wasn't interested in finding the murderer," said Marjorie, looking at Rachel.

"Wow," said Rachel. "Such a shame about her nan, though. I'm glad it worked out for her." Rachel yawned. "Sorry, it's been a long day. I think I need to go to bed."

As soon as they got outside the café, Marjorie nudged Rachel in the ribs. "What was that all about?"

"What?"

"You don't fool me with your 'I'm pleased for her' and the 'I'm tired' routine, Rachel. What's going on?"

"Don't you see? If Devon's telling the truth, and he's just a conman, not a killer, who do you think has the strongest motive? And who's been watching everybody since the day we boarded?"

Marjorie's mouth opened wide. "Of course. Olga Stone. You were right about her all along."

"It warrants further investigation, doesn't it?"

"Are we going to call on His Lordship?"

"Yes."

Chapter 31

Rachel phoned Jason to let him know she and Marjorie had new information, and he agreed to call Waverley. A short while later, they all sat down in Waverley's office with the chief looking far from happy.

"This had better be good." His voice betrayed how tired he was.

"It is, Chief Waverley, and I apologise for waking you, but I think we might have at last found our killer," said Rachel.

Waverley rubbed his eyes before flapping a hand, motioning for her to carry on. Rachel explained how she and Marjorie had come across Emma in a café, and what she had told them about Olga's grit and determination to prove Margaret a thief seeming to go against her nature.

"Emma has the distinct impression that Olga is workshy," said Rachel. She told them how Emma overheard the telephone call between Olga and the nursing agency, and how she had quizzed her afterwards. Jason leaned forward when Rachel got to the part about Olga's nan's lost fortune. "So Emma assumed Olga was working so hard because she needed the money, which I'm sure she does. But the key driver behind this dedication is more personal, and it's that which gives her motive."

When Rachel finished the story, Waverley was very much awake. His eyes were now alert when he looked at Jason.

"Get Ms Stone down here, Goodridge."

Jason looked at his watch. "Now?"

Waverley grinned. "It appears I won't be the only person being dragged from a good night's sleep tonight."

"Would you like us to leave?" Rachel asked after Jason had gone.

"And miss the finale? Certainly not," Waverley said.

Olga Stone looked almost as grumpy as Waverley had an hour earlier, but somehow, she had found the time to groom herself and apply a fresh layer of makeup. She glared at Rachel, then Marjorie, before addressing Waverley.

"What's this all about, Chief Waverley?"

"We have a few more questions for you, Ms Stone. Please take a seat."

Olga threw herself into a chair. "And these questions couldn't wait until morning?"

Rachel wondered whether she was always this moody when woken in the night or whether the casino tables hadn't brought her the fortune she had been hoping for.

"Some new information has come to light. Information you neglected to mention when you were here earlier."

"Don't tell me Myerscough's denying it now."

"No, it's nothing to do with Mr Myerscough. This information is about you, or rather, about a relative of yours."

"Oh?" Olga glowered at Rachel. "And how did you come by this information?"

Marjorie cut in. "We met Emma and shared a hot chocolate. She had some interesting things to say about your personal circumstances."

"Why would she do that?"

"Because she didn't realise the implications of what she was saying," said Rachel. "She meant you no harm."

"Humph," Olga blew air through her lips. "So you know my nan was cheated and lost everything? How that gives you the right to drag me down here in the middle of the night like some criminal is..." her eyes widened suddenly, "...unless you think... you can't believe I'm in league with these guys? Or..." the cogs were clearly turning.

"Whilst Devon Myerscough might be a thief, Ms Stone, he was a friend of the murdered woman, whereas you... well, let's face it, you had every reason to want her dead."

Panic filled Olga's eyes as they shot from one person to another. "You've gotta be kidding me? My nan loses everything and I'm forced to work like a dog instead of pursuing a modelling career. I didn't like the woman, that's for sure."

"Which adds to your reasons for wanting Miss Green dead," said Waverley, unmoved.

Olga put her head in her hands, laughing hysterically before lifting it and looking at the chief. "I admit I didn't shed any tears when Margaret died, but I'm not a murderer. Devon Myerscough must have argued with her and killed her for whatever reason, or maybe Stephen got his revenge. Hell… people must have been lining up to kill her, but I'm not one of them. I just wanted her to pay for what she'd done to my nan and countless others. If I'm honest, I'd have rather seen her inside a prison cell than a morgue, but hey… we don't always get what we want. Now, if you have any evidence for your insinuations, I'd be happy to see it. Otherwise, I'd like to go back to bed." Olga stood up, shaking with anger.

"Not so fast," said Waverley. "I'd like to ask if you have any evidence to the contrary?"

Olga snapped open her oversized handbag and pulled out a file. "You'll find everything I've been working on in there, including photos from the first night of the cruise. You'll also see that at the time Margaret was being strangled, I was with someone."

"Why didn't you mention that before?" Jason asked.

"Because I didn't think I'd need an alibi, and I didn't want people to assume that's how I normally behave. After seeing Margaret with Preston, I assumed the two of them went off together, so I went for a drink with a guy I'd met at the hotel the night before we boarded. I met a guy, all right? We spent the night together. End of story. When you've finished with that file, I'd like it back." With that, Olga tossed back her hair and, with head held high, stormed out of Waverley's office.

The four stared at each other. Waverley's face softened. "You weren't to know," he said to Rachel.

"Well," said Marjorie, "that was quite the departure. I think she's been taking lessons from Emma."

Jason's lips upturned, and even Rachel grinned.

"If you want to check through that lot, go ahead," said Waverley, "but I'm going to bed. Lock up when you leave, Goodridge."

"Yes, sir," said Jason.

After a few moments' silence, Rachel reached for the file. "I'd be interested to see what she's got in here. You never know, there might be something she's missed, seeing as she wasn't interested in finding the killer."

"Is that all right with you, Jason?" Marjorie asked.

"I'm on the night shift anyway, so yeah, why not?"

Rachel opened the file, and they each leaned forward to examine what was inside.

Chapter 32

It turned out Olga was a diligent private investigator who had been following various people who worked for the agency for several months before the cruise. Her alibi for the night Margaret was murdered checked out, with a few selfies of her with a man, including timestamps, that put her out of the frame. There was an array of good-quality photographs and some that were grainy. These had been taken using a phone at night, in dull conditions, or from a distance.

Rachel had moved on from examining the contents of a large Manilla envelope marked 'relevant' to one marked 'miscellaneous'. This envelope contained photos without handwritten notes. Olga clearly didn't deem these to be relevant to her investigation.

Marjorie squinted at one of the grainier photos, passing it to Rachel. "I think that's Margaret, but I can't see who she's with."

Rachel held the photo up to the light. Marjorie was right about it showing Margaret, who was striking an aggressive pose. It was dated a few weeks prior to the cruise and appeared to show Margaret arguing with a man whose face wasn't clear because of the poor quality. Something about him seemed familiar.

"See if there are any more photos like this one." Rachel handed it to Jason. They searched through the miscellaneous pile and found a few others from the same night, but in these, Margaret was alone.

"Hang on," said Rachel. "Look! There in the background. It's the same guy. He's following her."

"Who is he?" Jason asked. "These photos tell us nothing."

"Except that she had some unwanted attention," said Rachel.

"He might be a relative of someone she stole from, and have nothing to do with her death," Marjorie argued.

"Wait a minute," said Rachel. The fog in her brain was clearing as she recalled their first conversation with Olga in Waverley's office. "Something has been nagging at me since Marjorie and I were chatting at a café on Garden Island yesterday afternoon. Now it's come to me. I know who the killer is."

"Well don't keep us in suspense, dear. Who is it?"

"A devious perpetrator who has been extremely clever. If you're happy to, Jason, it's time to give someone else an early morning wake-up call."

"Before I wake the boss again, you're going to have to give me more information."

Rachel told them what she was thinking and how she had come to her conclusion. Jason and Marjorie were sceptical until they studied the grainy photograph with what Rachel had shared in mind.

"Okay," said Jason. "It's only my job on the line. I'll call the boss and make another early morning call. Wait here."

Rachel's heart was pounding so loud, she could hear it in her ears. This was the feeling she always got when she was about to catch a perpetrator who imagined they were invincible. But having made a wrong assumption about Olga earlier, she had to push down her doubts. While they were waiting, she received a call from Jason, who had cleverly gathered additional information that would help them put this man away.

Waverley arrived, looking brighter than when he had been woken before. "Hello again," he said.

"Good morning, Chief," said Marjorie.

Rachel couldn't speak. She was eager to bring everything together when Jason arrived with the man she was convinced was the bad guy.

"Here they are now," said Waverley.

An angry but confident-looking Brad Roberts entered the office with Jason. His arrogance melted briefly when he saw Rachel and Marjorie, but returned as he stood tall.

"I don't appreciate being woken up at this hour to answer questions. I assume this is about the killer you've arrested. Stephen told me about it, and I can tell you now, I don't know him, and have never met him."

"Take a seat, Mr Roberts," said Waverley.

"Why?"

"Because I'd like to speak to you," said Rachel.

Brad gave Rachel a sharp stare, but when Jason put a hand on his shoulder, he obeyed.

"Over to you, Rachel," said Waverley.

"Do you remember Olga mentioning something about Brad's father being rich enough to buy him out of trouble? Well, until now, we've ruled him out as a killer because of the plaster on his arm, but I've been asking myself: what if it's a clever cover-up?"

"That seems unlikely," said Waverley.

"Pure fantasy, if you ask me," Brad interjected, encouraged by Waverley's comment.

"It does seem unlikely, but think about it," Rachel pressed on. "Marjorie mentioned something when we were out yesterday that got me thinking. He never changes his shirt." Rachel ignored Brad, speaking directly to Waverley. "The same shirt he's wearing now, even after being woken in the early hours." The others looked at Brad's shirt while the man's face reddened.

"So I don't follow fashion," he snapped.

Still ignoring him, Rachel continued. "Marjorie and I laughed about it after seeing him and Olga flirting together. We mistakenly thought Olga was trying to rob him, but it turns out he was on her suspect list."

"She's not heard the last of that," muttered Brad.

"Marjorie then mentioned it was odd how he wears a long-sleeved shirt the whole time, even in this hot weather. Now I believe it's because he's trying to hide something."

All their heads swivelled Brad's way again. Rachel noticed him fidgeting and squirming. A lot less confident now than when he'd entered.

"Like what?" asked Jason, smiling. "We can all see he's wearing a plaster cast."

"And why would he fake an injury?" Marjorie asked, joining in the fun.

Rachel pretended to wrack her brains as if trying to remember something. "Got it!" she said. "Stephen told me that on the night Margaret died, he overheard her arguing with someone on the phone – he was convinced it was a man – and that she told this person to stop following her and to move on. What if that man is a loser? What if he – Brad, that is – was so desperate to get near her, he faked an injury to join the same cruise, and just so happened to hire a nurse so he could travel among the same party?

"Alas, the dream reunion he had imagined…" Rachel held Brad's gaze, "…this is where the fantasy comes in. So the dream reunion didn't transpire, and she rejected him again. Then, imagine his rage when he sees her with his own nurse, Preston Smith, later that night. The woman he's obsessed with is throwing herself at the man he himself had brought aboard. What if he then went into a fit of rage and strangled her?"

Rachel now addressed Brad. "Ever since that night, you've been covering your tracks, using the fact that everyone believes you have a plaster on your arm, so you're safe."

"Rachel, it's a bit far-fetched, don't you think?" Jason couldn't hide a smirk.

"Yeah, it is. In case you haven't noticed, Miss Clever Boots, I do have a cast." The arrogance returned and Brad held his left arm aloft.

"I'm coming to that," she said, turning back to Waverley. "If Devon isn't responsible, and it wasn't Preston because – unbeknown to you, Mr Roberts – he was locked in the brig when you slipped a threatening note under my door," Rachel wagged a finger at Brad, who was squirming again, "you see we can't afford to overlook the one person we haven't considered, no matter how unlikely it may seem."

"Not to mention if what you say is true, Rachel," said Marjorie, looking at Brad, who was now entering panic mode, "Brad might feel the need to punish Preston if he believed his nurse had succeeded with Margaret where he hadn't. Although he'd have to be a very sick man to do any of this."

As they pretend-mulled over Rachel's theory and Marjorie's summary in front of the perpetrator, the atmosphere changed. The two women sat back, each watching Brad for a reaction.

"Preston was with her that night. I saw them. Ask Olga, she'll tell you. It's him you're looking for, not me."

"He wasn't with her in the way you think," said Rachel. "He rejected her, but even if he had been with her, you had no right to do what you did. We have photos here showing you stalking her weeks before the cruise." Rachel held up the photos, more in hope than confidence that specialists could match the grainy images to Brad.

"Okay, so we went out for a while, but I finished with her. I didn't expect to see her on the same cruise. How could I strangle anyone with this?" He held the arm aloft again.

"Over to you, Jason," said Rachel.

"Before waking you, Mr Roberts, I called an old contact who works for the NYPD, Detective Celia O'Malley," he said. "They are six hours behind us, but she was working late. I don't know how you police do it, Rachel," he said before turning back to Brad. "It turns out that when she called a few of her colleagues and mentioned your name, one of them recognised it. You were accused of attacking a girlfriend at college."

Marjorie's eyes widened. "What happened?"

Jason continued. "This next part stands out: the young woman claimed they had been going out together, and when she ended the relationship because he was becoming too clingy, Brad tried to strangle her."

"Why didn't this come up when Olga did a background check?" Waverley asked.

"Because Brad got off scot-free. As Rachel mentioned, his old man's loaded, and the detective remembers he hired a high-priced lawyer who threatened to discredit the girl and her story, so they bought her off, and she dropped the charges. In return, he kept a clean record." Jason's fist clenched as anger filled his face.

"And now we have three more cases of strangulation, one fatal, because a father decided to protect his son rather than let him face justice," said Rachel, glaring at Brad.

"You can't prove anything. I have a clean record."

Rachel channelled her anger, replacing it with determination. "All we need now is to inspect that cast," she said, ready to uncover the truth.

"I'm sure you won't mind us taking a look, Mr Roberts," said Waverley.

Brad's right hand flew to the cast. "You have no right," he said.

"Ah, but that's where you're wrong. We have every right," said Waverley.

Jason didn't wait for an invitation. He pulled up Brad's shirt sleeve and they could all see that the cast was loose enough to pull off. With a gentle tug, it came away, revealing a healthy wrist which Jason wiggled around for good measure.

"I'm sure we'll get a DNA match from Mrs Hayes's stick, and when we request your medical records, I'm guessing they won't show any history of fracture," said Waverley.

Jason leapt up, pulling Brad to his feet and applied handcuffs.

"I need to phone my father," said Brad, looking down at his feet.

"Not this time, Mr Roberts," said Waverley. "Under maritime law, you don't get your phone call, but I'm sure the police back in Honolulu will give you that option. In the meantime your phone is evidence, because I expect the person Stephen heard Margaret speaking to on the night of the murder was you."

Brad's eyes were ice cold after Jason took the phone from his pocket. He glared at Rachel.

"Make sure you look over your shoulder, because one day, I'm coming for you."

Rachel held his gaze. "You'll have to get in line."

He turned his eyes towards Marjorie.

"Don't look at me," she said. "I'll be long gone by the time you get out of prison."

"Take him away," Waverley ordered.

"With pleasure, sir," said Jason, pushing the cuffed Brad out of the office.

"Phew," said Marjorie. "I can see what Olga meant when she said that man gave her the creeps."

Rachel shuddered. "Me too."

"Do you think he meant what he said?" asked Marjorie.

"Probably, but let's hope his long stay inside gives him time to reflect. Maybe he'll forget about me."

"I worry about you, Rachel."

Waverley cleared his throat. "Thanks again, Rachel. I don't suppose you're ready to take that job on the security team?"

"Not in this lifetime," said Rachel.

"Right now, we both need some sleep," said Marjorie. "Do you mind if we have a lazy day today?"

Rachel stood and took Marjorie's arm. "I insist upon it."

Chapter 33

Lounging on a Hawaiian island beach was just what they all needed, thought Rachel, as she listened to her three friends' banter.

Rachel and Marjorie had slept until lunchtime, and she was thrilled when Sarah called her to let her know that she and Jason had the afternoon off. Jason had already filled Sarah in on Brad's arrest, although he told Rachel he had omitted to mention how Brad had threatened to get her. A wise decision, as Sarah was prone to worry and had already seen what Rachel's enemies were capable of on past voyages.

As Rachel looked out at surfers riding the waves, the murder and the attacks, along with all things Bradley Roberts, seemed a lifetime away.

"I'd love to be able to do that," said Marjorie as they watched a slim woman scantily clad in a bikini riding the peak of one of the highest waves.

"Why don't you?" said Jason.

"Don't encourage her," said Sarah, giving him a playful thump on the arm.

"Otherwise you go with her," threatened Rachel.

"Excuse me, but I am here you know. If you're going to start that ageist nonsense again, I might just go over to the other side of the beach." Rachel could tell when Marjorie was feigning offence.

They giggled and chatted happily for a few hours, sitting comfortably under a beach parasol. When they reluctantly got up to leave, they saw Stephen, Emma, Preston, and Olga; the only four remaining from the party of eight that began the cruise. Emma waved.

"She looks so happy now, doesn't she?" Marjorie remarked.

Rachel nodded. "I'm pleased for her."

"We've got good news," called Stephen when they were a few feet away.

"Oh, please tell me Victoria's going to be all right," said Sarah.

"Not only that, she's rejoining the ship today for the last stop."

Rachel felt her eyes widen but didn't get to speak as Marjorie nudged her.

"You see, us oldies can hold our own, you know. We're made of sturdy stuff, and I was a war child, you have to remember."

"You might have been, but I doubt Victoria was," Rachel whispered and got another nudge for her cheek.

"She's doing fine. The swelling came down quicker than the medics expected. The quacks would rather she stayed in hospital for a few days to recover, but… well… she's a stubborn old girl." Stephen seemed almost proud of his old sparring partner.

Sarah beamed. "I'm pleased to hear it. Did she remember who attacked her?"

"Yeah," said Olga, grinning. "She also says she got a jab in."

Marjorie appeared confused.

"With her stick," said Rachel. "Does she know why he tried to strangle her?"

"Apparently somebody had vandalised the disabled cubicle just enough to be able to peep into the men's next door. The authorities reckon it was kids. Anyway, she was inquisitive and was shocked to see Brad removing the cast as he was about to shower, but her stick fell against the wall, alerting him. They're paper-thin. He turned and saw. He must have grabbed a towel and shot next door to check who it was. It was quick and random and she put up a good fight, crying out, which is why he couldn't finish the job." Stephen smiled happily after relating what Victoria had told him. "He obviously thought he'd done a good enough job, put the cast and its cover back in place, and when Preston saw him come out of the disabled cubicle, he called for help, soon after making up his story."

"Good for her, though," said Marjorie. "And I suppose he attacked me because he heard the rumour that we were investigating." Marjorie rubbed her neck where there was still some reddening.

Preston nodded. "Yeah, Brad must have guessed because you were asking a lot of questions."

Rachel swallowed hard. "At least two out of three escaped with their lives. I'm sorry about Margaret, but this time I don't think his father will be able to buy Brad out of trouble. He'll pay for his crimes."

"As me and Vicky didn't have a nurse," said Stephen, "I've taken Preston on until we get home."

Rachel smiled, pleased for Preston.

"As long as Victoria doesn't mind," said Preston.

"You leave Vicky to me. I'll handle her," said Stephen. "She's not as bad as she makes out, you'll see."

"And I've got an appointment with my agent the minute I get back to New York," said Emma. "He's got a prominent part for me – or so he says," she rolled her eyes.

"I'm thrilled. We must exchange email addresses and keep in touch," said Marjorie.

"I'd like that," said Emma. "If anything comes of it, you could come over for the premiere."

Marjorie's eyes lit up like a small child's. "I would be delighted."

"Enjoy the rest of your holiday," said Jason to Stephen and the others. "And in the nicest possible way, I hope our paths don't cross again in my professional capacity."

Stephen grinned. "I never liked that Brad fella. You make sure he gets locked up for a long time, otherwise you will see us again!"

Jason gave a mock salute. "Yes, sir."

As the group walked away, Rachel decided she would call Carlos that evening when she got back on board the *Coral Queen*. With a satisfied sigh, she smiled as her thoughts turned to going home.

THE END

Author's Note

Thank you for reading *Treacherous Cruise Flirtation*, the twelfth book in my Rachel Prince Mystery series. If you have enjoyed it, please leave an honest review on Amazon and/or any other platform you may use. I love receiving feedback from readers.

Keep in touch

Signup for my no-spam newsletter and receive a FREE novella. You will also receive news of new releases, special offers, and have the opportunity to enter competitions.

Join now:

https://www.dawnbrookespublishing.com

Follow me on Facebook:

https://www.facebook.com/dawnbrookespublishing/

Follow me on YouTube:

https://www.youtube.com/c/DawnBrookesPublishing

Books by Dawn Brookes

Rachel Prince Mysteries

A Cruise to Murder #1
Deadly Cruise #2
Killer Cruise #3
Dying to Cruise #4
A Christmas Cruise Murder #5
Murderous Cruise Habit #6
Honeymoon Cruise Murder #7
A Murder Mystery Cruise #8
Hazardous Cruise #9
Captain's Dinner Cruise Murder #10
Corporate Cruise Murder #11
Treacherous Cruise Flirtation #12
Toxic Cruise Cocktail #13

Lady Marjorie Snellthorpe Mysteries

Death of a Blogger (Prequel Novella)
Murder at the Opera House #1
Murder in the Highlands #2
Murder at the Christmas Market #3
Murder at a Wimbledon Mansion #4
Murder in a Care Home (Coming soon) #4

Carlos Jacobi PI

Body in the Woods #1
The Bradgate Park Murders #2
The Museum Murders (Coming soon 2023) #3

Memoirs

Hurry up Nurse: memoirs of nurse training in the 1970s #1
Hurry up Nurse 2: London calling #2
Hurry up Nurse 3: More adventures in the life of a student nurse #3

Picture Books for Children

Acknowledgements

Thank you to my editor Alison Jack, as always, for her kind comments about the book and for suggestions, corrections, and amendments that make it a more polished read.

Thanks to my beta readers for comments and suggestions, and for their time given to reading the early drafts, and to my ARC team – I couldn't do without you. And a big thank you to Alex Davis for the final proofread, picking up those punctuation errors and annoying typos!

I'm hugely grateful to my immediate circle of family and friends, who remain patient while I'm absorbed in my fictional world. Thanks for your continued support in all my endeavours.

I have to say thank you to my cruise-loving friends for joining me on some of the most precious experiences of my life, and to all the cruise lines for making every holiday a special one.

About the Author

Award-winning author Dawn Brookes holds an MA in Creative Writing with Distinction and is author of the Rachel Prince Mystery series, combining a unique blend of murder, cruising, and medicine with a touch of romance. A spinoff series with Lady Marjorie Snellthorpe taking the lead is in progress with the prequel novella *Death of a Blogger* available in eBook, paperback, and as an audiobook.

She also writes crime fiction featuring a tenacious PI which may be of interest to fans of Rachel Jacobi-Prince.

Dawn has a 39-year nursing pedigree and takes regular cruise holidays, which she says are for research purposes! She brings these passions together with a Christian background and a love of clean crime to her writing.

The surname of Rachel Prince is in honour of her childhood dog, Prince, who used to put his head on her knee while she lost herself in books.

Dawn's bestselling memoirs outlining her nurse training are available to buy. *Hurry up Nurse: memoirs of nurse training in the 1970s, Hurry up Nurse 2: London calling,* and *Hurry up*

Nurse 3: More adventures in the life of a student nurse. Dawn worked as a hospital nurse, midwife, district nurse, and community matron across her career. Before turning her hand to writing for a living, she had multiple articles published in professional journals and coedited a nursing textbook.

She grew up in Leicester, later moved to London and Berkshire, but now lives in Derby. Dawn holds a Bachelor's degree with Honours and a Master's degree in education. Writing across genres, she also writes for children. Dawn has a passion for nature and loves animals, especially dogs. Animals will continue to feature in her children's books, as she believes caring for animals and nature helps children to become kinder human beings.

Printed in Great Britain
by Amazon